Praise for the

series

'Totally **hilarious**, this boasts a **refreshingly relatable**
view of just **how tough motherhood can be**'
HEAT MAGAZINE

'**Utterly self-assured**, so, so, so **honest and
downright brave** . . . Every page is packed with
hard-earned wisdom, joy and truth'
LINDSEY KELK

'The latest adventures of Robin Wilde is sure to be a hit with
Louise Pentland's many fans. **Witty, fun, and full of warmth**
that will leave you with the feel-good factor'
FROST MAGAZINE

'You'll love this **funny**, warm and **relatable** read'
FABULOUS MAGAZINE

'A **refreshingly honest** take on life as a working single mother
. . . Its message resonates – life is messy and sometimes we just
have to embrace its unpredictability. **You'll be left empowered!**'
WOMAN MAGAZINE

'**Hilarious, moving** and **extremely well written**'
SUNDAY TIMES STYLE

Wilde Women

ABOUT THE AUTHOR

LOUISE PENTLAND is the *Sunday Times* bestselling author of the *Wilde* trilogy. She's the number one parenting vlogger in the UK, with 8 million combined followers across her social platforms. Louise is the host of the motherhood podcast *Mothers' Meeting*, she writes a monthly column for *Mother & Baby* magazine, and was crowned the Number 1 Mumfluencer in the magazine in 2019. Louise has filmed with the Pope at the Vatican to discuss the challenges facing young people today and HRH Prince Charles and HRH The Duchess of Cornwall to support Bookstart to encourage childhood literacy.

Wilde Women **is her third novel.**

🐦 @LouisePentland
📷 @LouisePentland
▶ SprinkleofGlitter
www.LouisePentlandNovel.com
#WildeLikeMe
#WildeAboutTheGirl
#WildeWomen

LOUISE PENTLAND

Wilde Women

ZAFFRE

First published in Great Britain in 2019
This edition published in 2020 by
ZAFFRE
80–81 Wimpole St, London WIG 9RE

Illustrations by Sophie McDonnell

A CIP catalogue record for this book is
available from the British Library.

Paperback ISBN: 978-1-83877-074-7
Hardback ISBN: 978-1-78576-930-6
Export ISBN: 978-1-78576-931-3

Also available as an ebook

1 3 5 7 9 10 8 6 4 2

Typeset by Palimpsest Book Production Ltd, Falkirk, Stirlingshire
Printed and bound in Great Britain by Clays Ltd, Elcograf S.p.A.

Zaffre is an imprint of Bonnier Books UK
www.bonnierbooks.co.uk

*For all the people who have ever seen a little bit
of Robin, Kath or Lacey in themselves,
this book is for you.*

Thank you for coming on this Wilde ride.

You are truly the best of eggs.

PROLOGUE

I F I'D KNOWN I'D be starting my morning running through Heathrow Airport with my whingeing eight-year-old daughter, my dithering auntie and my best friend heaving her new baby along in a sling, with more bags, bits of paper and snacks than you could shake a stick at, and sweat trickling down my back, I'd have worn my sleekest athleisure. This has to be the least enjoyable way to get on a plane to New York City, ever!

We were supposed to set off an hour earlier than we did, but I was up till the small hours writing lists, packing bags, obsessively checking I had the US visas, and ended up sleeping through my alarm. It wasn't until Auntie Kath let herself in with a 'yoo-hoo' that I shot out of bed in a panic. Lyla, who wouldn't know speed if it bit her on the bum, decided now was the time to tell me she had to say goodbye to every single toy in her bedroom, and Lacey (who had stayed over the night before for 'ease') chose that particular moment to wonder out loud if she would be allowed to take Willow's bottles through security, or if she could buy enough milk for Willow in the airside pharmacy. She seemed to have lost all sense of reality, and the fact that she could've googled this last week – we didn't have time for faffing, we had a plane to New York to catch!

Once we were finally in the car, some of us calmer than others ('I'm not worried, lovey, I've used my new lavender aromatherapy roll-on today so I feel very "zen", as you young ones would say,' Auntie Kath helpfully shared as I raced down the motorway), I started to feel that fizzy wave of excitement in my stomach.

And now, here we are, standing, panting like we've just run through a marathon finish line, at the check-in desk, with Willow loudly crying and Lyla asking me to open a packet of Skips, and what feels like every judging eye on us for being 'those people' who haven't organised themselves well enough to saunter up to the desk on time with happy children and snacks sorted. But I won't let this defeat me.

This is it: the trip of a lifetime. Everything is at stake, but equally and more promisingly, there is everything to play for, and I, Robin Wilde, the Total Badass Single Mum, am going to smash it!

I know this trip is important for me and my career, and I hope that the others will enjoy it too. But even I have no idea quite how much our lives are going to change before it's over.

Part One

EVERYTHING CHANGES BUT ME

ONE

MARCH

I T'S BEEN ONE OF those days where I almost can't believe how well it's gone. Two years ago, if you'd told me I'd be Creative Director at a major beauty agency, that I'd be coming home to my beautiful three-bedroom house and that I'd have a drop-dead gorgeous boyfriend and a bunch of friends who are the best squad you could wish for, I'd have laughed in your face. Or cried. Probably more likely the latter. Today though, wow – I've nailed it, and I am almost bursting to tell the aforementioned drop-dead gorgeous boyfriend all about my great day as soon as we sit down for dinner tonight.

But making dinner is easier said than done when you've got an eight-year-old with a loud voice and an active imagination to wrangle. We've barely got back from the school run when I hear the not-so-dulcet tones of my daughter from the living room.

'You. Are. A. Slimy. Worm!' Lyla spits with such venom I am actually a bit taken aback. I rush through to see what can be the cause of such fury.

'He's taking everything! This is MY house and that's MY Malteser and she is MY MUMMY!' she continues with the volume steadily increasing to a frantic shout at the end, and her usually perfectly milky skin turning pink in fury.

'Lyla, that's *enough*! First he put his shoes in *your* shoe cubby, then he sat in *your* chair at the table and now he's eaten *your* specific Malteser out of the box?' I ask, exasperated, trying to make sense of this, as Edward looks on with a tiny furrow in his usually calm brow and a now slightly melty Malteser pincered between his finger and thumb.

You don't need to be a child psychologist to see that this outburst isn't about the shoe spot or the chair or even the Malteser. It is about the final words my daughter had screamed at my new, and now probably-wondering-what-he-was-letting-himself-in-for boyfriend, Edward. It is about sharing me, her mummy.

They say you've got to pick your battles. I wonder if 'they' have ever been a single mum trying to squeeze a man into the mix without causing World War Three over a box of chocolates. Edward must see the cogs turning in my very tired brain as I sit down on the sofa next to him, because he puts his hand on my knee, unfurrows his brow and gently says, 'Lyla, I know this is your mummy. She's always going to be your mummy. It would be silly if she was my mummy, wouldn't it? She'd have to have grey hair and wear flowery blouses and smell a bit funny like my actual mum does, wouldn't she?'

This stops Lyla in her tracks.

She thinks about it for a moment, and then: 'What does your mum smell of?' A tiny smile curls at the edges of her little rosebud lips, only detectable to an eye fully trained in all things Lyla Blue Wilde.

'Hmmm,' says Edward. 'That's a very good question. She always just smells like my mum, but I suppose if I had to narrow it down I'd say she smells a bit like talcum powder, a bit like custard cream biscuits and, maybe, just a tiny bit . . .' and here he pauses for effect, with a big smile and mischievous glinting eyes, which are perhaps a bit contagious, 'a teeny-weeny bit like a . . . big, long, slimy worm!'

Despite desperately trying to remain cross, with narrowed eyes and lips forced together in a scowl, Lyla is failing miserably at maintaining her angry demeanour and giggles at the notion of an old lady smelling like a slimy worm.

'She'd have to smell a bit like a slimy worm since I'm a slimy worm, eh?' Edward continues, clamping his arms to his sides and slithering about on the sofa as though he really is a worm.

Finally giving in to the fun, Lyla throws herself over me to jump on Edward and tries to pull his hands out from by his sides. 'I was JOKING! You're not a worm! You're Edward! A MAN!'

'Help me!' he says in high-pitched mock distress. 'Help me, I'm just a big slimy worm that slimes about, worming my way through all the chocolates! A wiggly, slithery worm!'

Lyla squeals with delight at the new game, entirely forgetting her rage, hitting him with pillows and shouting, 'I'm going to squish the worm!'

I rescue the completely mushed chocolate from his hand, eat it (waste not, want not), put the rest of the box on the coffee table and decide I might as well join in. I pelt pillows at Lyla and tickle her while Edward fully takes on his slimy worm role and slithers onto the floor, leaving him more exposed to our cushion bombardment.

Twenty minutes later – with breath back in my body (wow, I'm unfit) and a film on Netflix about a princess who swaps lives with a bakery competition contestant at Christmas (it was Lyla's choice to watch a festive film, despite it being the first week in March), and half a box of chocolates now being shared nicely – normality (whatever that is) is restored. Phew. That could have gone really wrong, but thankfully Edward is basically the most perfect man I've ever met, and every time this kind of thing happens – which is a lot – he knows exactly what to say and how to defuse the situation. I often wonder if perhaps he should actually be a bomb disposal expert, or one of those people who negotiate the hostages out of banks, instead of the high-end furniture buyer that he is.

Don't get me wrong, he's very good at spotting the latest trends in interiors, but he's also pretty freaking amazing at managing our funny brand-new little family. Oh, that feels weird, calling it a 'family'. It always used to mean just me and Lyla, but then sometimes, especially when I think about what happened last year, I mean all three of us. Or should that be four? My brain and heart feel a bit discombobulated.

I've learnt lately that the most efficient thing to do is ignore that feeling and move on. Skye, my colleague and former frenemy, would say I need to speak to someone about all this. That I'm just suppressing my issues, and that if I really want to be 'woke' to the planet around me and the world within me then I can't just ignore it and 'crack on'. I've told her repeatedly that I am a 'cracker-on' and that I don't really want to be very 'woke'. Mostly I want to just be 'snoozed'.

We have a lovely family dinner in the end – although I decide my catch-up with Edward can wait until later. It takes longer to settle Lyla down for bed than usual because of all the slimy worm excitement, but I'd rather take an extra half hour with a happy daughter than delay bedtime to soothe a cross one.

Downstairs, I snuggle up to Edward on the sofa and pull his arm over me.

'Now, Edward, I need to discuss something really quite important with you,' I say in a serious tone, drawing little circles with my finger on his T-shirt, enjoying having a man to touch.

I feel his arm and shoulder stiffen around me. 'Oh yes?'

'I think we're going to have to call it a day . . .' I pause for painful effect.

'On . . . us?' he asks, sitting up and taking his arm away from me, looking alarmed.

'Yes. If you ever suggest I'm your mum again, or compare me to your mum or, obviously, a worm,' I say, climbing up onto my knees, straddling him and planting a big kiss on his oh-so-kissable lips.

'Right,' he says through my overenthusiastic kisses. 'Noted.' And then the kisses become more and more and more, and before we know it we're playing a very naked and very risky game right there on the sofa.

Sometimes life might be a challenge, but moments like this definitely help.

LIFE LATELY HAS BEEN pretty dreamy, though. My boyfriend (yes, hi, I recently added *official girlfriend* to my list of titles, and despite everything that has happened over the last couple of years, I'm weirdly OK with this), Edward, ended up camped out at my house for most of February, working from 'home' or commuting into London, and he doesn't have to go back to his life (his apartment, his job, etc.) in New York for a fortnight or two. He's intending on wrapping things up stateside (the business there will continue with him managing from afar), and he'll be concentrating on setting up a shiny new store in London – maybe on the King's Road – to entice a new crowd of interiors snobs. I say 'snobs', but it's just because I'm jealous that I don't know how to style a room or pick trendy greys and vibrant velvets that all just blend seamlessly. My idea of 'interiors' is a few cushions from Next, a candle and some fake succulents. Suddenly, a wave of doubt washes over me. I wonder if Edward ever secretly thinks I'm a bit crap and wants to change things in my house? No, I'm not going to let myself spiral. Maybe I should just broach this with him when we get a moment alone, which is almost never.

As the worm-fight proves, Lyla is still adjusting to me having a man in my life. It's been the Robin and Lyla Show for so long that it's strange to have another body in the room. We're used to Auntie Kath popping in almost daily, of course, but that's not the same as a great big man being here day and night. Plus, things with Kath and her new gentleman-friend Colin seem to be going so well that we don't see her as often. Lyla's adjusting to that, too, but Colin hasn't been called a 'slimy worm' in months now, so I think that's going OK and my daughter's defensive battles are being fought closer to home.

But I know Lyla, and what's more, she knows I love her. Even if it might take her a bit of time to come round, I have to let her see that a bigger family just means more love to go around, not smaller amounts to share. And for once, everyone else is loved-up and on cloud nine. Hurrah. Hur*rah*.

Now, if I can only stop myself getting distracted by his barely clad state, I can finally tell Edward what happened to me today.

TWO

M Y MORNING STARTED PRETTY joyfully.

'I've said it before and I'll say it again, I think she might just be perfect. A lot of them at this age look like a cross between old men and misshapen potatoes, but this one, she's absolutely perfect,' I swooned, breathing in that new baby smell that I wish stayed forever.

'Thanks, Robin,' laughed Lacey, new mum and my best friend, through a mouthful of McDonald's fries. 'I'm really glad you don't think my firstborn child looks like the elderly or carbs, that's really good of you.'

'You know what I mean! I just can't get over how utterly gorgeous she is. She's the best baby I've ever seen,' I said, carrying on gazing at her placidly staring up at me, as I sucked thick strawberry milkshake up my straw.

'You can't say that! What about Lyla?' Lacey was smiling, knowing full well a mother's heart always belongs to her own children.

'Aha! Well, obviously, Lyla is my number one, but can I make Willow joint fave? I love how gorgeous she is, and I love how I can hand her back.' I laughed. 'Do you remember how much of a mess I was when Lyla was born? You're absolutely acing it. You look so together,' I said, thinking back to eight years ago when my life was very different.

'I never saw you being a mess. I just saw you being incredible.' She's a good mum; she's already a diplomat.

'Mmm, Lacey,' I said, mock-hitting her arm. I never know what to do when people compliment me, especially when it's about motherhood. If she were complimenting my skirt, I'd just yell, 'It has pockets!' But instead I threw it back, classic coping mechanism 101. 'I think *you're* doing incredibly.'

Lacey Hunter is smashing it. Willow Faith, her newborn daughter, is three weeks old, her husband Karl has just gone back to work in the City after his paternity leave (after all these years of friendship, I still don't really know what he does, and it seems too far gone to ask now) so I popped round with a giant bagful of McDonald's and a spare four hours, expecting the house to be total carnage, the baby to be crying, Lacey to be looking like the 'mombie' we all become and me there ready to save the day. Instead, the house was tidier than mine even after my new cleaner's been, Lacey looked serene and I think she had even contoured (unless she'd replaced her pregnancy glow with fourth-trimester sculpt – is that a thing?) and the baby was, as well as being utterly perfect, swaddled in a clean, ironed muslin and sleeping soundly in her crib.

'Lacey, how have you made all this look so easy? I don't think I knew my arse from my elbow for about three months when Lyla was born,' I said in awe, moving on to my cheeseburger while Lacey rummages in the bag for more fries.

'It's really simple. I just don't go out, don't spend any time talking to anyone else, don't do any cooking, don't do any work and don't have any sleep. I just devote every waking second to keeping her alive and everything looking OK.' She laughed drily. 'I can't actually remember what life outside this house looks like, and I'm not sure my vagina will ever be the same again, but you know, it's worth it, and all that, isn't it . . . Isn't it?'

'Oh yes, especially if you're acing it like this. I mean, just look. You should take an Insta! Of the tidy lounge, I mean, not your slightly ravaged (but I promise it will get better) vagina.'

We both laughed and finished our food, knowing we were on borrowed time before Willow woke and I had to collect Lyla, wondering how time had gone so fast from her being this size to being in Year Four at school.

I hope Lacey will treasure these early moments with her beautiful daughter and all the possibilities she brings. Once the high of meeting your new baby vanishes, it's so damn hard to have the energy to do anything, let alone try to remember to be in the moment. So I figure that's one thing I can do – drink it all in so I can remind them both how flipping gorgeous they were in these crazy, magical first weeks.

I thought it would be hard for the day to get any better after a morning of Willow cuddles, but the afternoon had its own surprises.

'Oo-ooo, Robin, Robin! I was hoping to catch you!' called Gloria Straunston from across the junior school car park as her two children, Verity and Athena, trailed behind her, tired from a full day of learning, playing and now their mother's seemingly unending enthusiasm.

I turned round from the boot of my car, where I'd been piling in the roughly eight thousand bags of kit my small child seems to need for school these days, and smiled. Having hotfooted it from Lacey's just in time for pick-up, I was feeling frantic, but I like Gloria. She isn't like the other mums; she has never made me feel inferior or work for her approval. They're not all bad, of course. I have my gang, with Gillian and Finola, and mostly I think everyone has accepted me now, but when we joined Hesgrove, the highly sought-after private pre-prep school, two years ago (thanks to my inheritance from Granny), with, let's face it, my life at that point very firmly not together, it took me a long time to be brave enough to feel I could stand my ground with the Posh School Mums (PSMs).

A year serving on the PaGS (Parents and Guardians Society – I swear it took me a full school year just to learn all the acronyms), where I helped organise a spa night to raise money for the cancer charity supporting Mrs Barnstorm, a battleaxe but beloved teacher (now thankfully on the mend), a lot of small talk in the foyer, a victorious struggle with the school-mum-bully and keeping shtum when I found the head, Mr Ravelle, in a rather compromising position (with Gloria herself) in the school supply cupboard, and I think I've finally earnt my place among the PSMs and am now treated as 'one of them'. I feel like the confident bearded lady from *The Greatest Showman*. Here I am, this is me. Except sometimes I do still have very small and very quiet worries. I bet even she did from time to time.

Gloria's twins joined the school a year later than Lyla, and, like me, she is a bit different. Her husband doesn't fund her lunching/gymming/shopping life-style. In fact, like me, she doesn't even have a husband (she has an ex). And she doesn't abide by the Hunter-boots-and-Joules-navy-padded-gilet mumiform. She's a successful businesswoman with a penchant for vibrantly coloured velvet trousers, filthy jokes and an even filthier laugh. She originates from the States (Nashville), met her now ex-husband at a business conference ten years ago, had a whirlwind romance ('With all those men falling at my feet, I couldn't help it, Robin, I just had to have one of them,' she said in a Southern drawl once over a glass of Pinot, with such confidence I almost fell for her myself), moved to the UK to set up home in Kent, married in what I can only assume was the wedding of the century by the way she's described it, fell pregnant with the twins on her honeymoon (a three-week tour of Europe so she could see this side of the pond) and then, once the babies were born and reality set in, 'the magic just wore off'. He left and moved up to London to carry on as though nothing had ever happened, and she brought Verity and Athena up here to Cambridge for a completely fresh start. I asked her once why she'd stayed in the UK, and she talked about having roots here now and seemed uncharacteristically down-trodden, so I didn't push it. Gillian and I have wondered if the evil ex has tried to stop her taking the twins, even though he never sees them. Despite the upheaval and the heartache, she's continued to grow her freelance PR business, always talks to everyone as though they are her number one priority, is always up for a mums' night out, or a mums' night in, any night at all, and never seems to run out of steam. She is brilliant.

'Hellooo!' I trilled warmly. 'Haven't seen you in a while!' Lyla edged forward and waved a little hand at the twins, who were so engrossed in a clapping game with each other, they didn't really notice. Social interactions are hard at every age, I think.

Gloria started up again.

'Well, you're never here anymore! You're always swanning around at MADE IT, or loved-up with that new boyfriend of yours,' she said, as all three children mimed being sick at the idea of me with my new boyfriend.

'What can I say, Gloria? I'm just exceptionally fabulous now.' I mock-zhooshed my hair and laughed. 'I usually put Lyla in an after-school club so I can do a full working day, but my friend's just had a baby so I've taken a bit of time off to go and see her. Thought she'd be up to her eyeballs in nappies and hormones, but she seems to be one of those together women I'd have been supremely jealous of eight years ago. Actually, I'm still quite jealous!'

'Sounds like me too! It doesn't feel like five minutes ago that I was almost drowning in a sea of diapers and hormones! My ex was about as helpful as a bout of thrush, so my mom flew in and we tag-teamed for four months. It all just feels like a weird hazy blur now. Do you think you and the new beau will go for another?' she asked, smiling excitedly, not considering that Lyla was listening with fervency and not realising the poignancy of her question.

A little pang of pain whooshed through me as I blinked a couple of extra times to steady myself. This time last year I had no idea that I was about to lose the baby I hadn't even known I wanted. Sometimes I forget it happened, and then someone will say something innocent like Gloria did and the pain is sharp and raw and deep all over again.

'Aha! Nooo! We're doing fine for now! He's only staying with me for a few weeks, nothing official yet, taking it a day at a time, you know? Fine, it's fine for now!' I smiled as the words tumbled out, smothering any indication that anything might be less than OK. I'm very good at that. One day I'd love to have the courage to say, 'You know, it's not super-cool to ask someone if they're going to have a baby. So many people suffer losses or struggle to conceive, and the question just stabs all the harder if they're walking that journey alone', but I knew Gloria meant no harm and 'fine' felt so much easier. As always.

'Well, I'd say you're doing more than fine – you're absolutely killing it, and I need to talk to you about just that! I need your exceptional more-than-just-fine skills on my new project,' Gloria said with pomp and circumstance.

'Ooh, go on,' I replied, intrigued.

Gloria marched us away from the cars and across the road to the park, where the children could clamber over the climbing frame and give us a moment to talk.

'I'm starting a club, a network, called "Women Who Win",' she said with that self-assured confidence only Americans seem to have (judging by the ones I've met, anyway).

'I already like the sound of this!' I laughed.

'I want a way to connect local women who are building businesses, have awesome skills and smart ideas, or who want help to grow a project with other like-minded women. I want a place where we can openly shout about what we're good at without feeling like we need to apologise or humble ourselves. We can work together, build better businesses and share our experience, and I think the benefit to everyone involved could be incredible.'

Wow. 'Oh my God, yes! This sounds brilliant!'

See what I mean? She's awesome.

'I've spoken to Mr Ravelle. As you know, he's always very on board with what I have to offer, so is happy to let us use the hall for meetings and events,' she said with a raised brow and a wry smile.

'You know, I still haven't told anyone about that cupboard incident! It's absolutely killing me! It's the juiciest piece of school gossip anyone has ever had,' I said, nudging her in mock frustration.

'This is why I like you, Robin Wilde,' she told me, not even wincing at my tease. 'You've got integrity as well as a strong work ethic. This is why I want you to be Vice Chair of Women Who Win. You're a perfect fit. You're the ideal success story!'

I felt exhilarated. 'I don't think anyone has ever called me "the ideal success story", but I'll take it, and I'd love to help out. Tell me more! I don't know how good I'd be as Vice Chair. That sounds very official, but I'm definitely down for helping women, sharing skills and us all rising together. There's just one condition,' I added.

'Name it,' she replied eagerly.

'If I ever catch you and Ravelle snogging in a cupboard again, I'm not keeping it a secret. I'm telling everyone. I'm submitting it to the PaGS newsletter. I'm probably even telling Vicious Valerie!' I laughed.

'Deal!' she said, putting her hand out for me to shake. 'How about we go for coffee next Tuesday if you've got time after drop-off, and I'll tell you all my plans? And let's never speak of that cupboard again!'

'Great,' I said, still reeling that she'd asked *me* to help her set this up. 'Right, I need to round up Lyla, take her home, battle over getting the homework done and referee her next round in the ring with Edward.' I couldn't help but feel a little buzz of pleasure, knowing he'd be there when we get home.

'You're a boss!' Gloria called as I walked across the playground with a spring in my step to peel Lyla off the climbing frame. That's why I like Gloria so much. She didn't say 'boss lady', just 'boss'.

Well, you know what? Maybe I could be!

THREE

'SKYE, THESE DESIGNS ARE so good, you've totally nailed it. I love the gold leaf round the temples – they add such a lovely sprinkle of glitter. I think Natalie will love them. Would you like me to cast my eye over them properly before you send them across to her?' I ask from behind my desk. In my job as Creative Director at MADE IT, I now have sign-off on a number of quite big projects. The one we're working on at the moment is really exciting, and I'm watching Skye, our Head Make-Up Artist, thrive. I have a little sticker on my pencil pot that says *Empowered Women Empower Women*, so I'm trying to channel that and let Skye know I've got her back at all times. I think it's working and, like I said, she's thriving.

'Yeeaaahhh, it might be nice to have a second opinion,' Skye says breezily from her desk, which takes up one side of my office. OK, so when I say *thrive*, she's a lot more relaxed about it – and secure in her own genius – than I could ever be.

Last year, when I stepped up to a management role to cover for Natalie Wood, our CEO, while she took a much-needed sabbatical to spend time and reconnect with her lovely husband Martin, I had my own office. It was pretty great, but if I'm honest with myself, a bit lonely. I found myself secretly spending a lot of time staring gormlessly at memes on Twitter or flicking through the holiday photos of people I went to university with, and perhaps not using my time as wisely as I could.

So although Skye, as Head MUA, is usually out on bookings, when she's taking an office day to plan or put together creative proposals, she's got a desk in here to use if she needs it. She doesn't call it a 'desk', though. She calls it a 'space'. She also doesn't have a drawerful of sweets or an entire noticeboard of photos or funny postcards. She has two succulents (actual real ones that she keeps alive), a keep-cup and a candle made by women in Nigeria who are selling them to raise money for schools. I asked her once if she wanted a pen pot and some stationery, and she just replied, 'I have a laptop', as though this meant pen and paper were extinct. I felt instantly embarrassed that I'd shown my age, but then righted myself. It's an honour to age, and I won't be pen-pot-shamed. To age is a privilege; with it comes wisdom and experience, and without that, I wouldn't be where I am. So, pen pot and I, we're fine.

'OK, a second opinion and some security that you're not going to almost ruin my career again, eh?' I comment with an exaggerated eye-roll and a smile.

'You know I'm not ready to joke about that, and you know doing that weird eye-roll thing doesn't make it OK.' It's not that long since Skye's rather relaxed approach to business almost cost me my job. We found our way through it – and get on better than we used to – but sometimes there's a flash of nerves behind her laid-back gaze.

'Sorry, Skye. I'd love to read it anyway, so I can soak up some of your creative genius,' I say, doing an even more exaggerated eye-roll that involves my whole body and almost toppling off my chair as the wheels clunk under me.

'That chair. It's my mood,' Skye says with a completely impassive expression.

'What?' I ask.

'It's my mood,' she says, normally, as though she's not speaking in riddles.

'The chair is your mood? You're feeling . . . chair?' I question slowly, feeling perplexed.

'You're so old.'

'You're so baffling.' I've got good at ignoring Skye's lessons in what the cool kids say. 'Have you sent that proposal over? It's not in my inbox.' I try to change the subject back to concepts I can deal with.

'I made a board for it,' she offers, her voice a monotone.

'Is that in my emails?' I ask again.

'No, it's on Trello.'

Is she literally speaking another language?

'Is that the same as WeTransfer?' I try.

'No, I've tagged you in it,' she says with a hint of frustration.

'On Facebook?' Why is this so fucking hard?

'Oh my God, now the chair really is my mood,' she says, as though she's speaking to a moron.

'Jesus Christ, Skye, I don't know what you're talking about! Can you just print it and I'll read a piece of paper with writing on like they did in the olden times, while you can just carry on empathising with the emotional capacity of a bloody desk chair!' I vent, thinking Lyla was now the *second* most exasperating person in my life.

'Wow. Chill out. I've emailed it.'

'Thank you,' I say. My 'space' is now very un-zen, even with the succulents.

Skye flounces off to talk to Alice and Stuart, our lovely admin staff in the front office, about her holiday pay so she can have another day off to watch her uncomfortably macho boyfriend compete in one of his bodybuilding competitions. I read her proposals and am really impressed. Skye might be the epitome of coolness, deeply confusing with her young lingo and one of the most self-absorbed people I've ever met, but my goodness, she's got talent.

Last year (on the back of my idea for a natural beauty look, I'd just like to quietly add), we won the opportunity to style Mara Isso's London Fashion Week show. She is one of the UK's top fashion designers, and she broke all the boundaries last autumn by sending her entire collection down the runway on plus-size models. Not just one or two of them: all of them were beautiful women of every shape and size, nationality and ethnicity, and it was a roaring success. The press were enthralled, and women everywhere were thrilled to find they could be part of something that for years has been exclusive to one type of body. Don't get me wrong, I work with traditional models all the time on commercial or editorial make-up jobs, and I think they're beautiful, too, but it was amazing to see so much variation and inclusion. It was certainly the only time I've ever seen a body that I could recognise as something even slightly like my own on a catwalk.

So we bid for the job to do the hair and make-up and, by the skin of our teeth (let's not go too much into mine and Skye's blunder with the proposal that nearly cost me my entire career), we won! We sent those women down the runway highlighting what their mamas gave them. No muss, no fuss, just letting their natural beauty shine through. I mean, shine through a lot of carefully blended make-up and perfectly styled I-woke-up-like-this hair, of course. Being part of that, showcasing women we normally wouldn't, was amazing, a career and life highlight for me. Robin Wilde, at actual London Fashion Week – that was something I'll never forget. And watching it all come together actually made me believe in myself, and in my skills – for a while, at least. I mean, impostor syndrome never fully goes away, it seems, but you can certainly shut it up for a bit.

For her next collection, which launched just a few weeks back at the spring/summer LFW, Mara went with a rival make-up company to 'keep things fresh'. Obviously at MADE IT we all understood and graciously (aka through gritted teeth and, for my boss Natalie and me, some anxieties about meeting our budget) sent her a bouquet of flowers to congratulate her on another winning season. We had to assume that was our lot with Mara, and that we should carry on bidding for other work in the catwalk arena because it was such a success for us last time and Natalie – savvy businesswoman that she is – is so keen to keep expanding our portfolio.

You can imagine how thrilled (and relieved) we were when Mara's team called and said they loved us so much they wanted to work with us again. Could we 'put something together'? Natalie told me to keep it on the down-low that, although they said they needed an official proposal, we were the front runners. The theme for their spring/summer collection will be 'Not of This World', so of course, our Queen of Special Effects is finally having her moment. No one does a holographic eye or a strobed cheekbone like Skye.

Skye is brilliant at breathing life and energy into a big, creative concept. She instinctively knows how to add pizzazz. I know we've come a long way in the last year because I can actually tell her this comfortably without feeling a touch bitter and like I want to eat my feelings afterwards. Maybe this is growth?

While Skye is buzzing over the new Mara Isso project, I've been working alongside my boss and all-round absolute hero, Natalie, to explore other areas that MADE IT can expand into. I love that she trusts me to help with this, and as much as I enjoy going out on my usual MUA jobs and working with regular clients, I'm really coming to love the business side of things and feel the thrill of it.

I surprised myself a couple of years ago when I assisted Natalie on a horror film shoot in New York.

I'd never travelled for work before, and I thought I'd be a wreck, but after a shaky first night, I got into my stride, found my confidence and totally excelled. The franchise is British, produced by an American company, and we won the ongoing contract. I'm so proud of the role I played in winning the five-film contract, and my job started to grow from that day onwards. The production company had assured us the next film would be in progress within twenty-four months and would be shot here in the UK. Being known for regular feature film work would be a huge feather in our cap. However, things are looking a bit rocky on that front just now, as it's all gone a bit quiet. When Natalie and I grab a moment to chat, I can tell she is worrying about it too – but she dismisses my anxiety with: 'I'm sure it's nothing, these things take time', and after we send a polite 'check-in' email, we move on to what I really want to talk about: my new idea to expand the MADE IT business.

Ever since seeing my PSM friend Finola blossom after a mini-makeover and pamper session at the PaGS charity spa night last year, I'd been thinking how many women there are like her out there who would love some support and guidance with their make-up.

My idea is to set up a studio where men or women could book slots of time to come and have an expert beauty lesson from a qualified make-up artist. They'd be shown what colours and textures suit them, and we could offer tutorials on any kind of look (casual day, glitzy night), and then the client would go home with a clear idea of how to do their own make-up well and feel their absolute best. I'm a big believer in people feeling good about themselves regardless, but I also know that when I've applied the perfect strong brow I feel like an utter badass.

I explain my ideas to Natalie and she thinks it's a great plan. With so many freelance MUAs on our books, as well as Natalie, Skye and I employed full-time, there's more than enough expertise to hand. Stuart and Alice could manage the logistics of it – we'd just need to think about hiring studio space or venues and marketing it right. Natalie tells me to go out there and bring in the business. Right. Well. I will, then!

Once I've had my meeting with Natalie, read through more of Skye's unsurprisingly amazing creative ideas for Mara (think Swarovski crystals, think coloured lashes, think holographic body art), organised which MUAs are on which jobs next week, worked on creative ideas for my own upcoming book-ings, spent a healthy amount of time scrolling through Insta when nobody's looking (it's research, honest!), and texted Edward what I'd like to do with him once Lyla's in bed (oh, how I've missed filthy messages popping up on my phone that aren't gross dating app dick pics), it's time to pack up and head to school to collect my girlie.

I close my laptop with a satisfying thud, throw all my sweet wrappers and debris into the bin (wrappers first, notes/screwed up paper on top so nobody can judge me), pick up my trusty giant bag and head out of the office, saying my goodbyes cheerily as I go.

Life feels good right now. At last. I'm where I've always wanted to be. Further than that, in fact. Am I a bit out of my depth? Maybe. Would I change it for the world? Hell, no!

FOUR

APRIL

'I've got something to ask you,' Edward announces the next Friday night as I flump down on the sofa next to him with a glass of wine that, held deftly aloft, I don't spill a drop of. As Skye would say, 'Hashtag: skills'.

I feel an instant prickle of panic on the back of my neck. I don't want to deal with any more hard stuff; I just want to collapse on the sofa with wine, and maybe share some light gossip or happy news, like when I finally got to tell him about Gloria picking me to help her set up Women Who Win. But immediately my brain starts shuffling through all the bad things he might be preparing to say. Before he's said a word, I'm convinced he's leaving, or that he must have some terrible illness, or he's about to tell me he's a member of one of those cults where you have to get up before 4 a.m. every day. Then I take a breath, steady myself and regain control of my mind.

I'm a very able woman; whatever he has to say, I can handle it, and respond.

'Oh, right?' Nailed it.

'I still don't know what to do about the move, and I've only got a few days left here,' Edward says, staring ahead, flicking through the Netflix options.

He's being very casual. Maybe he's felt the panic prickle, too, and is trying to de-escalate the situation.

'What do you mean? I thought you were going back to wrap things up a bit in the US and then base yourself here for a while? Has the plan changed? Are you not going back? Have things fallen through with the business over there? Have they fallen through with the store here? Did you—'

'Oh my God, did your brain just throw up on me?' Edward asks, pulling his attention away from the TV and looking at me in surprise.

Oops, lost control. That steadiness might have gone . . .

'Erm. Yes. What I meant was, lol, I'm so casual, lol, and breezy too, lol, what's up?'

Edward laughs. I love it when he laughs. His jaw sort of drops down a tiny bit as he smiles and looks all chiselled and strong, but his eyes go all crinkly round the edges and make him look kind. It makes me want to curl up into a ball and at the same time cuddle him, but then also to straddle him. It's very confusing in a very wonderful way. I've been thinking about this a lot, and should probably be paying attention to what he's saying, but it's very difficult when he's this delicious, dammit. I could literally just stare at him all day, remarking on how attractive this man is and how I can't quite believe he's here with me.

'Oh yes. I knew deep down my girlfriend was ultra-chilled and would never get wound up over her boy-friend potentially uprooting his entire life and moving across the planet for her,' he continues, chuckling.

It's ridiculous at this age, but I still feel a bit of a tingle down my spine when he says 'boyfriend' or 'girlfriend'. It's a weird validation every time that I love, but also feel a tiny bit unsettled by. It's all a bit much. Or maybe it's not. He's so lovely. I'm over-whelmed. No, no, I'm fine. Totally fine.

'For him too, not just for her, let's be clear. And no!' I exclaim. 'I would never think that after being solo for about five hundred years, a man changing what side of the world he lives on is a big deal. It's nothing, really. On a par with deciding between chips or salad in a restaurant. Just a teeny thing, you know?' I try to laugh back with as much breeze as possible, but I still feel tense and the overwhelm is increasing. These are big issues.

'So, when this man who thinks you and your daughter are amazing (even though she hid my laptop in the recycling bin this morning)—'

'Yes, sorry about that, I—'

'When this man wants to wake up next to you each morning, but needs to decide if he's going to rent a place in London or commute from here, what should he do?' Edward says, his eyes looking straight into mine.

Wow, his eyes are soft. It's like the edges of his pupils just blend with the speckles of brown and it's almost blurred. His eyes always look kind and gentle. In fact, he's always been kind and gentle. I realise I've totally lost track of the question.

'Hmm?' I say, playing for more time.

'Should he rent his own place, or live here?' He tilts his head slightly with the last word.

'Oh.' Suddenly things have gone from sofa bants to sofa serious. This feels like too much to put all on me! For the last two years (and more, in some respects), I've been making huge decisions. What school to put Lyla in, how to bring her up alone, saying yes to Natalie's promotion, walking away from Theo (my Turned-Out-to-be-a-Total-Bastard ex), choosing a new place to live. I've also been the only one making all the little decisions, like what to put in Lyla's lunch box, and where to grab a coffee, and is it time to call a plumber about the weird knocking noise in the airing cupboard pipes. I'm done with deciding things. This *is* too much!

'I . . . I like things as they are.' Everything is fine as it is. I like having Edward around, and I definitely don't want him to go, but if I make the decision that he should live here and then it all goes wrong, once again a great big mess will be all my fault.

Edward pushes on, thankfully not hearing my over-whelming inner monologue.

'"Things as they are", as in me living here with you

and Lyla, or "things as they are", as in going with the flow?' he asks, still gently.

'I don't really know. Do you want to live here?' I ask tentatively, putting it back on him. I need to know what he wants, too.

'Well, there's the space,' he says suggestively.

'That's not a good enough reason! I need more than that, please!' I laugh nervously.

'Well, I love falling asleep holding you, and spending evenings on this bloody awful sofa arguing about what to watch with you.' He shifts about on the brown leather as though this proves it.

I'm nervously floating on cloud nine when I think about how much I've wanted a man to say something like that to me for so long, followed very rapidly by a wave of indignation. I'm utterly incensed that he could insult my beloved sofa.

'This sofa is not awful! I've had it forever!' In fact, I inherited the sofa from my granny when I moved into her old house. This sofa is special. It's full of soul. Not *her* soul. My sofa isn't haunted by an old woman, but, you know, it's a good one. An oldie but goldie.

'Yeah. I can tell.' He ramps up the sarcasm.

'Cheeky sod. Now I'm definitely not asking you to

live with me.' I hit him with one of my many cushions that, if I'm really honest, I bought to try to improve the sofa.

'But you were going to, before I dissed your awful sofa?' he asks with a grin.

I pause. 'I was going to say you could live with me if you thought you could handle it. We're not perfect, in this house. Or super-stylish. And sometimes when Lyla's at her dad's I like to walk around in a face mask and giant pants and just *be*, yanno?'

'If I can handle being called a worm, a pimple, Mr Nits and Edward Poo Head, as well as having my laptop hidden in the recycling, my keys buried in the shrubs and bogies wiped on my phone, then I can absolutely handle you in big pants. I might actually join you!' he says, leaning in for a little kiss, sending me into a bit of a tizz about whether I should just rip his clothes off here and now or continue this very adult conversation.

God, he's lovely. And now, yes yes yes, it looks like he's going to live here! Fuck me, this is turning out very well indeed. And, even more amazingly, after that initial panic I feel quite happy about it. I'm not freaking out!

Deciding (see? Always making choices) not to convey what I'd actually like to do to him on the sofa (I'll save it for later, and maybe then he'll come to love the sofa more), I continue our chat and move very firmly away from sexual antics on the sofa not filled with Granny's soul.

'I'm sorry Lyla's being like this. She will come round. She just needs to feel safe. It'll be fine.'

'I know. I get it. I'm not at all cross. I want to make her feel safe, too. I want to be a family. I wanted us to be a family last year,' Edward says, the tone changing in his last sentence as he feels the loss of the miscarriage.

Although it hurts, I love that he still talks about it. Miscarriage is so rarely spoken about, and when it is, it always seems to just be a 'woman's problem', as though it's only the woman who hurts. But seeing Edward grieve too helps me feel we're in it together, and that the little life we didn't get to bring into the world wasn't nothing. It was something, and it was loved, and there is still love there.

I take a big breath. 'I'd love you to move in. Things are getting so busy at work, and at home now Kath isn't on hand as much, and with Lyla – who I swear has a more active social life than me – that you living somewhere else and us having to schlep about wouldn't make any sense at all. We'll talk to Lyla in the morning, and reassure her that everything's going to be fine, but in the meantime, keep an eye on your valuables. I've seen her eyeing up your sunglasses as her next target.'

Edward laughs, nods, clinks his wine glass against mine, and I decide that actually now *is* the time to show him what I'd like to do to him on this sofa, because if you can't celebrate with sex in the lounge when your boyfriend says he wants to be a family, when can you?

FIVE

TWO WEEKS LATER, HALFWAY through April, Edward goes back to New York with all of his possessions intact and no new nicknames from Lyla. After a lot of reassuring chats and, I'm ashamed to admit it, a lot of bribery (in the form of buying way more LOL Dolls than was strictly necessary), I think maybe Lyla has not only accepted but started to really enjoy Edward's company. One night they sat up way past her bedtime (it was a Friday, don't judge me) and carefully constructed a cardboard doll's house out of an old box, complete with furniture and an added garage. I came downstairs and watched them for a moment, without them knowing I was there. Seeing Edward in his element (designing, styling, guiding, caring) and Lyla following on so beautifully made me feel overcome. It felt like I was finally getting the family unit I'd always wanted. Part of me couldn't believe any of this was happening. I took a stealthy photo on my phone and texted it to Lacey.

Looks like we're both living our family dreams, eh? How are you three getting on? Not heard from you in a few days. Did you ever go to that baby yoga group? Xxx

Moments later, my phone pinged with a reply.

Awww, they look so cute together. No. Felt too much, and I don't like taking Willow out in the cold xxx

It's April – she'll be OK if you put a little coat on her. Babies are more resilient than you think! Xxxxxxxxx

I added extra kisses so she didn't think I was telling her off or being high and mighty; Lacey is a sensitive soul. And I remembered how I'd felt as a new mum – as if I was looking for an instruction manual that never arrived.

> *Yeah. I'll go next week. Just a bit tired at the moment. All worth it though! I love her to bits! She's my absolute world! Xxx*

> *I know – she's the best <3. Do you want to pop over tomorrow after Lyla's finished school? We'd love to see you! Xxx*

> *Mmm, I'm not sure I can. I think Willow might be a bit too snuffly to come out. You could come here though. Xxx*

> *Poor thing. We'll come over at 4-ish xxxx*

I switched out of my chat with Lacey and sent the same photo to Auntie Kath, who sent a heart and happy face emoji back. I'd normally get more out of her, but I expect she was busy with her lavender crafts (she tells me business is booming with her hand-blended oils and soaps, and so on) or with Colin. Or both. I quickly put the thought of the supposed 'sensual versatility' of her favourite body lotion creation out of my mind. I'd pop in on her during the week, too. I wonder if Edward would like me in lavender?

IT'S SCHOOL PICK-UP TIME, and I'm in my usual spot with Gillian and Finola in the foyer by the main entrance. I've learnt that we all have our spots. You don't change your spot. If you do, you'll upset the entire dynamic of where people stand, mothers and children will be lost to one another, families will break down instantly and governments will collapse. OK, maybe I'm going a bit far, but seriously, nobody ever stands in a new place. Once you're in, you're fixed, and I'm not rebel enough to go against the unspoken pick-up spot rules, that's for sure.

'Now look, my dear, I've been having a think about your grand plans with Gloria, and I'd like to sign up!' Finola says in her usual authoritative tone.

'Great! But Women Who Win isn't going to be a sign-up thing. You can just let us know you're going to come along, and then chat through ideas and see where you can get some advice and help others in turn. For example, I want to figure out how best to push forward with my style tuition idea for MADE IT, and offer any help to anyone who needs it. We've been doing some great work on setting it up. Gloria came round last night and we went through the plans over a glass of wine – she's so nice. Gloria thinks it's a great chance for everyone to make really good connections. Are you wanting to offer help, or do you have a sneaky little idea up your sleeve?' I ask teasingly.

'I'm not a sneaky woman, Robin. Sneak up on a horse and he'll kick you in the chest. I like to come at you face forward,' Finola says, pausing for breath.

'Yes, sorry, I didn't mean it in a bad way,' I add, my brain taking me to an unwanted image of her going at her husband 'face forward'.

'Do you have an idea, Finola? I'd love to hear it,' Gillian encourages gently. Sometimes I think Gillian is so nice that I'm actually jealous of Clara, her daughter, because I want Gillian to be my mum. My own mother rarely leaves Cornwall to visit us here in Cambridge, and is about as encouraging as a wisdom tooth infection.

'I do, Gillian. I'd like to start offering riding lessons

at the stables. Honor and Roo can ride wonderfully now, and I have found myself at a loose end during the days. Sometimes it's a little, well, lonely with Edgar at work all day and just the horses and dogs for company. I'm not looking to change the world, but perhaps I could teach other people to enjoy animals, too. Maybe I could start with the women in this network, and then . . . maybe someone could show me how to do all the advertising and whatnot,' Finola explains, with just a shred less certainty than usual.

'Finola, that sounds like a fantastic idea! I know Lyla could be your first customer! She loved that day at the yard last year. I bet you'll be inundated!' I say happily, wondering why she hasn't done this sooner. It's probably best if I don't remind her of Lyla's reaction the first time I took her riding – 'I bloody hate ponies' – because, you know, empowered women empower women.

'Well. Yes. Quite right. The sticky wicket is, I'm not really what you'd call a people person. I like the horses and dogs, and my two and I just get on. I need to know how to handle the whosits and whatsits of a business, as it were.'

'What sort of thing do you need?' Gillian offers,

faltering slightly. 'Maybe I could help you. I've started looking for things to do during the day now that Clara is a bit older and I don't have so much to do at home.' Gillian looks briefly at her shoes. 'I'm glad Clara doesn't need me as much – she's not a baby, is she? She's a big girl, and that's lovely!'

I must check in with Gillian properly soon and see how she really is. Last year we talked about her wanting more babies and struggling, so perhaps it's hard to see Clara grow. I'll invite her and Clara over for a play date and chat as soon as everything settles down a bit.

'You should both come along to Women Who Win. You've both got questions, and answers, and we'd all benefit. Our first meeting is in a couple of weeks. I'll send you the details. I'd love to stop and talk more, but I promised I'd pop in on Lacey. She's being a bit weird about taking the baby out,' I say, looking at the time on my phone and wondering why the children haven't been released yet. Mrs Barnstorm, who has returned to work for afternoons only while she's recovering, is usually alarmingly prompt. Previously Head of Pastoral Care in Pre-Prep, she's never been my favourite teacher, thanks to her stern words about missing bits of ballet kit, or me sending Lyla in with the wrong colour hair ribbon, but since her recovery she's softened a bit, and moved up to Juniors, where she's occasionally given me a tight smile and a nod. After all we've been through, I take this as firm friendship.

'Oh dear, that sounds like the baby blues to me,' Finola says with a wise nod, bringing me back to the present.

'Does it? I think she's just being a bit anxious,' I respond, surprised that she's jumped on 'baby blues' so quickly.

'Mark my words, deary, that's not just anxiety or paranoia. We had a mother and foal who wouldn't leave the stable. Very depressed, she was. Ordinarily up for a sterling hack, but as soon as her foal arrived she wouldn't leave its side or the stable for love nor money.'

'Well, my friend Lacey is a woman, not a horse, and she has wanted this baby for years, so I can't imagine she feels blue at all – in fact, she seems really happy and together. I feel a bit jealous. I was such a wreck with Lyla. Lacey's quite the opposite of blue, I expect,' I say indignantly.

'I'm sure Lacey will be glad to see you either way,' adds Gillian, sensing the tension and bringing her supreme diplomat's skills to the table. She'll be ace in WWW, I think. Or the UN . . .

'I'm so pleased you'll be there at Women Who Win. I'm supposed to be making some opening remarks, so it will be great to see friendly faces.'

As soon as I finish speaking, all the children come running out. Amazingly, Lyla is holding hands with Corinthia, the class bully. There's no time to delve into this now, though, and who am I to get in the way of world peace?

TWENTY MINUTES LATER, WE are knocking on Lacey's door with three Happy Meals and three McFlurries. The golden arches went down so well last time, and why fix what isn't broken?

'Ah, we've got to stop meeting like this!' Lacey says as she opens the door, perfectly made up (though sporting some heavy-duty concealer, to my expert eye) and beaming at the goodies.

'I know! I don't have a fast food loyalty card, I just remember how it is in the early days – a hot meal isn't always on the agenda when you're up to your eyes in mess and nap—' I stop dead as I take in my surroundings. Lacey's perfectly refurbished Victorian town house is absolutely immaculate. The ornate tiles in the hall are gleaming, her white quartz countertops in the kitchen are sparkling and there is a brand-new White Company candle lit on the mantelpiece. She isn't up to her eyes in anything except Insta-perfect interiors. Even the cushions have the karate chop thing in them that everyone's doing these days.

'Wow, Lace, you're so on top of things,' I say incredulously.

'Well, I don't want anyone to think I've let myself go,' she replies, walking on into the kitchen where Willow is asleep in her vibrating bouncer. Oh, to be a baby, when you're encouraged to snooze all day.

'Nobody could ever think that about you, but you are allowed to let things go a little bit. You've had a baby, literally only weeks ago!' I say, leaning over said two-month-old and deeply inhaling that gorgeous baby smell. Gosh, she is scrummy. Lacey has dressed her in a pale peach romper with tiny ducks embroidered on the chest and a perfectly ironed white collar tucked under her chubby cheeks. I stand and watch her face snuffle about as she breathes deeply in her sleep, and reach out a hand to softly stroke her perfect little face.

'Don't wake her up,' says Lacey, a little sharply. I step back in surprise.

'Willow came out of your vagina, Lacey, didn't she?' Lyla interjects helpfully, reaching across the counter for her strawberry milkshake as if she hasn't said anything at all shocking or interrupted a slightly weird moment there.

'God, sorry, she's started getting to grips with these things,' I say to Lacey, who is laughing now I've moved away from Willow. 'Yes, Lyla, Willow did come out of Lacey's vagina.' Gillian said Clara's been asking all sorts of questions, and the best thing to do is give a frank and succinct answer. I think that did the job. She knows what's what.

'Is it still on?' Lyla says, looking at Lacey.

Oh.

'Is what still on? My vagina?' Lacey asks, trying not to laugh, and looking as if she's taking the matter very seriously.

'Yes, when she came out, did it come out or snap off too?' Lyla continues, deadpan.

'Oh. No. Willow came out of my vagina, and my

vagina stayed attached to my body. She just came *through* it.' Lacey looks over at me with eyes that say, 'What the eff do I say now?' but I am too stunned to know what to say.

'Like when sick comes out of your mouth?' Lyla clarifies. Good job, Lyla.

'Yes, Lyla. Robin, did your daughter just compare the birth of my precious baby to vomiting?' Lacey asks with a smile, though a shadow crosses her face as Willow begins to gurgle and wake.

'Yes. Yes, she did. You've got all this to come. Now give me that baby, eat this burger and try not to snap your vag off!' Note to self: have another, more detailed birds-and-bees chat with Lyla at some point soon.

It is lovely, squishing Willow and stroking her velvety little cheeks, running my fingers across her bunched-up little fists, stroking the back of her hair with its wisps of blonde stuck up in squiffy tufts where she's been lying down and telling Lacey repeatedly how gorgeous she is, but wow, I'd forgotten how much hard work a baby is.

She's currently on a three-hour schedule of feed, burp, change, cuddle time, sleep, repeat. No sooner have you sat down than you need to get up again.

Despite her mum, Terri from Dovington's (the family florist's Lacey runs) and Kath (I tried not to be a tiny bit stung that Kath seems to have time for Lacey but not for us) offering to babysit, Lacey hasn't been out of the house sans Willow yet (in fact, she doesn't seem to be going out much *with* Willow either), and says she feels guilty at the mere thought of needing time to herself.

I wonder if I'm a crappy mum for enjoying my time away from Lyla so much these days, or if I've just forgotten feeling the way Lacey does.

'It's OK to want time for you, Lace,' I say. 'There's not a mum in the world who doesn't need a break. You can't pour from an empty cup, can you?' I add as encouragingly as I can.

'I know, I know, and I don't begrudge the other mums who have breaks, but Willow's different. We tried for so long, all those desperate months, and now she's here. What kind of person goes on and on and on about wanting something so very much and then when she gets it, wants time out?'

'A really normal person, Lacey, a really normal mum,' I reassure.

We chat on about what's normal and what's not,

and end up on a tangent about half the girls we used to go to school with, followed by a joyful forty-five-minute Facebook stalk while Lyla sits in the back room playing on Karl's Nintendo Wii. God bless modern technology, eh?

WE STAY TILL KARL gets home from work at around seven, just in time to give his baby girl a cuddle before Lacey whisks her off to bed.

'What do you think to family life then, Karl?' I ask as Lacey comes downstairs again with, I notice, a freshly applied slick of lip gloss. I also notice she's reapplied concealer over the big bags under her eyes.

'It's pretty amazing! Willow is the best baby I've ever seen, and Lacey is a fantastic mum. It's pretty easy, really, isn't it, Lace?' Karl replies, beaming at his clearly shattered wife.

'Yep! Totally! Willow is amazing. Couldn't be happier,' Lacey says, walking over to squeeze her husband, with what I think might be the fakest smile I've ever seen her do in over twenty years of friendship. She didn't even smile that falsely when she fell flat on her face on the tennis courts at school, and pretended she'd done it on purpose to get out of PE!

On the drive home I can't stop thinking about Lacey. Her house is perfect, Willow is a contented and cheery baby, but she's not really going out and she looks beyond tired. Every time I try to broach the possibility that she doesn't have to be perfect, she talks about Willow being worth it all and everything being fine. But the more she says it, the more it sounds like a script. Since Finola planted that seed in my head, I've started to wonder if it is the 'baby blues'. I hope Karl has noticed. I'll drop him a message and keep an eye on her. This week's a bit manic with work bookings and Edward coming home (to my home – our home? – to live. *Whaaat?*) next week, but I could ask Kath to have Lyla after Homework Club on Wednesday and pop in on Lacey. Yes. Good. It's on the To Do list. It feels good to be this buzzy and busy. I feel like super-woman. After so many years floating through The Emptiness, where I felt far from busy and able, I'm going to hang onto this feeling with both hands!

When I pull up onto the drive and look in my rear-view mirror, I see that Lyla has already fallen asleep. I can't believe I've been a mother to her for eight years. Holding Willow tonight reminded me of how far we've come. From those intense first months to the lonely toddler years and now this, an almost-family unit. I think of Edward and how easily he's slotting into my life, and I pull my phone out of my bag while Lyla continues to sleep peacefully in her booster seat.

How's it going over there? Are you enjoying your freedom and not having soil put in your shoes?

I press send, scroll through Insta for a few seconds and a message pings back. This is what I like about Edward – no games.

It's fantastic. I've been hanging out with my American girlfriends all week but I asked one of them to put soil in my shoes to help me feel at home. How are you, gorgeous?

Ha ha. So this is fully 'home' now, is it? X

You know what they say.

What's that?

Home is where the heart is.

*I heard it was where the slimy worm is. I miss
you. And your worm. Your slimy worm.*

*I know it was meant to be sexy but
that got really gross.*

I know. Let's never speak of this again.

And with that cringeworthy faux pas, I smile and click
my phone shut, climbing out of the car, opening Lyla's
door and carrying her very heavy no-longer-a-tiny-
little-girl body into the house and up to bed.

Aside from not seeing as much of Kath as I'd like,
Lyla occasionally destroying Edward's things (but I
think – I hope – she's starting to come round . . .),
Lacey maybe struggling a bit and work being a tad
full-on, we're all ticking along nicely. And now for
some long-awaited me time, I think as I flump into
my apparently ugly sofa with a fresh bar of fruit and
nut and the TV all to myself.

SIX

THE NEXT MORNING, AS I pad around the kitchen bleary-eyed, pouring a bowl of cereal for Lyla and a cup of strong coffee for me, she drops a clanger.

'So is Edward my new dad, then?' she asks through a mouthful of Rice Krispies.

Oh my God, it's too early for this. I don't think she got the memo that I was awake till 1 a.m. worrying about Lacey feeling low and Kath being distant and all the tasks I need to do, plus work being intense and planning for the first ever WWW meeting, *and* about how maybe I need two laundry baskets now that Edward is going to live here. Or will we merge all of our dirty clothes together, and will he see my dirty knickers and will I touch his dirty socks and—

'Mu-um. Is Edward my new dad or my stepdad or my adopted dad?' Lyla asks again impatiently, and with a tiny hint of anxiety in her voice.

'He's none of those. He's just my boyfriend, so he doesn't need to have a dad title. Your dad is your dad. That's not going to change.' Maybe I haven't dealt with this as well as I thought. We've had numerous chats over the last few weeks, and I hate to see her struggle to understand what's going to happen this week but I don't know what to do. Am I moving too fast with Edward? Is it wrong to want him here with us? I wish Kath was more available to help. She's always so good at things like this. I'm going to give her a call later. If she's not too busy to chat, that is . . .

'I know Dad is Dad, but now Edward's going to come and live with us and I have to be kind to him, what will he be to me?' Lyla says plainly. She doesn't seem deeply distressed or psychologically damaged, which is good, but I can't imagine that spate of destroying Edward's things was a particularly good sign.

'He'll be your friend, I hope.' That sounds like a good answer, and she seems sold on that.

Gillian told me recently, when I offloaded the Lyla vs Edward situation over coffee, 'Children are not little adults, they don't just have our emotions but smaller.' Apparently you have to be short and simple with your responses to allow them to process the information. So, that was pretty short and sweet, I think. Look at me go, winning at MumLife.

'Corinthia's mum is getting a new daddy,' Lyla continues.

'Do you mean Corinthia's getting a new daddy?' I ask, knowing that her mum, my school nemesis, Valerie, is separated and going through a divorce.

'No. Corinthia said her mum was on FaceTime to her auntie and said, "What I need is a sugar daddy", so now Corinthia knows her mum is getting a new dad. Durrr,' Lyla adds at the end for my benefit, as if I'm being completely ridiculous not understanding all this immediately. 'And he's going to give her loads of sweets.'

Trust Valerie to actively search for a man

specifically to pay her way. I really can't bear that woman.

'Also, I actually know what a sugar daddy is,' Lyla says triumphantly.

'Do you now?' I say, outwardly confident. Children are like wolves – you can't let them smell your fear.

'Yep. Corinthia asked, and her mum said it was a man to make her very happy indeed.' She nods firmly, as though that is the case closed.

'Well. Fabulous. Good for Corinthia and her mum, then. Now, shall we hurry up with this breakfast so we can get going, please?'

'Edward makes you very happy indeed. Is he your sugar daddy?' Lyla says, ignoring my plea for us to 'get going'.

'No, he's my boyfriend.'

'And not my sugar daddy?'

'No, Daddy Simon is your dad. You have one dad, and that's him. Edward is not your dad. If one day in the far, far future we decided to get married, then he'd be your stepdad. But Simon, your dad, will always be your dad. I don't want or need a sugar daddy, and my real dad is Grandad Wilde in Cornwall.' Good, keeping things short and simple. Nobody is confused at all.

'But Grandad Wilde, who is your actual dad, isn't your sugar daddy, because he is not a man that makes you very happy indeed, is he?' Lyla says, still not eating her cereal. My God, we're going to be so late, and I'm going to be on the Shit Mum list again.

'Grandad Wilde is my dad and he's very nice.' There. Pulling it back. Closing it down.

'But he never comes to see us, and Grandma Wilde is horrible and thinks you're fat, and when you're on the phone to them your eyebrows do this.' She mimics me frowning. 'And I heard you tell Lacey that Grandma is a self-absorbed, middle-class arsehole,' she finishes, with a massive smile on her face as though she's Sherlock Holmes and she's just cracked the case of the century.

'Oh my God, Lyla Blue Wilde! First, you listen too much, and second, I did not say that about Grandma, and third, we are now running very late, so eat that cereal in silence and let's get bloody going!' I say, not calmly, shortly or sweetly.

'You *tell* me to listen, and you definitely did say that,' she sniggers into her Rice Krispies.

Good grief, motherhood is a hoot today. But my little Lyla Blue seems happy with the fact that no one is going to try to be her new daddy, and that's OK with me! I take a breath and feel a tiny knot of worry start to unravel a little.

THAT LITTLE WORRY KNOT might have unravelled a bit as far as Lyla and her woes go, but now I've got my own set of panics and preoccupations to think about. Edward has been here a week, and I love it. It's really good. Really, um, cosy.

On Official Arrival Day Lyla and I made him a banner for the front door saying: WELCOME HOME EDWARD, with pictures of hearts and butterflies and just one or two slimy worms (Lyla assured me these were for comedy effect), and I cleared out space in my wardrobe and a few drawers in the bathroom unit. Obviously I was happy to do that, because for such a long time I've thought about what it would be like to have a man living with me, with *us*. And not just any man, of course, a lovely man like Edward. It was actually good to go through my possessions and do all those things everyone tells you to do these days: decide which sparked joy and which didn't and thank them, and then fold things so that they stand up. I'm on board with all that.

I'm just not sure I'm on board with all the other changes, but if I say something I'll sound like I'm moaning, which I'm not. Just, you know, maybe drawing his attention to the fact that nobody needs to leave shaving hairs in the sink, or that he has a box file neatly set aside for him in the office downstairs (I've glorified that a bit – we have a little box room/playroom to the side of the house that we use for the dusty old desktop, my work kit and a few of Lyla's bigger toys), so he doesn't need to leave his letters or paperwork all over the kitchen worktops. It's no big deal, so I'm really trying to be chilled about it all. But who takes their socks off in bed and leaves them floating around the bottom of the duvet? And also, good God, I've never known anyone to have showers as long as he does!

I've decided I'm not going to say anything about it because it's early days – and anyway, he probably has a list of things I do that make him bite his tongue. But after waiting, and thinking so hard about if this is right for me and Lyla, I'm not going to spoil it by getting het up over a bit of housekeeping. It's not a big deal. Honest.

Plus, there have been some really lovely moments, too. Like when I got home and found Edward reading to Lyla. Sometimes she tells me she's too big to have stories read to her, now she can read so well herself, but I know there's still magic in someone telling you a story, so it was beautiful to catch them curled up together with a book.

'Penny for them?' Edward says as he walks over to the bed, leaving his towel on the floor. Breezy, I'm breezy, I remind myself.

'I was just thinking how lucky I am to have a man like you here all the time,' I say, smiling. In fairness, as a very attractive, very naked (no socks!) Edward gets into my bed, I don't feel quite so annoyed by a few abandoned towels and messy desks.

'Not as lucky as I am to be lying next to this beautiful woman,' he says, moving on top of me.

We hear a creak on the landing and pause. I'm convinced it's Lyla waking up and about to wander in. I'll have to make up some excuse, and fret for six months that she can't unsee her mother being straddled by her new boyfriend, but no, it's not. The door stays shut; no more floorboards creak. Maybe it was just the wind. And so a rather wonderful time ensues with no interruptions, no annoyance about sharing my space and a pretty smug confidence that everything's coming up roses.

SEVEN

MAY

'BEING TOO BUSY IS a luxury problem,' my mum used to say as she paraded around telling everyone she was 'far too busy to sit down', despite not having a job, her daughter being fairly self-sufficient (out of necessity) and my dad basically living in the shed or at work. But as April turns to May, my superwoman vibe is fading, and I'm not sure 'luxurious' is the word I'd choose to describe my life.

I'm going to have to call Mum soon for our catch-up. We don't speak much, but if I don't keep her up to date on things she rings me, annoyed, so it's better to get in there first. She and Dad moved to Cornwall when Lyla was only a baby, to 'get away from it all'. Thanks, Mum. She's engrossed in the Women's Institute and the Rotary Club, and Dad has retired to tinker about in his shed. Last I heard he was building a boat. Mum called it a 'sea vessel' repeatedly.

Mum and I have never really seen eye to eye. She's like a short, stocky army officer, barking orders and feeling constantly disappointed that her only child never got a 'real job', and just 'floats about fluffing hair and blushing on powders'. I think my splitting up with Simon, Lyla's dad, was the final straw for her, despite the fact that he cheated on me. According to her he was 'having a blip, as all men do', and I should have spent my days working out where I went wrong to cause him to 'turn his eye'. Boys will be boys after all, eh?

A couple of years ago, on a rare weekend visit down to them, Lyla announced that she was a feminist. While I high-fived my daughter, Mum said, 'Good God, Robin, do you want her to be one of these overweight lesbian girls with no hope?' and as you can imagine, a flaming row broke out. I wish I could say that was the most offensive thing she's ever said to me, but it's not. Dad doesn't say anything quite as hideous, but he doesn't stop her. I think over the years she's ground him down so far that he doesn't actually have any opinions anymore. His father was a domineering, formidable character, so it makes sense that he's a bit, well, useless.

You can see why we keep our distance. I find a monthly phone call usually does the trick. I think Kath fills Dad in (Dad is Kath's older brother) here and there, but they haven't been close for as long as I can remember. Ironically, childless Kath has always been the most nurturing of all of them.

Anyway, life is busy. Edward's been back for about a month now, and every time he suggests I slow down or relax, I remind him that I don't need to: I like being this busy. There was a time – a couple of difficult years – when all my days were sad and empty and I felt like Lyla was the only person that needed me. Now, though, it's quite the opposite. And I never, ever want to go back to The Emptiness again.

I'm doing what I can for Lacey. Honestly, she is becoming more and more withdrawn. I've been over twice to see her and Willow in the last few weeks, and it just seems like Lacey spends all her time keeping her house spotless, making sure Willow is cared for and always in a beautiful outfit, plastering a smile on her face and feeling like she has to be perfect. But she's spending no time on herself. She tells me she's been out and about with Willow, but I'm starting to wonder if she's telling the truth. She's fragile under that smooth facade. I've asked her over here twice, and offered to go to the baby groups with her, but she finds reasons not to. Last week I told her it might be worth mentioning to her health visitor that she's being a bit hard on herself, but she brushed me off crossly, pointed at a placid and smiling Willow, and firmly said she was fine.

If all the women in the world set up a bank account and put a pound in every time they used the word 'fine' to mean 'alone', 'sad', 'afraid', 'stressed', 'tired', 'angry', 'struggling', 'anxious' or 'downright bloody dreadful', that would be world poverty solved in a fortnight.

I spoke to Edward about my concerns last night over dinner, which in itself is a bit of a rarity because I've spent most evenings working at home (cleaning my kit from a job that day or sorting it for the next, looking into venues for our new live beauty tutorials project, working on proposals to expand our use of social media to raise MADE IT's profile and exploring creative ideas for forthcoming jobs. It's getting harder and harder to squeeze my job in around school hours, and it's spilling into the evenings a bit. I don't mind, though, not too much, anyway). But when I told Edward about Lacey, he listened, because he's wonderful, and then suggested a night out with her to spark her back to life.

I couldn't imagine she'd be up for a full night out, but maybe just getting her out of the house would be a start. It was a good plan. Then I remembered we were supposed to be having 'us' time. I switched my focus on to our new living situation.

'How are you finding it so far?' I asked nervously. 'You know, living here. With us. Are you enjoying it?' I was sipping a glass of wine at the breakfast bar as Edward stirred the tagliatelle and Lyla sat in the front room rotting her brain with TV.

'Yeah. It's much like it was before, except you've kindly donated me an extra drawer in the bathroom and eight inches of wardrobe,' he teased. 'I might need a couple more inches when I bring the rest of my stuff over from New York.'

He always knows how to keep things light, which I like. I'm all for a bit of the serious stuff here and there, but last year was so intense this is definitely what we need, for now. Lightness and laughter.

'I promise you, once I sort more of my stuff out there'll be more space. I've made a good start with my special folding.' I laughed.

'No, no, I get it. I can see why you need an entire drawer full of ski stuff when you hit the slopes so often,' he said, stirring the crème fraiche in with the onions and garlic.

'Look! I don't know when I'll need that again! I went skiing at uni, and was amazing at it!'

'Best on the green slopes, I'd imagine! I can't wait to take you back there one day and you can show me your moves.'

'I'll show you my moves later, if you're lucky,' I said, crossing to the stove and leaning up behind him with my hands round his waist.

'What moves, Mummy? Can I see them too?' Lyla asked as she stood at the door. 'Stop touching him so much, Mummy. Can I have a biscuit?'

'Ah. Ha, ha. No moves. My ski moves. Yes, here you go,' I said, passing her a pink wafer and shuffling her back off to the lounge.

'Why did you give her that when I'm cooking

dinner?' Edward asked with a slight note of annoyance to his voice.

'I just wanted her to toddle off so we can carry on with this nice moment.' I slid my hand back round his waist. 'She's not going to fill up on one wafer.'

'I know, but you're satiating every demand she makes,' he said, not really going with the flow of the 'nice moment'.

'It wasn't a demand,' I retorted, removing my hand and taking up my spot by the breakfast bar. 'And I'm not ready to discuss my parenting decisions with you yet, Edward. She asked to have one biscuit, and I decided to let her.'

'OK. Yep. I'm sorry, Robin. Of course. You're the boss.' Edward didn't look up from the saucepan.

Jeez. Whenever I cook, I nibble bits here and there and don't fill up. I mean, I suppose she's smaller than me, and she probably didn't need to have a biscuit, but I was doing it for us, so we could have a moment together. There's no need for him to be such an arse. At least he apologised.

Not wanting to make a meal of it, ho, ho, excuse the pun, I let it go, called Lyla in to help set the table (see, Edward? She's a well-adjusted, helpful, responsible child and I'm not a shit biscuit-dishing-out mother) and, tensions forgotten, we all sat round the table to eat Edward's 'signature tagliatelle', garlic bread and salad like a proper little family. It was bliss.

'What do you think, Lyla? Yummy?' Edward asked optimistically. He was probably just hoping not to be called a worm/rat/mole/ant again.

'I think it's better than Mummy's cooking!' she said with a glint in her eye as she looked at me over her fork.

'Ha! I've made it!' Edward cheered, raising his glass of Malbec high in the air in celebration.

'But not as good as Auntie Kath's,' she added coolly.

'Aha! Close, but no cigar, my friend! Auntie Kath's cooking is the best in all the land, isn't it, Lyla?' I declared happily. The tagliatelle was phenomenal. Having this man in my life really is excellent.

'Yes, but we never see her anymore because she loves Colin so much and only ever wants to make lavender things and see him,' she said sadly.

'Oh Lyla, that's not quite true. I saw her the other day. We went to visit Lacey together and she gave Willow a cuddle. I think she pops in on Lacey quite a lot, actually.'

'Why doesn't she pop in on us then?'

'Well, I'm at work all day, and then, in the after-noons, Colin finishes at his flower warehouse and comes to see her, and they have yummy dinners and work on her lavender creations. And she knows we're settling Edward in with us,' I said in sing-songy primary school tones, even though I'm also feeling a bit stung that Kath makes time for the baby and not for us, or not as much as she used to.

'Settling him in? He's not a dog, Mummy!' Lyla giggled through a mouthful of garlic bread.

'Woof!' barked Edward, and the whole 'serious chat' fell to bits and mass woofing and dog impressions ensued. It wasn't romantic, exactly, but it was lovely.

EIGHT

THE DAY HAS COME. Tonight is the inaugural meeting of Women Who Win. I'm going to stand up in front of everyone, with Gloria, and say a few words. I feel a tense pang in my stomach. A solid twenty to twenty-five women are attending, which is a lot more than you'd usually expect for an event in the school hall, and certainly more people than I've ever spoken in front of before. I'm not a painfully shy person, but I've never been one for public speaking, so I'm feeling that sick swirl of dread in my stomach but trying really hard to suppress it and focus on setting up.

Gloria is one of those women who give off good vibes – who make you want to try things, do things, be things you thought you couldn't. And what's more, she manages to be inspirational without being preachy, or making you feel like you're not good enough as you are. She's a total beauty, and 95 per cent of that is her attitude. She isn't tall and sinewy like the models I work with, and she doesn't have huge, full lips and lashes longer than a giraffe's, but my God she is absolutely stunning. Gloria is average height, very full-figured, with dyed platinum-blonde hair the shade my mum would say 'nobody can take seriously', bright pink nails, always a bit (or a lot) of cleavage, the most fabulously bold-coloured wardrobe you've ever seen and a walk absolutely dripping with confidence. If you were my mum, you'd look at her and think: 'chubby blonde bimbo'. If you met her and had half a minute of conversation with her, you'd think: 'smart, assertive, warm, badass boss'! She's actually inspired me a little bit to break out of the jeans-and-top mould (which I've been really stretching these days with jeans and a jazzy, tucked-in shirt) and go for some short tea dresses with tights. Tonight I'm actually wearing a short leopard-print dress, black tights, black biker boots encrusted with pearls instead of studs, gold hoop earrings and red lipstick. I feel utterly brilliant, and judging by Edward's rather keen response (and the subsequent quickie we had, pushed up against the towel rail in the en suite), he thinks I look pretty brilliant too.

The tension I'm feeling isn't appearance-based (I've got my armour on), but intelligence-based. Gloria says I'm a boss, Natalie says she's thrilled with our progress, Edward marvels and Kath says (when we had a nice chat on the phone the other day to catch up – I hope we can do that face-to-face soon) what I'm doing is 'lovely' (though frankly, I could take to crafting necklaces out of dried cow dung and she'd call them 'lovely' – Kath is always my cheer squad, whatever I do). Even Lyla sometimes says, 'Oh Mum, you're so awesome', which makes me melt from the inside out. The thing is, it's really hard to let yourself think you're awesome, isn't it? I'm worried someone will ask me a question I can't answer, or will start talking to me and I'll have no clue at all what to say. I feel better than I've felt for ages, but I still feel like I'm constantly just blagging it – both WWW and life.

Does anyone else feel like that, I wonder? Or is it just me?

'Right!' calls Gloria assertively with her hair and boobs bouncing at once. 'The chairs are laid out, we've got twenty-two booked in to come and I've got a stack of clipboards and pens for you to dish out when people arrive. That OK?' she asks.

'Yes! Totally. What will we be doing with them?'

'Well, after the intros and ice-breaking chit-chat, I thought we could all write down and share our goal, give us all something to hook our coat on, you know?'

'Yes,' I say, wondering what my goal will be. 'What if you don't have a goal?'

'Everyone who is moving forward has a goal.' Gloria sashays off to put the sign outside that will usher people through to the hall. 'If you're not sure, someone in this room will inspire you. You'll see.'

I've been in the school hall my fair share of times for carol services, end-of-year plays, parents' evenings and the charity spa night I helped run last year (still proud of that), but there's something nostalgic about it, nevertheless. It doesn't matter what primary school you're in, there's always that smell of poster paints and rubber-soled PE shoes. The hall feels so homey and wholesome, with one wall covered in paintings 'inspired by our garden', and another with those great pieces of hinged gym apparatus that have coloured metal hoops or climbing ladders embedded into them.

The chairs, instead of standing in their usual rows facing the stage, have been moved by the caretakers into little groups with a small coffee table in the middle, and on each table is a stack of pieces of A5 paper emblazoned with 'What is your goal?', a roll of large stickers saying 'Hello! My name is—', a few glasses of water and, rather sweetly, a small vase holding a single pink or white carnation.

Showtime. The hall starts filling up, and I give people their clipboards and ask them to find a seat. As you'd imagine, there's much dithering over which cluster to sit in, and I feel for the lone women who have to join a group that's already seated, but I'm pleased to see that everyone is being really friendly. Some are starting to stick their name badges on and introduce themselves. I always think these moments are anxiety-inducing, so I feel weirdly proud of all these brave women who have stepped into the unknown and attended our event tonight. Gloria comes over to tell me that she'll tackle the intros, so

I don't need to give my 'few remarks' this time. She tells me this in a very apologetic tone, but I'm secretly pleased, like when a friend cancels a night out that you didn't really want to go on anyway. Although a (tiny) part of me was looking forward to overcoming my fear.

I find Finola and Gillian in a group of four seats at the back and join them, saving the last seat for Gloria. I know she is going to be running a quick-fire Q&A, so I'm not sure if she'll need a seat, but saving one on her behalf feels like the role of a Vice President. I look up and see her at the front, striding about with total confidence, as though this is a very comfortable environment for her. Her old job was in international PR, and since she moved here she's freelanced in the same field, so I know she's a capable woman, but right now I'm in total awe of her! The room's as full as it is going to get and Gloria takes a sip of water to clear her throat, when one last person opens the heavy hall doors to come in.

'Golly me! Sorry I'm late!' Storie, Simon's girlfriend, whispers as she hurries over towards the spare seat next to me, but I divert her to the welcome table with the attendee list. 'I've banned electrical timepieces from the house, you know, because of the radiation energy, so we're relying on solar and it just didn't happen today.'

I've no idea where to even begin with that sentence. Why has she banned 'electrical timepieces'? How did the sun 'not happen'?

'Storie! I didn't have you on our sign-up sheet,' I whisper back as Gloria starts her welcoming speech.

'I don't agree with forms and unnecessary commitments. I commit with my heart,' Storie says loftily, removing her patchwork bag and pulling it on the floor with her stainless steel eco bottle.

'OK, we just need to know who's coming for the numbers,' I say, gesturing to the sheet.

'I am.'

'Yes, I know that now. Welcome,' I add, so I don't seem bitter or petulant.

I'm not bitter, I'm fully and totally over it, but that still doesn't mean I like Storie. When Lyla was born, her dad, Simon, didn't cope well. It's a shock to anyone's system having a baby, but Simon really struggled. He spent more and more time at work and less and less time with me. Feeling isolated, I slowly but steadily slipped into depression, and he announced that he needed to 'find himself' with a three-month trip to Tibet.

Looking back, I don't know why I didn't kick up a huge fuss and fight this, but at the time I was lost, deep, deep in The Emptiness. The depression meant that I just didn't have the strength in me to care about anything. My only focus was getting up each day and faking normality for Lyla. I'd go through the motions of motherhood, take her to the park to feed the ducks, smile at old ladies who cooed over her in the super-market, post the adorable pictures of her in her wellies and bobble hat on Facebook, but then spend my evenings alone, lying in the bath or under my duvet, wondering if I would ever feel that fizz of joy again.

I did feel it again. It took a while, but I found that the only one who was going to rescue me from that hole was me, and I'm bloody proud of myself for it. Simon, though, found another way to be rescued from his own hole and that was courtesy of a Mother Earth-obsessed nineteen-year-old backpacker from Peterborough called Caroline, who insists on being called Storie ('with an "ie", please').

I don't blame Storie for breaking up my engagement to Simon – it was dead in the water way before she

e

came along – but it's her total lack of acknowledge-
ment that I might not want to be friends with her
that irks me. To her, we're all just children of the
earth, free to waft around together, eating nuts and
seeds or something.

Thinking about it a moment longer, she might well
be right there: perhaps we should all feel peace in
our hearts and connect on a deeper level. But then I
remember that last year she let my daughter eat
unidentified foliage on a wild mushroom foraging
trip and Lyla was sick for days, so fuck that, I'm not
her buddy. I leave her by the welcome table and go
back to my seat with Gillian and Finola.

Gloria finishes welcoming us all and moves the talk
on to how the quick-fire Q&A part of the evening will
work. Essentially we're all going to have a couple of
minutes in our seated groups to introduce ourselves,
share one of our ideas or goals or reasons for coming
tonight, and then we can decide if we want to share
a 'Q' and the rest of the room are welcome to offer
suggestions to 'A' it. I am quite excited to be the
teacher's pet, and write down my goals and ideas.

I like writing things down, but the politely reserved
Brit in me feels highly uncomfortable with the

thought of sharing a problem or offering to help someone else. I don't think I'm alone in feeling dread at the words 'icebreaker' – it seems to wipe my mind. There is *nothing* interesting to say about me. What if everyone thinks I'm stupid? What if I answer something and someone thinks I'm being really patronising? And why am I doing this to myself again when I should be remembering that Gloria chose me because I'm not any of those things? Come on, Robin, stop putting yourself down. Instead I'm going to take a leaf out of Gloria's confident American book and get stuck in!

I wave Gloria over to come and sit with us now she's finished her talk, but she declines, saying she's going to circulate round the groups, and ushers Storie, who's been floating about looking at the pictures of gardens on the wall, to come and sit in the seat I've saved. Inwardly I'm horrified, but outwardly force a smile. I'm not going to be unkind to her. Not out loud, anyway.

'Hey, guys,' she says, sitting down and offering a wave to Gillian and Finola, who of course already know who she is and offer hellos and how-are-yous in return. I notice with annoyance that she has peeled off the name label I gave her. Maybe she doesn't believe in labels. Or names. Who bloody knows.

'So . . .' I decide to lead, because I'm VP and because I'm a strong, confident woman who will not be intimidated by the woman who shagged my fiancé on a mountainside in Tibet while I was at home looking after our daughter and suffering from post-natal depression. I'm bigger and better than this.

'So,' I start again, 'Storie, this is Finola. She has a goal of setting up an equestrian business and has two children here at the school. This is Gillian, a problem-solver extraordinaire who has a lovely little girl at the school. And you already know me. Everyone, this is Storie, Lyla's dad's girlfriend.'

We all take a moment to say hello again because we're British and so must be overly polite at all times.

'I think Gloria was hoping we'd have a chat about our aims for a few minutes,' I lead. 'I'm mainly hoping to learn from everyone else and perhaps find a bit of inspiration on how to balance everything, because I'm finding that quite pressing at the moment. Not impos-sible or too tough, though,' I add quickly. 'Just, you know, with the gorgeous Edward wanting to spend so much time with me . . .' I say, looking at Storie, even though I know it's a really weak and petty dig. 'On top of all my work stuff and motherhood, it's quite the juggling act.'

'I know exactly what you mean, because I'm sort of the opposite – I'd like to have more in my life to balance,' says Gillian diplomatically, with a sweet smile but a hint of sadness behind the eyes.

'Well, dearie, perhaps you can be the one to help me, because I haven't the foggiest how to get my lessons off the ground! I've got the horses, the stables, the time and the oomph, but I don't know how to get the customers and then sort all the finances and other affairs, as it were,' Finola says with dismay.

'Maybe I am the person for you, then, Finola,' Gillian says calmly. 'Perhaps we could get together and work out your rates and availability, and I could start marketing you a little bit to local schools or clubs. I've dabbled in social media a bit, too, so I think I could manage a Facebook page or something,' she finishes with a big smile.

'This is amazing! This is exactly the kind of thing we wanted to see coming from Women Who Win!' I say, thrilled to see positivity and collaboration happening right in front of me.

'I think it's really important to fully blend yourself with the horse's spirit,' Storie says slowly, staring meaningfully into the distance.

'I'm sorry, dear?' Finola says, confused. She is the most black and white, matter-of-fact woman you'll ever meet. She often compares mothering to looking after dogs, and her husband regularly looks a little bit afraid of her.

'Working with animals. You are intertwining your spirit with theirs in a way you simply cannot with other humans,' Storie clarifies.

Finola blinks at her as though she's just spoken in an entirely different language. I know Storie, so I can just about follow what she means, but I know Finola as well, so I can imagine she'll be wanting to throw up at the idea of blending spirits with your horse.

'I think that sounds really lovely, Storie,' Gillian says, rescuing the situation as always.

'Yes. Not at all like utter poppycock!' Finola says, trying to be agreeable but failing entirely.

'Thanks, Storie, that's a really, er, different take on things,' I say, regretting my jibe earlier and trying to let her have her moment and be nice. 'Did you have anything you wanted to bring to the group?'

'Ah no, not really,' she wafts. 'I just like to be in rooms full of thinking women. The energy in here is so vibrant,' she says airily, gazing round the hall. 'I'd love to try some gong bath healing in here.'

I am actually feeling quite enamoured by her purity and simple love for others, but then she brings out the gong bath chat and we are back to square one. Before I can reply, Gloria has taken her place at the front of the room again and is about to ask us to start sharing our in-group chats with the wider audience.

It's amazing how quickly the hour passes. People are a bit timid to share at the start, but soon everyone is chipping in and contributing. A brilliant evening of women talking, sharing, problem-solving and connecting, and by the end, after my free glass of room-temperature white wine, I'm completely buzzing with inspiration. Sometimes it takes an evening like this not just to celebrate our differences, but also to realise the struggles we all share. It's reassuring to see that behind everyone's glitzy Instas or stories of their booming businesses, these women are juggling, struggling and winging it at times, too. But somehow, bring us all together in a room and we'll find answers, friends, mentors and goals.

And while I might have had my doubts that I was a Woman Who Wins, tonight I'm feeling it.

As everyone files out, I watch Gloria take the time to chat to every woman, thank her for coming and make her feel amazing. I busy myself stacking up the chairs and moving all the little vases of flowers onto one table.

'Well, I'd call that a success!' Gloria calls over to me as the last woman leaves.

'So would I! It's amazing what you can do with two child-free hours and some good thinking time,' I say, utterly enthused.

'Oh yeah?' Gloria pushes.

'Yep! Gillian and Finola are basically going into business, and I didn't push my ex-fiancé's new girl-friend off a chair, sooo . . .' I trail off.

'So pretty successful then!' We both laugh.

'I thought you welcomed everyone so beautifully, made them feel at ease and ran your group really well,' Gloria says. 'Next time you'll have to come up front with me!'

After the success of the evening, my nerves have vanished and I actually feel like I could do it; I feel so far away from that secretly-glad-she-cancelled vibe.

'Gloria, I bloody well will!' I say with a big nod.

'There she is! Ms Wilde has ar*rived*!' Gloria cheers.

We carry on talking about some of the other goals, some of our own goals and what we want from the group, until it gets dark. As I walk out to my car, I can feel a bubble of excitement in my tummy and drive home feeling lighter than I have in ages.

NINE

FTER MY CHAT WITH Gloria, I don't actually get home till gone 10 p.m. As soon as I walk in, I get my kit out and start making sure I have everything for my MUA job tomorrow. It's only a local shoot, but I still want to make sure I have anything they might ask for. Quite often we'll get booked to do a couple of hours on an individual shoot, and although we're now moving into much bigger projects like London Fashion Week or film work, we're never too big for our boots to say yes to a local blogger who wants hair and make-up for some lovely outfit shots, or for bread and butter jobs like weddings and school proms. Tomorrow I'm doing some make-up work for a local model who is having new headshots taken, and I'm looking forward to a more relaxed afternoon with the kind of job I started out on.

'Are you going to come up and watch *Luther* with me?' Edward calls softly from the bedroom. We've been working our way through all the seasons. We've both already watched it, but not together, so it feels nice to have a 'thing'. Is there anything more joyous than shared love for a box set?

'I will, but I just need to sort my kit, make Lyla's packed lunch for tomorrow, check her uniform's ironed and quickly do my Insta,' I shout up. I'm so pumped from my evening I feel totally like I can ace that list.

'Sign her up for school lunches and sack off the Insta!' he calls back.

'I can't! It's not my personal one, it's my work one. You know I'm growing my MUA profile to boost MADE IT, and I was told to post three times a day for maximum results, so I want to post me sorting my kit,' I call up again, getting a bit frustrated now that I'm having to explain all this, and feeling like I have to rush.

Silence. Either he's totally accepting of me pouring myself into my extracurriculars and my job and my child, or he's sulking. Jolly good.

'Do you want me to make Lyla's lunch?' he calls down, breaking the silence.

'No, it's all right, I can handle it. I know how she likes the sandwiches cut. She won't eat them if I don't do them a certain way. Thank you, though!' I semi-yell back up, forgetting about my sleeping child as I try to convince myself as much as him that I have everything under control.

I rush through my tasks, shoving Lyla's packed lunch in the fridge ready for tomorrow (yes, I have perfected the art of the 'morning routine' by organ-ising the night before, and yes, I am officially a goddess), take a grid shot of my kit and do a few stories about its contents (oh yesss, double goddess now) and find that Lyla's uniform from today is clean enough to just have a shake and a quick squirt of Febreze (you can't be a goddess at everything). Lovely.

I creep upstairs ready to give my handsome man a big squeeze, tell him about Women Who Win and to shout at Luther for being such a brilliant but bent police officer, but he's asleep (Edward, that is, not

Luther!). Well, that's taken the wind out of my sails. But to be honest, I'm so knackered I don't really mind.

TODAY IS GIRLS' DAY! We've been longing for it. Edward had booked to go down to London this weekend to scout out designers at an interiors fair, and then to stay with his parents in Hampshire. I'll miss him, of course, but Lyla and I are so, so excited about a whole day with Auntie Kath. It's been so long since we've had a proper, full day together and I think Lyla and I have both been feeling a bit empty for it. Don't get me wrong, I'm pleased that Kath's found love with Colin and fulfilment with her indie lavender business, but I do miss having her around so much. Still, life goes on, and the right thing is to be happy for her.

'I'm going to miss you,' I say to Edward as he puts on his shoes, sitting at the bottom of the stairs by the front door.

'I know, but it's only a few days, and absence makes the heart grow fonder,' he says, tying the laces.

'No it doesn't. Sex and wine and gifts make it fonder,' I joke, trying to sit on his lap, preventing any further shoe-putting-on and leaning in for a kiss.

'Urgh, Mummy, you're so gross!' Lyla announces, suddenly appearing at the top of the stairs. Honestly, she's like a truffle pig. If ever there's even a whiff of me having a nice adult moment with Edward, she's there.

'It's not gross, it's lovely! You'll feel like this about someone one day,' I reply huffily, heaving myself off Edward with a bit less grace than I'd have hoped.

'I won't. It's gross!' And with that, she floats off back to her room. By now Edward has his shoes on and is picking up his bag.

'You can sit on my lap again when I'm back. But naked. And not on the stairs,' he whispers as we sneak a cuddle by the door.

'Well, there's something to look forward to then. Perhaps if you're really lucky, I'll—'

'Oo-ooo, only me!' sing-songs Kath as she opens the door and comes right in, bashing her bag into Edward's back, sending him crashing over me and me into the wall mirror.

'Oh my bloody God! Can I ever just have a moment!' I say, exasperated.

'Nice to see you too, lovey!' Kath replies. 'I'll give you two lovebirds a minute.' She plods off through to the kitchen.

'KAAATTHHH!!' Lyla screams with utter joy as she hears her at the door and thunders down the stairs, barrelling past us into the kitchen to say hello to her, entirely ignoring Edward.

There's no time for me to finish telling Edward just what I had in mind for him, and anyway, the moment has passed. But I still get goosebumps as he leans in close.

'I love that you tried,' he says in a voice that just melts me. 'We'll get our quiet moment soon, I'm sure . . . goodbye,' Edward says all in one breath as he reaches for his suede weekender bag, slings it over his shoulder, gives me a quick peck of a kiss and walks out the door.

I join Lyla and Kath in the kitchen.

'Sorry, Kath, it's all go this morning – well, every morning! I'm glad you're here, I've missed you!' I say, giving her a hug and then feeling the thud of Lyla falling into my side to join in.

'We've both missed you!' Lyla adds.

'I've missed you all, too! I kept meaning to come

over, and it's not because I don't love you both, you know that. I've just had every day full! I've been helping Colly at the warehouse first thing in the morning. He takes the first delivery at five a.m., so it's a brisk start! Then I nip home and cook everyone some bacon sandwiches and bring them back. They're all so lovely over there. Then in the afternoon, after I've walked Mollie, I set to with my lavender creations! I've met loads of florists and shop owners through the warehouse, and a lot of them are stocking my bath bombs, creams, bubbles and whatnot. It's quite amazing, really, at my age! I'm actually starting to make a bit of money. Look at these fancy business cards Colly had made for me.'

'They're amazing! You're amazing, and make amazing things! They'll be stocking Lavender Lovies in Harrods before you know it!' I enthuse.

'I know!' says Kath, putting the kettle on and then reaching into her bag for the cake tin she's brought with her. 'Moira said she's never had so much intimacy since using my body creams. She said I should call it "Lovemaking Lavender Cream" and apply to one of those Dragons' Dens on the telly! Who doesn't want a bottle of lovemaking, eh?' She chuckles to herself.

I feel a bit disturbed thinking about her and Moira discussing their sex lives, but thankfully Lyla saves me.

'Auntie Kath, I've missed you so much. Are you going to stay all day today, please? Are we going to make things? Did you bring cake in that tin?' Lyla gabbles all three questions hopefully.

'I know! I'm sorry! I'd love to stay all day. We can make whatever you like, and yes, I've brought a whole chocolate orange cake,' Kath says with her usual warm smile.

'Are there proper slices of chocolate orange on top?' Lyla asks now, actually jumping up and down perilously on her bar stool. I lunge across the room to put my hands round her waist.

Kath takes the tin over and, very slowly, lifts the lid and voila! There are swirls made of chocolate orange slices and the sweet, chocolatey smell of freshly baked cake.

'Yesss!' whoops Lyla, jumping into my arms and nearly causing me to topple over for the second time this morning.

'That looks like an utter triumph, Kath!' I say, already wanting a piece.

'Well, it's the weekend, and I'm with some of my best girls, so let's have cake for breakfast!' Kath says in celebration.

Just as I'm about to ask what on earth she means by 'some of' (I mean, surely we're *the* best girls to her), my phone buzzes. I look down at the screen to see 'Lacey' flashing up and take it into the other room. It's so nice to hear from her. I'll invite her over to join us for our breakfast cake feast.

'Helloo-ooo, Ms Robin Wilde, BFF Extraordinaaa-aire,' I say in my poshest and, in my opinion, most comedy gold tone.

'Robiiinnn,' sobs Lacey.

'Oh, no! Sorry for the silly voice. Are you OK? What's wrong?' I prattle, instantly panicked, as Lacey's not the sort to phone me crying.

'I can't, I can't, I-I don't know, I just . . .' she sobs between each word, trying to catch her breath and compose herself.

'Lacey, is Willow OK?'

'Ye-esss,' she blubs.

'OK. That's good. Are *you* all right?' Kath has clearly heard the serious tone and comes into the lounge. She is mouthing and gesturing like one of those

American baseball coaches. I have literally no idea what she is trying to communicate to me, but it is really off-putting.

'I am, but honest to God, I can't fucking believe it.' Lacey's voice has gone from utter despair to anger, so I know she is physically safe at least. I can hear Willow starting to cry in the background and then Lacey's sobs begin all over again.

'Lacey, do you want me to come over?' I ask softly.

'No, I'm fine. You're having a lovely morning with Edward and Lyla. I'm fine,' she says through the sound of her own and Willow's increasingly ear-piercing cries.

'OK, well, it isn't true, is it? You're not fine, you've rung me crying. Edward isn't here. It's just me, Lyla and Kath, and you sound like you're in a real state. I'm going to get myself together and then I'm going to come over, even if it's just for an hour to hold Willow while you have a nice bath, OK?' I say in my sternest but kindest mummy voice.

'OK,' she almost whispers. 'Thank you.'

I hang up and turn to both Kath and Lyla, who are standing there, agog, waiting to hear what's going on.

'Mummy, are you missing our fun Kath day?' Lyla says, panicked.

'Was that Lacey? Is she all right? She seemed a bit low when I saw her on Thursday but I thought it was just tiredness,' Kath adds.

Just how often is Kath going over to see Lacey and Willow? I don't have time to go into that – I just know I need to get proper clothes on (I'm still in an old tee and velour joggers) and get to my best friend.

'Right, Lacey's upset and we've got three options,' I say firmly.

Kath and Lyla look at me, ready for orders.

'Either we all go round and cheer her up, just me and Lyla go over and cheer her up, or I leave Lyla here with you, Kath, and I go on my own and cheer her up. Which shall we do?'

'I want to see the baby!' Lyla says instantly, jigging about on the spot.

'No, she's been a bit flat the last few times I've been round. She just needs her friend. You go on your own, lovey, and I'll stay here with my best girl. We can make fairy cakes with blobs of jam in them and then if there's time we can go for a walk by the river and pick some nice flowers to make little posies,'

Kath says, looking at Lyla, who looks suddenly delighted.

Wow, that sounds so freaking wholesome I'm sad to be missing out. Also, what does she mean, the 'last few times' she's been? I need to find a moment to get to the bottom of all this, but now isn't it. Now is the time for jeans and a top that isn't 2013 vintage Primarni with pasta sauce stains down the front. I get myself together and dash out the door.

TEN

'OH, LACEY.' I ENVELOP her and a screaming Willow in the biggest cuddle I can give as soon as she opens the door. Lacey looks atrocious. I have to hide my shock. Her hair is greasy, her under-eye bags are puffy, her skin is grey and even her silk jimjams have seen better days. Willow's cheeks are flushed and her eyes are watery.

'I think she's got a cold or she's teething, or she just basically hates me,' Lacey says bitterly as she thrusts her daughter into my arms. She's clearly noticed me looking at Willow with concern. The house is still oddly immaculate as we head through to the lounge.

'OK, well, I'm going to throw this out there, my love: your three-month-old baby girl does not hate you. I don't think they start hating you until the teenage hormones kick in, so we've both got a few years ahead of us before we can enjoy all of that. She might be teething – some start really young – or she might just have a bit of a snuffle. We can sort both of those out with lovely, lovely Calpol, which solves all your problems and makes the world right again. It's a bit like gin and Chinese takeaway, but for babies, you know?' I keep my voice light as I shift the warm bundle that is Willow from my chest onto my lap.

Lacey sits bolt upright across from me on one of her beautifully upholstered high-back chairs, fidgeting with the waist strings of her pyjama bottoms and holding her phone so tightly I can see the whites of her knuckles.

'Lacey, has something happened? Whatever it is, tell me and I can help you,' I say as softly as I can, not making any sudden movements.

'It's going to sound so silly.' The tears well up again.

'I promise you, whatever it is, I won't think it's silly.

You're my best friend and I love you,' I say calmly, and then, holding Willow's tiny arm and wiggling it about, with a high-pitched voice I add, 'and you're my best mummy!' which makes Lacey smile weakly, so is a success of sorts.

'You're going to think I'm such an idiot,' Lacey continues, pushing the hair back off her face.

She was making such a fuss I was starting to get a little frustrated, but like I've seen it done on the six hundred police interview programmes I've watched with Edward, I stay calm and continue to probe.

'Lacey, it's me. I've known you since we were in lower school. We've helped each other through thick and thin, and we've seen each other at our very worst. I've held your hair while you sicked up in Rebels nightclub, that time when you'd just met Karl and then lied and said it was me that was vomming, and that's why we were so long in there, so he would still fancy you. There is no judgement here – as always, I'm on your side, but unless you tell me what's going on, I can't help you. If it's something about Willow or Karl, I'm here. You've literally just had a baby, it's hard, I get it. Now, take a deep breath,' I say, breathing in deeply myself, 'and let it all out.'

'It's Rosalind Shah,' Lacey blurts out quickly.

'Huh?' I'm racking my brains for who the hell this is and what it is she could have done.

'Netball Rosalind. From school. You know,' Lacey coaxes.

'Oh yes, OK. What about her?' I can't work out the connection. I don't think we've seen her in about twelve years, apart from that time we ran into her in Next a few years back and literally just said a few hellos and that was that. Why is she bringing this woman up now?

'Earlier this week I finally went to one of those mother and baby groups.'

'That's fantastic, Lace! Well done!' This feels like a big step for her, so I'm bracing myself, hoping nothing went wrong.

'Well, Rosalind was there with her son – he's four months older than Willow, according to Facebook – so I said hello and we had a chat about the old days at school, and I asked if she's still playing netball and stuff,' Lacey sobs.

'Right, right, this all sounds totally OK.' I'm still baffled by the tears.

'Anyway, I go online this morning to send her a

private message on Facebook, maybe see if she wants to go to another group next week.' Lacey pauses, drawing in breath.

'OK, yes, that's nice, well done,' I encourage.

'And she's unfriended me!' she says, sniffing. 'I never even liked her much, but I can't even get being baby group friends right. Why am I such a fucking failure?' she wails.

'Oh, Lacey! Please, don't get upset,' I say, standing up to go and hug her, still holding Willow in one arm, who's starting to squirm a bit. 'Come on, now. You don't need Rosalind Shah! This really isn't as big a deal as it feels.'

'*Everything* feels like a big deal,' Lacey snaps. 'Everything is so fucking hard, Robin. I've tried and tried, but I just can't be like one of those proper mums, who has a perfect home and makes perfect meals and dresses the baby in perfect outfits and has a baby who doesn't cry *all the fucking time* and has perfect winged eyeliner and has the exact right shade of dark grey skirting boards and the correct opinions on feminism, and makes a million fucking friends at fucking baby fucking groups, and—'

I stop her before the descent spirals out of control.

I think once you're interspersing each word with 'fucking', you need an intervention.

'Lacey, are you joking me? Those mums aren't real! No mum excels in the ways you've suggested! You're setting yourself painfully unrealistic standards,' I say, wishing I could crawl into her brain and make her realise this.

'Look at this absolute corker of a baby,' I say, giving Willow, who is nodding off in my arms, an extra squish. 'You are totally acing motherhood. She's happy, mostly, and safe and growing and healthy. It's been *three months*. Of course it's hard. You're not getting much sleep, Karl's out of the house all day, you're not going out much, you're focusing a lot on things that don't really matter. Like, you do not need to worry about your eyeliner being perfectly winged. If you wear no eyeliner at all, that's OK, you know?'

'I know. I do know that Rosalind not being my friend on Facebook isn't a big deal. We weren't close at school, and it's just that I saw her and thought I should offer a play date, but it stung. It made me feel like I'd failed. You see all these other perfect mums, and I just can't be like them.'

'My lovely, wonderful Lacey, where are you seeing these "perfect mums", please?' I ask.

'Everywhere! At the group I went to, on Instagram, my mum friends on Facebook, you!' she says, crying again. I can tell she's just not thinking rationally.

'Lacey, I'm going to tell you something now, from one mum to another, and I want you to listen really carefully, OK?'

'OK.'

'None of those mums is perfect. They *all* feel stressed that they're not giving their child the right food, or worried that their baby isn't developing as well as the baby next to it at the group. The mums on Insta are showing you one carefully composed shot of one second of their day. Behind the camera they too have sweaty underboobs from all that feeding, or the Guilt with a capital G for bottle-feeding, even though "breast is best". Your mummy friends on Facebook are the same. Nobody is going to post a status about their episiotomy stitches being infected and their partner having to help them up off the toilet. None of them is going to say, "You know what? Maybe right now, with my ripped-up fanny and cracked nipples and eye bags I could pack my whole house into, maybe this baby isn't worth it – maybe I feel like utter shit and I'm wondering why the fuck I did this", are they?'

'Robin! Nobody thinks their baby isn't worth it. That's awful,' Lacey reels, sounding utterly horrified.

'No, it's not! It's human! You are allowed to look at Willow, love her with all of your heart and still think that right now motherhood is crap and you don't like it much. It's OK to not love motherhood sometimes. Can I tell you something? I didn't have that "ahhh, this is so worth it" moment until Lyla was about two years old. You must remember that! She had become a really funny, caring little being in my life, but up until then it was pretty one-sided, with me slaving away for her and her not letting me sleep,' I say, nodding, willing her to take this in.

'But that's babies,' Lacey says, starting to sound like she might believe me.

'Yes, and I loved her. I'd have run through a burning building for her. That doesn't mean I wanted to shout "I love being a mother!" from the rooftops, though.'

'Robin, I feel so ashamed.' She tears up again.

'No, Lacey, why? You mustn't.'

'I wanted this baby, my gorgeous Willow, for so, so,

so long, and I thought I'd be living the absolute dream, but this is like a nightmare. I'm so tired my thoughts don't make sense. All I do all day is feed her and burp her and change her and rock her and try desperately to keep this house clean and tidy. Going to that group felt as big a deal as going on a four-month backpacking trip round Asia. I wanted to go so you and Kath would stop going on at me. I don't care about Rosalind, and she was shit at netball, but it just all felt too much, and this morning, even though I told him I felt so rubbish, Karl went out to play a "quick" nine holes, and I know he'll be gone all day. Why did he leave us on our own? Why didn't he just take her with him? Just this once? I'm so tired, Robin. I shouldn't resent him but he gets to go out *all day, every day*. I should be glad to have Willow, but I'm just not. I feel horrible for saying all this because it's like I don't love my baby, and I feel even worse saying it to you because of what happened last year. I'm so sorry, you must hate me for it. Kath came over last week and said having babies isn't always what you think it will be like, but this *really* isn't. I hate it. I'm so miserable . . .' And the tears are like a flood now.

'Oh, Lacey, I'm so sorry you're going through this,

and I'm sorry Karl's gone out today. I don't hate you. What happened with my . . . with my loss' – saying 'miscarriage' is still too much sometimes – 'is awful, but it's not for you to worry about. It's OK. I'm going to stay with you, we're not going to think about house-work, we're going to use the expressed milk you've squeezed out into those baggies – well done on that, by the way, I'd given up on breastfeeding before Lyla was a month old – and you're going to go upstairs and have a bath and a nap and read a book and ignore your life.'

'Ignoring my life sounds amazing right now,' Lacey agrees with a sniff, sounding the most 'her' she has in weeks.

'Then, when you're downstairs again, we're going to order a Chinese takeaway for lunch, nobody is going to be wearing a bra – we'll be taking our fashion inspiration from Willow here in her Babygro – and let's have a think about maybe talking to your GP or health visitor about how you're feeling, OK?' I say as casually as I can because I don't want to worry her.

'I'm exhausted. I'm beyond tired. I feel like I'm a shell of a woman going through the motions of life and my brain isn't quite plugged in. She never sleeps for more than forty-five minutes, day or night. But I love Willow so much. As long as she's healthy, that's all that matters,' she says weakly, as though she's a robot reciting what she thinks she should say. We've all been there.

'Willow being healthy is not *all* that matters. You need to be OK, too, mentally and physically. She needs a healthy mummy, doesn't she? If you broke your arm and had to have it in a cast, would that mean you didn't love her?' I say.

'No, obviously not,' she agrees.

'And if you thought you had a fracture in your arm, would you go straight to the doctor to have it checked out, even if you weren't fully sure it was broken?'

'Yes,' she says, still following along.

'This is the same. We can go and see the GP and have a chat. They can help you, and if they say there's nothing to worry about, there's no harm done, you can tick that errand off your list. Let me just be really firm here, because it matters to my mummy heart too, after how terrible I've felt over the years with Lyla. Having a blip in mental health does not equal a blip in your love for your baby. It's more loving to your baby to go and talk to someone because you're taking care of yourself and you're the person who takes care of Willow!' I feel emotional saying all this. I wish someone had said this to me when I had Lyla. I remember Kath talking to me a lot about the baby blues and depression, but the words that rang loudest in my ears were from my mother telling me to pull myself together before Simon came home and found his fiancée a 'pathetic, crying mess'.

I take a deep breath at the same time as Lacey does and we sit in silence for a few moments, letting it all sink in.

'I love you, Lacey,' I say, tilting my head to one side.

'I love you too, Robin,' she says, mirroring me. 'Thank you.'

'Any time. Now, tell me how long I microwave your boob milkshake for, and go upstairs for the longest bath of your life.'

I SPEND THE REST of the morning and afternoon at Lacey's. She has a bath and a long sleep and I don't disturb her once. I remember the feeling of being desperate for a few moments of freedom. Freedom from the baby you love so much, but who affords you absolutely no let-up and who, in your darkest moments (in which I found myself regularly), you deeply, but secretly, resent.

As it's a novelty for me, Willow is a delight to spend time with. I mean, she doesn't do an awful lot at three months old, but we have a lot of cuddles, a lot of milk, a couple of squidgy, sludgy pooey nappy changes (I'd forgotten the joy of pre-solid-food changes) and some time in her all-singing, all-dancing baby bouncer. I used to be so jealous of mums who had all these things for their babies. Simon and I were on the tightest of budgets and had the bare essentials, so our bouncer was one of those basic wire and fabric ones. This one makes music, swerves from side to side and vibrates. I'd quite like to have a chair like that for myself!

Spending time with Willow also makes me think of the baby Edward and I lost. He or she would only have been a few weeks older than Willow, and would probably have had a snazzy bouncer, too. I spend some time wondering if I would have been a different sort of mother this time round, and if being financially secure would have made much difference to my mental health. Can money buy you happiness? Thankfully Willow doesn't leave me much time to spiral into this thought vortex or feel sad about my angel baby because she's on a three-hourly schedule, and by the time I've put her down for a little snooze, washed the bottles, made myself a cup of tea and taken forty-five pictures of her sleeping and looking so freaking adorable, I need to start all over again.

It is gone three o'clock by the time Karl comes home. I take him aside for a quiet word and try not to let my anger at him show. Lacey has been doing such a good job of pretending she's fine that he's just been admiring of her and letting her get on with it, as she insisted she wanted to. He is pretty chastened by my words, but promises to be more hands-on. Good.

When I finally get up to leave, it's nearly four o'clock, and so naturally I have the Mum Guilts about not having seen Lyla much. I could focus on the fact that I've helped my friend and looked after a baby all day, but no, the Mum Guilt is banging on the door again.

At the door, Lacey is crying again. Today I've told her over and over it is just Mum Guilt, and that she needs to ignore it, but I'm not even taking my own advice. She's promised me she'll book in with her GP. I wish I could go with her, but Karl will, and there's a bit of me that's secretly relieved because I didn't want to have to tell her that next week is crazy busy and that I am feeling a touch tense that Natalie has suggested we have a 'review meeting' soon. I hug Lacey hard and tell her I am here for her night and day, and that she is a good mum, a good woman, that she just needs to open up to Karl a bit more and that it is all going to be all right.

It is. It *is* all going to be all right.

ELEVEN

STEPPING THROUGH THE DOOR is like old times, with the smell of home cooking wafting through, and as I walk into my kitchen, a table full of productivity.

'Mummy, we're working on Auntie Kath's new line – lavender phone cases!' Lyla declares, standing up on her chair to greet me and nearly toppling off.

'Steady, love! And yes, we are! Colly thinks I need to get with the times and appeal to the younger market now that I'm up and running with all my other lavender creations, so that's what I'm doing. We're pressing purple pansy petals and lavender sprigs into these phone case whatsits, and then you young folk obsessed with your gadgets can attach them to the back of your phone and have a calming bit of nature wherever you go,' she says, smiling and gesturing a clear phone case around.

'That's such a good idea!' I say, plonking my bag on the worktop by the kettle and going over to look at all of them.

'Yeah, and each one is unique, just like us,' adds Lyla with an adorable attempt to wink at Kath.

'You should take her with you round the stockists as a sales assistant,' I laugh to Kath, leaning over to give Lyla a big squish and a cuddle.

'I might have to! I'm not really sure where to see about stocking these,' Kath says, surveying the table full of materials. 'Colly's set me up with some floristry friends, who have put a few pots of my lotions and bath bombs by their tills, so I think they might take a couple, but where could I put these where the young-sters will see them?'

'What about selling them online and using social media to promote them? Or seeing if there are any local bloggers who could help spread the word?' I suggest, admiring a couple of them. They really are good. I'd buy one!

'I don't know how to do any of that internet malarkey, and Colly has a girl to do his computer bits at work. Oooh, could you set me up?' she adds, as though a light bulb just pinged on in her head.

'Oh Kath, I'm beyond busy at the moment, with work and Lyla and Edward and now Lacey, but I might have just the solution for you! There's a group started at our school called Women Who Win, and it's full of smart women with smart ideas. Some of them want to start something, and some of them just want to be part of something. I bet there would be someone there who would love to help out on this sort of thing,' I say eagerly.

'Oh, would they? That's very nice of them! Will there be someone who can set it all up on the websites?' she asks, starting to clear her things away while Lyla fiddles with some loose petals and watches the back-and-forth with interest. She takes everything in these days.

'I'm sure there would. Plus, on sites like Etsy you don't really have to set up a website, they have templates and steps you follow to make it all really simple. Then maybe you could set up an Instagram account or go on Facebook to share what you do a bit, and promote it. You'd be a worldwide hit in no time!' I say, flourishing the phone case elaborately, making Lyla giggle.

'Well, I've no idea what she just said, but oh my giddy aunt, your mummy's got all the ideas, hasn't she?' Kath says joyfully to Lyla, who's loving this family time.

'You're my giddy aunt!' she says, standing up on her chair again and giving us a little dance. How do children have this much energy *all* the time? I can't remember the last time I wanted to stand on a chair and shimmy about, but it's almost a daily occurrence with her. They say men are a mystery, but I'm adding children to this list, too.

We clear the beautiful debris away into Kath's array of old biscuit tins, floral boxes, jiffy bag envelopes and ziplock baggies, and I make a mental note to order her a label maker and stackable storage boxes. While I've been out, Kath and Lyla have popped to the shops for 'the essentials' and whipped up a chicken and veggie bake and an apple crumble. Our Kath does not do things by halves.

We sit down around my big old oak table that has seen me through many years and tuck in.

'This is lovely! It feels like the olden days,' I say, putting my fork down and taking stock of my gorgeous family.

'What, like when you were little and you didn't have electricity or cars?' Lyla asks, with full cheeks like a hamster.

'Please don't talk with your mouth full, and I'm not that old. I was a child in the 1980s. We had everything you have now!' I retort.

'You didn't have the internet or Netflix or Kylie Jenner Lip Kits,' she says without missing a beat.

'When did you get so sassy, please?' I ask, laughing at her.

'I dunno. Corinthia thinks I'm *really* cool. She's asked to come for a sleepover. I said she could because it's OK, isn't it?'

'Oh. Well. You've got closer friends than Corinthia, haven't you?' I ask hopefully. I really want to avoid any contact I might have to have with her horrid mother, Valerie. We've never really seen eye to eye and have had one or two 'stern words' (aka she was nasty about Lyla a couple of years ago so I called her a bitch), so I can't imagine she'll be thrilled to have her daughter stay here. Although she hasn't been much of a problem these last few months, so maybe she's turned over a new leaf.

'So can we?' Lyla interrupts my thoughts.

'I think it sounds nice for Lyla to be having friends for sleepovers,' Kath says warmly. 'You used to love having sleepovers at my house when you were little. Do you remember, we used to make biscuits together and you and your friends would save them till really late for a midnight feast.'

'I do! They were such lovely nights! And Derek would steal them away, leaving clues for us to find and rescue them!' I reminisce excitedly.

'That's right, he did! He was such a good egg, wasn't he?' Kath smiles with sad eyes.

'He really was. The very best egg.' I reach out and put my hand on hers.

'But can Corinthia come, though?' Lyla badgers.

'Go on, then. It's lovely to make friends, so if her mum says yes then we'll arrange a date,' I concede.

'Woohoooo! Yasss queen!' Lyla cheers. She'll be as bad as Skye soon with her youthful lingo.

Once Lyla is in bed, I know it's my opportunity to talk to Kath about bigger topics.

I make us both a big mug of sweet tea and plonk down on the brown leather couch. I don't care what Edward says; it's part of my freaking soul, dammit.

'Oo-eee, what a day!' Kath says, taking a cautious sip in case it's too hot. Kath, as always, looks amazing. I think if anyone else wore some of the outfits she does, they'd look utterly gaga, but not Kath: she is the definition of rocking your look. Today she has on cerise-pink pedal pushers with little blue forget-me-nots embroidered (potentially by her) on the legs and matching blue tiny pompoms stitched around the hem (definitely by her), a floaty white cotton blouse, four or five chunky glass bead necklaces of varying colours, one with a selection of shells interspersed, a pair of tortoiseshell glasses (even though she doesn't need them) nestled in her well-coiffed hair (Kath used to be a salon stylist, so her hair is always on point) and a rainbow of eyeshadow shades on her eyelids. She's always been eclectic with fashion, but the eyeshadow is new.

'I like your make-up, Kath, it's really bold,' I start.

'Thank you! Colin says he loves how colourful I am, so I started making a bit more of an effort. I found a lovely kit in Boots that has a hundred and twenty

eyeshadow colours and I'm trying out each one. I'll
be taking over your job soon!' she jokes.

'Crikey! I'd best warn Natalie,' I says. 'I'm glad
things are going well with Colin. Are you as happy
as I hope you are?' I ask.

'I really am, lovey,' Kath says, reaching for my hand
to reassure me. 'He'll never be your wonderful uncle,
but he's a good man and I know Derek will be looking
down on us, smiling at how well we're getting on and
how happy we are. We've all got what we wanted.
You've got Edward, I've got Colly and Lacey's got
Willow – it's perfect!' she says cheerily.

'Are you sure you're OK, Kath?' Despite her cheer-
iness, I know something isn't quite right. I can tell.
She's been distant for weeks, and I am actually starting
to feel a bit worried now.

'Oh yes, lovey, I've got everything I need,' she says
brightly. 'No need to worry about me.'

When you're really worried about someone, and
they tell you not to worry, even though you know you
should carry on worrying, you feel a guilty relief. I've
got so many things to worry about, I'm getting a bit
overloaded: that upcoming work meeting with Natalie,
Kath being distant, Lacey being down, Lyla getting on

with Edward, bloody Valerie and I having to arrange a play date, being part of WWW and introducing Kath's lavender business at the next session. It's all a bit much. I can feel myself getting warm and itchy round my neck. Urgh! This is horrible.

'Are you all right, love?' Kath asks, watching me scratch at my chest and get up to open a window.

'Yep! Fine,' I say. There it is again, that magical word 'fine' that we use to shut out any help or show any shred of emotion. When does fine ever mean fine?

'You don't look fine. I'm your auntie – I know when you're not yourself. Maybe I can help,' she coaxes, really in her element now the emotional weight has shifted from me looking in on her, to her helping me.

I decide it's now or never.

'OK, I'm not *super*-fine. I'm *mostly* fine.' Can anyone ever just say they are not fine?

'That's a good start. What's not super-fine, then? Is it Edward?' she offers.

'No, it's not Edward. He's been so, so good with us, both Lyla and me. It's, well, it's lots of things – like work, and Lacey, and I've missed you. Lacey said you'd been visiting her, but you've been too busy to visit us properly,' I say, embarrassingly, like a whiny child. I need to get a grip.

'I have visited you! I popped in with the extra lavender bags last week, and you saw me out and about the week before when I was in M&S with my friend from crochet group!' she protests.

'It's not like it used to be, though! Popping in one week and bumping into you in M&S the week before? I used to come in and find you decluttering the airing cupboard, or Lyla would go to yours for whole afternoons to play,' I carry on needily. I don't think I've realised how much I've missed her until I've let all this out.

'Well, life's a bit busy at the moment, isn't it, pet? You've got your Edward and I've got my Colin and Lyla's getting bigger at school and wanting to spend more time with all of her little friends, isn't she?' Kath tries, weakly.

'I do have Edward, but you were here first. And you have Colin, but . . . you still have time to see Lacey,' I whisper quietly, looking into my cup as I say the last bit.

Kath pauses and looks into her cup, too.

'Willow is very special. And we can both see that

Lacey needs help, even though she's not been admitting it to anyone. And being with Willow, well . . . it's . . . healing, isn't it?' Kath says, still looking down.

'I know what you mean. My heart breaks for how long Lacey and Karl waited for her, so having her here is wonderful. I think once Lacey's back on her feet, she'll feel wonderful, too.'

Kath lifts her head and looks into my eyes for a moment. Kath might be fifty-four, but her eyes are so young. I always think it's a bit cringey when people say eyes 'sparkle', but Kath's really do.

'She will. Willow is so special. All babies are special, wherever they are,' she concludes eventually after a few seconds of silence, looking a bit teary. I think she might be gently referring to my miscarriage last year.

'They are,' I say. 'I would like to see you more, though. Maybe I can work around your schedule a bit, now you're doing more,' I offer.

'That'd be lovely. I don't want you or Lyla to think I don't love you. I do, very, very, very much. I've just had such a lot to do lately, and . . . such a lot to think about,' she says again, a bit wobbly.

'Is it all getting a bit much with the lavender

business?' I ask, sensing she might have bitten off more than she can chew.

'Yes, it might have done.' She nods.

'Well, we love you and we want to help. Why don't you bring some more of the cases over tomorrow night, and Lyla and I will help you put them all together? We can make an assembly line and have you up to speed in no time! Meanwhile, I'll add you to my WWW group mailing list, and everything, I promise, will be OK,' I say triumphantly.

'Thank you, my gorgeous girl, I'm so glad to have you in my life. You and Lyla are so special,' she says, misty-eyed. Usually it's me with the surplus of emotions, but tonight Kath's on form.

To lighten the mood, I spend the rest of the evening introducing Kath to the joys of reality TV on Netflix.

'So, they're all going to stay at this villa for a whole summer and try to fall in love with each other?' and, 'They're a bit flighty, aren't they? One chap one day and another the next, but all sleeping in the same bedroom! In my day if you so much as disappeared into another room for more than five minutes, your mother would have your guts for garters!' were some of my favourite moments of outrage from her.

'I thought you were a modern woman, Kath!' I laugh, reaching for my phone so I can send a check-in text to Lacey.

'I am! You know I'm very liberal, I just wasn't prepared for this. I'd love to be young and single in this day and age. I'd have an absolute ball on those dating agency sites you used to use!' she says, still glued to the TV.

'Apps, Kath, dating apps. And yes, I think you'd be brilliant on a show like this. Perhaps they could have you and Colin on!' I chuckle.

'Well, we'd certainly show them a thing or two,' she laughs with raised eyebrows.

'Eww, too far! No, you wouldn't. Time to turn this off – it's past your bedtime!'

And I have to confess, it's felt like the most special treat to have had my Auntie Kath all to myself tonight.

TWELVE

JUNE

A FEW WEEKS LATER, I'M driving into work after a little stop at Starbucks, and my mind is a whirl of anxiety. I went round to Lacey's yesterday and the house still looks weirdly immaculate. Every time I see Willow, I'm amazed at how much she's changed. I tried to have a proper chat with Lacey, but she seemed a bit out of it. I know all new parents are tired, and she said she was feeling much better, but I don't think I believe her. I asked her about going to see the doctor, and she said she hadn't had a chance to yet but promised me she would sort it soon . . . I must remember to check in and see how it goes. I know she needs real help, but you can't make someone do it if they really don't want to, can you? Lead a horse to water, and all that jazz.

I haven't seen Kath for a few weeks. When I last did it was lovely, but I still wish we saw more of her. I can tell she's really happy with Colin, and I'm glad there are no issues between us, but I can't help thinking there's still something lingering. I mentioned it to Lacey and she said she'd sensed something too. We think maybe it's a menopause thing and she'll get back to herself again eventually, but have both vowed to keep an eye on her.

Last night, Edward came home to a clean house and a beautifully cooked Chicken Cacciatore courtesy of his very loving girlfriend and Lyla only growled at him once, so I think that's a solid result. I'm trying not to fret over the whole boyfriend/daughter situation, but I know there's still a bit of resistance I need to work out. Maybe some more mummy time is needed, or maybe I could arrange this dreaded sleepover with Corinthia so she has a bit of distraction. Since having Kath round 'like old times', I've realised how much I really, really miss her and worry that Lyla's feeling the same. I don't want my little girl to be missing her auntie, to not like the man living in her house and to feel her mummy doesn't care. We didn't do our Sunday-night production line in the end because Colin wanted to go out for dinner. We've said we'll make it happen some time soon, but I'll admit I felt a little bit disappointed and weirdly guilty even though it wasn't my fault. It'll be OK, though, I tell myself. If there's one thing climbing out of the black hole of The Emptiness has taught me, I remind myself, almost as though it's my bloody life mantra, it's to have a little faith, a little patience and a little trust, and that you can get through almost anything. I'll add them to my life admin To Do list: sleepovers and Kath time for Lyla.

I mentally scan the rest of my To Do list. I still need to work out what's bothering Kath. And help Lacey admit that she needs help. And be a great girlfriend to Edward. And a loving, present mother to Lyla. First, though, I need to get out of the car and go into the office. Today is the day of my meeting with Natalie. She suggested we have a 'proper chat'. When does that ever bode well? I've been low-level dreading it since she emailed.

* * *

'Morning!' I say fake breezily as I push open the door into the boiling hot office. It's June, and while most people are rejoicing for the soaring temperatures, waving their barbecue tongs about with glee and skipping around in light cotton playsuits, I'm just sticky. It's 9.20 a.m., and the sticky has already begun.

Naturally Alice and Stuart, our admin and booking support, look perfect and shine-free with their desk fans blowing, and Skye has managed to squeeze her perfectly tanned body into an even-more-cropped-than-usual crop top and what I think she'd call a skirt but what I'd call a strip of jersey wrapped round her bottom. To top the look off she has the Baby Spice trainers I pined for as an eleven-year-old. If I wore this ensemble I'd be sectioned. When Skye wears it, she looks like she's Insta-famous.

I've also tried to get on-trend with the 1990s vibe, despite feeling utterly triggered because I looked as crap in it the first time round as I do now. But I have tried to make it work for me. I've gone for a knee-length ditsy-print button-down dress, a tan cross-body bag and white Converse.

'You look nice, Skye. Very glam,' I say, trying to

start the week on a good footing and with positive vibes, even though I am really not in the mood.

'Thanks. You . . . I like your bag. Also, you know they can make vegan leather from mushrooms, right? That way we don't have to slaughter animals and ruin the biosphere for you to feel good,' she adds, in front of Stuart and Alice, who, as usual, are pretending not to listen but are acutely aware that there could be a showdown any moment.

'I know, Skye. I did it on purpose. I deliberately want to spoil the planet,' I retort, mentally kicking myself for not saying something more cutting. I may as well just have said, 'I know you are, but what am I?'

'Wow,' Skye said as she carried on walking towards Natalie's office.

To save face in front of Alice and Stuart I do a laugh and an eye-roll that convinces literally nobody of anything, and then saunter to our office with my head held high.

Wow indeed. I shut the office door behind me – I'm not in the mood to share space right now – walk the five steps over to my window (which offers a stunning view of the car park and bins) and open it as wide as

I can, robbers and intruders be damned. I'm het up over Skye's nitpicking, annoyed at myself for not being sustainable (I do care, really) and I'm starting to have a tight feeling in my tummy over this morning's meeting with Natalie.

I hope it will be fine. I've hit all my targets, I've worked hard on our expansion projects, there haven't been any complaints and I've not had to take any time off for Lyla being sick or me not being well. It's fine, it's fine, it's fine. I keep telling myself this until, once again, 'fine' means nothing.

After a brief play around my laptop – pretending I'm busy but really looking at memes and having a quick scroll through the boohoo clothing sale to see if I can find anything that looks trendy *and* covers all my fleshy bits – I pick up my pad, pen and phone and head across the corridor (gratefully noting that Skye is working/sulking in the kitchen space), to the meeting room where Natalie is hot-desking.

Two steps from the door, and my phone buzzes. I could do without this right now, but it's Edward and I have the tingle of joy you only get with a new boyfriend, so I quickly answer.

'Hello, Robin Wilde, Professional Lady About to Go Into a Meeting, how can I help you?' I say in my best phone voice.

'Oh, hello, Robin Wilde, Professional Lady, this is Edward Frey, about to ask you if you'd like to go out for dinner tonight,' he says, playing along with my game, which I love him for.

'Mr Frey, I would love to have dinner with you, but I have a child I need to feed, bathe and generally nurture,' I quip back.

'Ms Wilde, I have spoken to the delight that is Auntie Kath and that's all taken care of,' he says assertively. God, I love his voice. It melts me. I don't feel like I'm standing in the corridor about to have a meeting with Natalie, I feel like I'm floating in a calm void where everything is, indeed, taken care of. Maybe I need to book in for one of those saline-water-immersion-tank jobbies.

'Ah, that's nice then. Are we celebrating something?' I ask, feeling so happy to have a boyfriend who organises little things like this for us.

'Well, I want to spend time with you, and also . . .' his voice changes, only a tiny bit but noticeably to me, 'I'd like to speak to you about something. It's not really an over-the-phone thing, and I don't want us to be distracted.'

My heart tightens. The last time I did this I was trying to tell him that I'd lost the baby neither of us had planned but had started to love. And the last time he said this, he asked me if he could move in. So either this is very, very good or very, very bad.

'Oh.' I don't really know what to say.

'Robin, are you coming in?' Natalie pops her head out of the door with a smile on her face but an impatient voice. That blissful, calm feeling has evaporated entirely.

'Robin, are you there?' Edward prompts. I want to run away from work and find out what he wants right now. Is he sick of family life already? Have I pushed him too far with having to always consider Lyla? Is he bored with things? Maybe he's not moving back to the UK after all. Maybe he wants to end things. My mind whirs faster than I can keep up, and I have to reach out to hold the wall as my legs feel like jelly. Deep breath in, fake it till you make it, I tell myself.

'Yes! Sorry! Dinner sounds great! Can't wait. I'll meet you at home. Obviously. We both live there, ha,'

I start to babble as I gesture to Natalie that I'll be just one minute.

'OK. Missing you,' he finishes.

'Missing you too. Have to go now. Sorry!' I press end.

So here goes. Time to stop second-guessing what Natalie wants and face the music.

THIRTEEN

'SORRY, NATALIE, EDWARD RANG, and I thought it might be important. It wasn't, though. Well, it was but it wasn't. It might be, later.' I gabble again, a bit short of breath.

'Take a moment, sit down and have some water,' Natalie says in a firm but motherly tone. 'You're flustered.'

'Sorry,' I say, taking a sip from the glass of water she's poured for me from the jug on the big black meeting table. 'Bleurgh, you know what it's like.'

'I do, I do. The juggle is real!' she laughs, shuffling all her papers into one pile. She has everything, from printed spreadsheets to magazine clippings of models we've worked on to notepads full of ideas and her laptop open on her inbox.

'So, is everything OK?' I venture, pretending to feel confident.

'Really cutting to the chase there,' Natalie says, smiling and looking up from her papers. 'I like it!'

'Ha! Well, I'm eager to get going on whatever it is you wanted to see me about. I've made good progress on the tutorials project. I've had a bit of an idea for a beautiful space we could use at my friend's florist's – remember, where I had my birthday?' I say, easing into the conversation, my faked confidence starting to turn into actual, real confidence as I think about my ideas.

'I do! And I do want to talk about that and lots of other things – we're long overdue a proper catch-up – but we need to talk about this first,' she says, placing a hand on a paper folder.

'OK – what's that?'

'Remember the movie job in New York?'

'I'll never forget it! For a hundred different reasons,' I laugh knowingly.

'Aha, no, I didn't think you would. Nor will I. I don't think I've had a bug that bad since!' she says, recalling how she got ill and left me in the driving seat. She laughs and takes a deep breath. 'I'm worried. We agreed a five-year contract in principle, with them filming over here at Pinewood and on location in the UK last year, this year and over the next two years. Clearly, though, this hasn't happened. They haven't gone with anyone else, and they haven't been shooting in the States.'

'OK . . .' I nod, not sure where this is leading.

'After the shake-up with Langston . . .' She pauses, looking at me.

'Mmm,' I say, feeling guilty but proud. Langston was the set director who I'd exposed for sexually and physically abusing a young actress called Marnie. As you can imagine, it was a Big Thing.

'After the shake-up, they decided to restructure the team, and that must have caused delays. Add to that the #MeToo movement, which I'm so proud we were a part of, exposing that vile man, plus a relook at the budget with the new structure, Brexit and European work licences, it's all gone a bit quiet.'

'Wow. Yes. God.' I don't really know what to say to any of this. It sounds too much. 'So, have we lost it, do you think?' I ask tentatively.

'I don't think it's a lost cause, but I think we need

to remind them who we are, what they agreed with us and what we can do.' She pauses, and for a moment I'm not sure if I want to hear what she's going to say next. 'When they offered the contract in principle, I budgeted that money straight into the business. It's allocated to all kinds of things like kits and equipment and expenses for travel, but also the big things – the tutorials expansion and, most pressingly, people's salaries.' Natalie pauses again. 'We all need this contract to come through,' she continues, looking directly at me with a hint of fear in her face.

'OK,' I say, letting the gravity of the situation sink in and feeling a wave of anxiety wash over my whole body, leaving the hairs standing up on my arms. Working at MADE IT is more than a job. The thought of losing staff, the thought of – I can hardly bear to give it headspace – losing my job, makes me feel faint. But then the feeling passes, and is replaced by something like rage, or energy. I won't let MADE IT suffer – I won't ever let it go without a fight.

'There must be something we can do. Are they making another movie?' I ask, suddenly feeling stupid, because if they were then we'd be recommissioned and paid for our contract.

'Good question.' Natalie's such a builder-upper. 'I have already been in touch, thinking that while they're not shooting a big project right now, we could go and do a bit of PR, like the old days. Head over there, offer free makeovers for the staff in the office, see if they're working on any smaller movies or commercial shoots that we could assist on, wine them and dine them a bit, win them over again.'

'Natalie, I want to be you when I grow up. That's such a fabulous idea. Do you want me to find out what shoots they have coming up?' I offer, totally geed up and motivated by her idea. Of course Natalie has a plan. It's going to be fine, I tell myself.

'Thank you, Robin, but it turns out it's not that simple. They're working on a national sportswear TV ad that – wait for it – incorporates the hero from the horror film *we* worked on. They're shooting in a few weeks. They'd already started talking to other agencies, but when I said that should be our gig, signed and sealed, they blustered. Said something about a Skype meeting to talk about it. But you and I know that if we sit here talking at our laptops while they sit there in New York with local agencies knocking on their door, we'll lose the work. They said they thought it was too far for us to want to travel for a three-day shoot for an ad. Well, let's show them the full MADE IT service. I'm not phoning this one in – I'm going to New York, and I want you there with me. We're going to wow them, and when the week is done, we'll be the ones in pole position for their next feature films.

'Silver screen, here we come!' she finishes triumphantly.

'Wow! I mean, I don't know what I'll do with Lyla, but yes, I am always here for MADE IT, and yeah. Wow. OK!' I say, tapping the table and nodding but feeling overwhelmed at the thought. And not just because of Lyla. What about Lacey? Would Gloria mind if I miss a WWW meeting? And will I be good enough to pull off this deal?

But Natalie carries on. 'I know it's a big ask, and yes, it's a big idea. So, it's a three-day project, but I figured we could spend an extra few days going on the charm offensive, then update the contract and sign on the dotted line before we go home. Pretty simple, really, aside from flying across the world with all our kit and camping out in the Big Apple!' she says, putting the lid on her pen as though that's that.

I'm still trying to take it all in, but as I hesitate, thinking of the right thing to say, I end up saying nothing at all.

Sensing my concern, Natalie says, 'Are you up for it? I considered taking Skye, but you were what sealed the deal last time and you're the absolute best fit for this.'

'I am up for it, I'm always up for a challenge.' As I say it, I realise I mean it. A few years ago, I'd have backed out immediately. I used to say no to every opportunity out of fear – then this year I've found myself saying yes to everything and taking on too much, but I'm determined to find a middle path. I decide honesty is the best policy. 'I'm totally on board. I'm just a bit worried about Lyla. It'll be nearly her summer holidays, and she's been struggling a bit lately with Edward moving in, so I don't know, I feel like I need to be with her a lot right now. I'm sorry. I'm not being very helpful, am I?'

I start to worry I'm not being the employee Natalie wants and needs, and I so badly want to please her. I really want to be the best mum, but I also really want to be the best *me*. I'll feel torn and guilty whatever I do.

'Robin, stop always torturing yourself and putting yourself down. You are amazing at what you do, and the fact that you think so much of Lyla and her well-being shows me what a conscientious woman you are. You're exactly the kind of woman I want on my team. You've worked your absolute arse off these last few months – we've all noticed. I know last year's loss must still hurt, and having Edward move in is great, but it's a monumental new life chapter. Maybe we just need to look at this differently. Why don't you bring Lyla with you? I was thinking of bringing Martin anyway, and you know we love her. Instead of ludicrously priced hotels we could rent a house and all share. We'd cover Lyla's flight as your expenses. In fact, could you ask Kath to come too? Didn't you say she was quite the traveller? If MADE IT's paying for the house, she'd just need her flights. Then she could take care of Lyla while we're working,' Natalie says smoothly and matter-of-factly.

'How do you do that?' I say, incredulous.

'Do what?'

'Just solve everything so easily.'

'Aha! Years of mistakes I've learnt from. I know what's important in life, and how to master that juggle.

You need your family. That sabbatical last year taught me that. Time spent together is the most priceless of all things. We need to get this job secured, but that doesn't mean we can't still be badass wives and girl-friends and amazing mothers. We're Natalie and Robin. We're smashing it!'

'We've MADE IT!' I say jubilantly.

We both fall about laughing. I don't think it's cheesy enough to warrant full hysteria, but I think the notion of a huge trip to New York in only a couple of weeks is all a bit much and we have to laugh like hyenas to get it out of our systems.

Once we've calmed down (which takes Natalie about four seconds because she's the kind of woman who can take immediate control over her emotions, whereas I'm a total mess most the time and feel almost sick once we've stopped laughing), talk things through a bit and tick off a couple of tasks I need to power through this afternoon, I go back to my desk and text Edward excitedly: *Really can't wait for dinner now! I've got something to tell you, too! xx* At least whatever he has to say, I have some news of my own.

FOURTEEN

RIVING HOME THAT NIGHT, I hadn't really expected to be feeling so emotional. It's as though all the things I've had on my shoulders that I felt like I was managing really well, have all become rather heavy and I want to take some of it off.

It's such a relief to pull onto the drive and see not only Edward's car but also Kath's parked up, too. Edward is my strong, handsome hero, but Kath, she's my forever hero, and on a heavy day, I want her the most.

'Oo-ooo, I'm home!' I call as I step in the door and push my shoes off.

'Oo-ooo,' Kath sings back. 'We're in here, all at work!' she calls.

I pad through to the kitchen and there, at my great big oak table, are my three most favourite people (don't tell Lacey – she and Willow make the top five!) in all the world.

'Well, this is the best thing I've seen all day!' I say to Kath, Lyla and Edward, who are all sitting round the table gluing lavender sprigs, sparkly stars and scraps of lace into phone cases.

'We're helping make things for Kath's shop!' Lyla calls.

'Whether we like it or not!' Edward jokes.

'I love it! I want to sit and join you,' I say excitedly.

'Well, my gorgeous girlfriend, you can't. There's a date night with your name on it, and I want to whisk you away to talk of many things!' Edward coos.

'Same to you too! I have things to tell as well,' I say mysteriously as I shimmy out of the room, giggling.

'You two lovebirds,' I hear Kath say. 'I love to see my girls happy.'

'So, I've got news,' Edward begins as I push my fork into a tiny but delicious pork dumpling. We've come to a new Asian fusion restaurant that opened in town last week. Normally I'd be really excited to be out having a meal at a place that doesn't serve a packet of crayons with the menu, but tonight, knowing Edward has *something* to talk about with me, I feel like there's a hard knot in my tummy again. Not ideal, now that I've seen the rather appealing food offerings.

I nod nervously. 'OK . . . I'm just glad you're speaking your truth,' I say, reaching my hands across the table and resting them on his, which are, awkwardly, still holding cutlery.

'I appreciate that you're taking this seriously and I certainly will "speak my truth",' he says with a wry smile.

'Sorry. I've been with Skye all day. Picking up the lingo is an occupational hazard. Whatever it is, though, I'm ready.' I smile while mentally bracing myself for whatever it is, and kind of hoping it's not a proposal because a) I don't think I'm ready for that yet, and b) my nails are a bit scraggly, so I wouldn't be able to get a good Insta shot of the ring tonight.

'You know the London store?' he begins.

'Well, no, I've not been there, but yes, I know you're opening next month,' I say.

'Right, well, now it's not opening next month. It's been delayed. The staffing fell through in New York and they need someone experienced to look after it, tide them over and help hire a new manager,' he blurts out in a rush while nodding as though I'm very slow.

'Oh dear,' I say, nodding back, probably looking even more slow.

'So, *I'm* that person,' he says bluntly.

'OK,' I respond, not really seeing what the Big Announcement is here.

'So I'm going to be heading back out to the States for at least a month. In two weeks' time. I won't be here with you for four weeks,' he says, putting his cutlery down now and looking me squarely in the eyes.

'This. Is. Amazing!' I exclaim, almost looking around for the waiter to order some champagne to celebrate.

'Robin, are you all right? You were sad when I went away for the weekend last month. This means I'll be going away in two weeks – to New York.' Edward's usually steady face is completely baffled.

'Guess what, my most gorgeous boyfriend?' I say,

swirling my chopsticks (that I have no intention of using but feel I look cool gesturing with) at him in little circles.

'What? You've gone mad?'

'Nope! I'm going to be in New York next month, too!' I say with utter glee at how well this has worked out.

We spend the rest of our starters with me explaining the situation with MADE IT and how I'm taking Lyla out too (though I realise I still have to get this squared with school. I can imagine it will set the PSMs' tongues wagging). By the time the mains have arrived, we've decided that when Natalie and Martin head home, me, Kath and Lyla will keep the house on for an extra fortnight (providing we can afford it and Natalie lets me have the annual leave – but I think she will because I haven't had a holiday in about forever), and we'll all have the most magical time together.

'I'll have time to show you everywhere. I'll take you to shows and bars and every shop you could ever want to spend far too much time in. I'll take you and Lyla to Coney Island, I'll buy her cotton candy that you won't approve of and I'll find Kath shells on the beach to add to her collection, and then I'll whisk you back to my place – thank God I have the lease till autumn – and absolutely ravage you, and show you how much I—'

'I can't believe how amazingly this has all turned out! What are the actual odds of two people going to the same city, at the same time, for totally different reasons? You always see these things in films, and I never think they can happen to someone like me, but they are!' I gush.

'It is going to be amazing . . . Because you are amazing,' Edward says quietly, smiling at me with his eyes all soft and crinkly in that way that makes my tummy flip. I smile back at him and breathe in deeply. Wow, I'm relieved this is working out so well.

We spend dessert talking about how fun it will be to have Kath in New York, the parks and museums Lyla will love and the bars we could meet up with Piper in. Piper, Lacey's little sister, lives out in New York and, after all, it's thanks to her that I have Edward. She's the one who dared me to go over and talk to him on a night out. It'll be like old times again, except with Lyla and Kath in tow. I can't wait!

* * *

As soon as we get in, I feel like I might explode if I don't blurt everything out to Kath. We find her in the kitchen, clearing her supplies into the little acrylic boxes I bought and labelled for her.

'Did you have a nice time?' she says, not looking up from her work.

'We did! Was Lyla good for you?' I ask politely, even though I'm desperate to jump on a chair à la Ms Wilde Junior and dance around. Maybe she feels this great all the time, and that's why she's always skipping about. That's a nice thought.

'She was good as gold. Read me a lovely story and went off to sleep, no problems at all.' Kath looks up and smiles.

'Oh, good!' I say, beaming.

'You look very happy. What's happened? He's not proposed, has he?!' Kath starts excitedly, standing up straight.

'No, he hasn't.' Edward, with his perfect timing, comes into the room smiling after taking his shoes off.

'What is it then?' she says, fully picking up on the vibe.

'How would you feel about coming to New York

163

with us for three weeks next month?' I ask, clasping my hands together and standing right up on my tiptoes.

'What?!' Kath squeals.

'I need to be out there with MADE IT. We'll rent a big house – don't worry about the cost, we've got it, you'd just need to cover flights – Natalie and I have to work for a week so I need some help with Lyla, and Edward has to be out there for work too, so I figured we could stay on a bit when Natalie's gone home, have a bit of a family adventure!' I almost shriek at the end.

'Yaahooo!' Kath cries. 'An adventure! With my girls! Yaa*hooo*!!'

'So that's a yes, then, I think,' Edward says, going over to give Kath a hug. I love how good he is with my family.

'I always say yes to adventure, Edward! My Derek and I travelled the world. Adventure is in my blood!' She cheers as I open the fridge and pop the cork on a bottle of Prosecco to celebrate.

WHAT A DIFFERENCE A day makes. Yesterday I was driving to work feeling anxious and overthinking whether I'd mucked something up badly enough to warrant a Proper Chat with Natalie, and now I'm driving to work almost speeding to get there so I can tell her I'm fully on board with what's shaping up to be a month-long trip to America, pretty much. And, by the way, my amazing boyfriend will be there too!

I'm not even feeling anxious over requesting an extra two weeks off after Natalie's empowering speech yesterday about family being the most important thing in life.

I pull into the car park and almost skip into work.

'Well done on not ruining the planet today, bae,' Skye comments as I walk in happily, this time with a canvas tote instead of my slouchy leather cross-body.

'Thanks, Skye. I took your advice and decided I will only ever use sustainable bags until the day I die.' I smile back at her.

Skye is sitting on Alice's desk (who hasn't arrived yet) chatting to Stuart, and looks gobsmacked. Luckily she senses my tone isn't malicious.

'You're so weird. Do you want me to hot-desk out here today? Alice is away, and I want to respect your space,' she says, offering what I can only assume is an olive branch.

'Ahh, thanks, Skye. You're very welcome to sit in the back office with me, but I don't mind if you want to keep Stuart company. I think I'll be with Natalie most of the morning, so it's up to you,' I say, offering an olive branch in return by calling it the 'back office' and not 'my office'. We have our scraps, but Skye's all right really.

'OK, cool. I'll float,' she says, plopping delicately down into Alice's seat and taking things out of her trendy backpack. I wonder if I could rock a backpack?

I dump my bits in the 'back office' and head straight to Natalie's.

'Yoo-hoo, only me.'

'Hi. So, tell me, how did Edward take it? Is Kath up for it? Can Lyla even contain her excitement?' Natalie asks, more animated than I've seen her in a long time.

'Edward is more on board than we could have anticipated, Kath screamed with joy and I haven't told Lyla yet because I just need to check something with you,' I venture.

TWO HOURS LATER, AND everything is done, dusted, signed and delivered! With Stuart's administrative support (that man is absolutely incredible – he's sourced a three-bedroom town house in the West Village, a car for Natalie and Martin, who want to have a couple of weekends exploring the state, and flights for all of us in less time than most people take to find their passport). Natalie has OK'd the extended trip (I'll be covering the last fortnight, rent-wise) and she's been in touch with the film company about offering our services and spending some time with them.

I sit in my office taking some deep breaths before giving Mrs Barnstorm at Hesgrove a call to discuss taking Lyla out of school a week early. I thought she'd be reluctant, but she's much gentler with me than she usually is (I think it was thanks to last year's PaGS spa night), and has said that they don't get much work done in the last week of the year. She's said the trip sounds like a 'wonderful experience of culture and adventure for Lyla'. Fabulous, then!

So: Natalie's fine with the extra leave, the school have given me permission to take Lyla out, and I do need to chat to Gloria about our second WWW meeting, but I'm too fizzy right now to worry about that because this all just feels so amazing. I can't wait to tell Lyla – she'll be so excited. I can't wait to show her the Statue of Liberty, the Empire State Building, Coney Island – oh, who am I kidding? I'm the one who's excited!

New York, are you ready for us?

FIFTEEN

S ETTING UP FOR THE second WWW meeting feels just as exciting as the first. Once again, the diligent caretakers have grouped the seats around coffee tables, and again, each one has a small vase, this time with a yellow rose in it – we've gone up in the world, I muse to myself.

'All set?' asks Gloria, striding over, looking magnificent as usual. It's a warm evening and Gloria has dressed for the weather in beige tailored knee-length shorts, a floaty silk shirt with pearl buttons and light brown wedges. With her hair in a high pony with soft blonde tendrils bouncing around her face and the glowiest make-up you've ever seen, she looks like an assertive goddess.

'Yep! Going to smash it!' I say, much more convincingly than I thought I would.

'That's what he said.' Gloria gives a laugh. Then, placing her hand on my arm, she says, 'Just gotta keep it from the heart and you'll do fine!' The door opens and we shift our attention to it. People have started to come in and, remembering the system from last time, are heading over to the welcome desk for their name label.

Gloria walks over to greet them and I, somewhat nervously, go to the front of the room to make sure everything is as it should be.

Old wooden podium Mr Ravelle uses for assemblies? Check. Chair for model? Check. Trolley with all my kit? Check. Tripod, camera and live screen all hooked up? Check.

I can do this. I've done so much already this year, I can easily do this, I repeat in my head, wiping my palms down my skirt. I too have a bit of a spring in my step from the hot weather and joy-inducing sunshine, so I've gone for a mustard-yellow jersey maxi skirt and then, because today's session is all about confidence and I'm trying to really get on board with that, I've worn a denim shirt with the sleeves rolled up but instead of tucking it in, I've undone a few of the bottom buttons and tied it up in a little knot. It's not Skye crop-top level, since you can't actually see any tummy skin, but it's a nod to it, and that's confidence in my book!

Tonight I'm opening the meeting with a brief word or two, handing over to Gloria, who's going to be sharing her top three tips for confidence, and then I'm going to demonstrate (with confidence) a few make-up techniques that we can use to help build us up a bit and feel our best. And what's more, it's going to be filmed, so people not only see in close-up what I'm doing, but they can go back over what they see tonight. I'm super-excited to be doing a bit of what I love with the make-up, but I've never had a camera trained on me – I'm much more comfortable the other side of one. Still, it'll be amazing practice for my live tutorials project with MADE IT, and after the whirlwind of a fortnight I've had prepping for New York, I haven't really had a chance to get nervous.

I stand at the podium and watch everyone file in and take their seats around the tables. The hall feels a lot more full than last time – word must be spreading. I feel a little tingle of what might be pride. Gillian and Finola take the same table (it's much like the foyer mentality, where once you have a space, that's it until you die), and they give me a little wave. Well, Finola gives a stony nod and Gillian gives a big smile and a thumbs up. In each of their languages they've basically said, 'Good luck, babe!'

I keep an eager eye out for Kath, who said she was coming, and just as I think we're going to start, I hear, 'Oo-eee, sorry I'm late! I was talking to Moira, who's been having a hell of a time with her joints.' Kath has started talking to Gloria, who's trying to guide her to a table but having no luck, because once Kath starts, it's hard for her to stop. Ever the small-time hero, Gillian jumps up, heads over and says hello, having seen Kath at the school gates a few times with me, and takes her over to their table. Storie is nowhere to be seen, and I can't say I'm too disappointed.

With a nod and a massive smile from Gloria from the back of the room, it's my moment.

I lean into the mic. 'Hel-hello everyone, tonight!' Hmm, OK, weird start but not too bad.

There's a very faint murmur of hellos from around

the room and I lock eyes with Gloria, who is opening her arms, lifting her chest high and smiling, like one of those mums who stand at the back of child beauty pageants, encouraging her over-tanned four-year-old to smile and win the tiara. I take it and throw myself in. From the heart. Here we go.

'Thank you for coming to our second meeting of Women Who Win. For those of you I've not yet met, I'm Robin. I know that coming to things like this can be difficult, not just with logistics and childcare, but it can also be an emotional hurdle.' I notice a few people look up from their clipboards as if agreeing.

'When my daughter first started here, at the school, I didn't know anybody and I was in a bit of a bleak place. I found it really hard to make small talk in the foyer, let alone have the confidence to form relation-ships or share goals and ideas with any of you lovely ladies,' I continue, gesturing around the room.

'It's taken me a few years to realise that it was never because I didn't have any good ideas, or because I wasn't worthy of having friendships, but rather, I totally lacked the confidence to put myself out there. It's not easy! It's not easy to share parts of yourself you feel insecure about, and it's not always easy to come to events like this, so before we even hear the amazing tips and hacks Gloria has put together, I just wanted to tell you, I think you're already Women Who Win, and I'm so honoured to be here tonight.'

To my shock, the women in the room clap. Not a standing ovation, and not Oscar-winner-level cheering (although Kath is actually cheering, 'That's right, lovey! You're our winner!'), but it feels amazing. How far have things come, eh?

'So in a moment, I'm going to pass you over to Gloria, but before I do that, I wanted to let you know we'll be looking for a volunteer model so I can demonstrate some simple but effective make-up techniques that might help you feel a bit more confident. For those who don't know, I am a professional make-up artist at a local company called MADE IT, and I have worked on film sets, at London Fashion Week and on an array of commercial sets, as well as offering wedding and event sessions and private bookings.'

I say the last bit about myself with so much confidence I can see Gloria at the back making silent whooping gestures. That's right, kids, I am a proper professional make-up artist and I'm not afraid to say it. Mum's opinions be damned: I am worthy.

'While I let you all think about whether you'd like to volunteer, I'd love to welcome Gloria Straunston to the front of the room to share with us her incredible tips for confidence!'

Gloria bounds up to the front and stands there in silence, smiling for a few moments. We're all a bit bemused, until she tells us we'll understand what she did when she gets to point three of her 'top tips'.

She has the whole room under her spell as she lists them.

'If you don't ask, you won't get' is her first tip, and I have to admit she's right. I've always been afraid of asking for what I want, waiting for someone to offer me things instead, but I can see it ties in perfectly with her second tip: 'What's the worst that could happen?' As she explains how the fears that hold us back are so often only in our heads, I can see the audience all sitting up straighter, a wave of self-belief spreading through the room. And when she gets to her last point, her intro suddenly makes sense. 'To project confidence, simply don't say anything at all,' Gloria tells us. 'Silence is one of the highest-status tools in your arsenal. You don't have to fill every gap.

Believe in yourself and your value and take your time, own your space, your right to be in the room.'

Gloria elaborates on her tips for a few minutes, and takes some questions from the room. Everyone is engaged. It's a pleasure to hear her insights, and I can tell the rest of the attendees feel the same. I'm riding on such a high from my intro, and her amazing talk, that I barely notice it is coming to the point in the evening where I have to showcase my make-up skills.

'And now, please welcome back to the podium Robin Wilde, who I just know is going to wow us with some fantastic make-up artistry!' Gloria beckons to me, the women clapping again.

If ever there was a time to feel confident, it's now. Channelling Gloria's three tips, I walk to the front of the room, where one of the other mums is wheeling out the little trolley I set up all my make-up on earlier.

While all this is happening, I take a moment to gather myself. I look out over the room, and everyone is looking back, ready for me to speak. I have commanded their attention with my confident silence. I'm acing this already!

'Hello. Again. Aha. As I mentioned earlier, I am a fully qualified make-up artist. I'd love to show you some techniques I use to portray that mask of confidence for the days when I'm not quite feeling it on the inside, and trust me, there've been a lot of those. Is there anyone who'd like to volunteer?' I ask, secretly hoping it will be somebody I know.

A few women meekly put their hands up. Just as I'm about to pick Gillian (because I know her and feel really confident working on her), I decide to push my comfort zone. I've already done so much this evening I wouldn't normally do, so why not go a bit further?

'Yes, the lady in the front, I think it's Amrita?' I say to a mum I've seen around but haven't ever really spoken to much.

Amrita nods and comes up 'on stage' (it's not a stage, it's a little area at the front of the hall, but it feels special to be there).

'Before I begin working on Amrita's lovely face,' I say with a smile that makes Amrita smile too, 'I just wanted to mention that you don't need make-up to feel confident. Every face is beautiful and strong and confident, and make-up is really just the icing on the cake. But I also wanted to say that if you're having one of those days, or like I have, one of those years, it's OK to let make-up help you. For a long time I felt quite shy and nervous, but by making sure my skin was glowy and my lips were bright, it sort of helped me feel a bit brighter, too,' I finish.

I notice a lot of nods around the room, and feel geed on by the support.

'OK, so tonight I thought I'd show you something that we can all do but that I often hear people saying they don't have the confidence to try. As Gloria has said, though, what's the worst that can happen? You can relate that to make-up. If it all goes horribly wrong, just wipe it off! I'm going to demonstrate here, on Amrita, how to apply the perfect red power lip.'

The next ten minutes are a blur of being in my happy place, applying precise red lip liner, filling in with one of my favourite MAC lipsticks in 'Russian Red' and finishing off with a little concealer around the mouth to give it that powerful, crisp outline. I find myself relaxing more and more, and having such a fabulous time thinking about how exciting it will be when my MADE IT live tutorial project is off the ground.

Once finished, I receive another round of applause

and Gloria takes over, thanking me for my efforts and urging everyone to book me the next time they need a make-up artist.

As I go back to my seat, my heart is racing, but I realise that I'm ten times more nervous thinking about doing new things than I am when I'm actually doing them. All hail the red lip!

SIXTEEN

AFTER THE SUCCESS OF the second WWW night, I'm on a high. I feel so good about sharing some of the tricks of the trade that the glow stays with me all the next day at work. But as the end of the day approaches, the glow changes to nerves. There's something I have to do.

Biting the bullet, I drive straight to Lacey's after work to tell her what's going on. There's no doubt in my mind – she's not going to be OK about this. I haven't seen her OK about anything for a really long time, so I'm dreading how this is going to go.

Twenty minutes later, Lacey opens the door of her stylish Victorian terrace with tears running down her cheeks and a screaming, red-faced baby in her arms. Not a good start, but, I tell myself, it's better than Lacey still pretending everything is 'fine'.

'OK, the cavalry has arrived. Let me take Willow, you go and take fifteen. Wash your face, scroll through your phone, scream into a pillow – we've all been there, and you are going to be all right,' I say in my most confident tone.

Lacey doesn't say much but hands me a very cross Willow, a damp, crumpled muslin square and a bottle of milk and thuds upstairs with heavy feet. I park myself in the unusually untidy lounge (not that I'm judging, but for four to five months it's been show-home standards), and put the bottle to Willow's lips. Instant contentment. Oh, wow, I've missed holding a baby like this. Her warm little body rests against mine and she holds onto the end of the muslin as she drinks, keeping her eyes locked on me, as if to say, 'Who is this woman? She's not my mummy but she's feeding me and she seems nice.' At least, I hope that's what she'd say if she could. For a couple of moments I think again about the baby Edward and I lost last year. I wonder if I'll ever stop silently comparing. I wonder if I'll ever be able to talk about it with Lacey, or if it's too morbid to compare your friend's beautifully thriving child to your baby that never was. With miscarriage affecting so many of us, why do we live in a secret world of grief? I lose myself in my thoughts, not feeling sad or angry but melancholy for the way things are, until I hear footsteps in the hall and Lacey comes into the lounge in fresh PJs, her hair brushed and a weak smile on her face.

'God, sorry about that. I'm a mess. Ha. I'm always a bloody mess. I just had a big horrible chat with Mum about breastfeeding,' she says, flopping down onto her stylish grey sofa and moving the plump crushed velvet silver cushions out of the way to get comfy.

'Really? I always thought Tina was super-supportive? I used to be so jealous of you and Piper having such a chilled-out mum when mine was so, well, like mine,' I say, still looking at Willow's face. She's mesmerisingly beautiful. Bright blue eyes almost the same as Lyla's, but white-blonde, fluffy hair like a duckling's feathers and big pillowy cheeks that you can't help but want to stroke.

'She is. She's great. She's done loads for me, but she's old school. She never worked, it was always Dad, and so she's made motherhood her profession and bloody aced it. You remember what she was like, don't you? Cooked everything from scratch, baked for every school fete, read us a story each night, mended our carefully ironed matching dresses – all of that lovely mum stuff. She thinks I should stick at breastfeeding and "push through" for Willow's sake. I just can't. I feel utterly drained in every single way.' She starts to tear up again, distracting herself by plumping the already plumped cushions. I can see how the cleaning thing got out of control.

'Lacey, you are an amazing mum. It's so lovely that your mum enjoyed the whole homemaker side of things, but it's OK if you don't. You've done so, so well with breastfeeding this far! Willow's already bene-fited, and now if you feel it's time to move to a bottle, that's perfectly OK,' I reassure her.

'I know. I know you're right, and I'd say the same to you. It's just that her words seem so powerful and I feel so crap. She just kept saying: "Breast is best,

Lacey", over and over, and I'm so tired. I don't sleep because I can't fill her. Karl offers to help all the time but it's me she needs. I'm just done.' The tears start falling again.

'No! I will not let you be upset over this. You're a brilliant mother! Let Karl help. If you feel ready for the bottle, it's OK. You know what's best? A mother who feels well and rested and in good spirits. Once you find your footing with this new feeding and you're sleeping a bit more, and Karl's taking on some night feeds, you're going to feel so much better. It's going to be OK, I totally promise you.'

'OK,' she says, wiping her eyes. 'I'm so glad I have you, and that you get it.'

We sit in silence for a few minutes, just looking at Willow while I sit her up and burp her.

'Lacey, I need to tell you something,' I start.

'Oh God, it's bad news, isn't it?' she jumps in, instantly looking panicked. This is going to be hard.

'It's not bad news. It's good news for me, but I don't know . . .' I trail off, suddenly wishing this wasn't happening and I could stay looking after Lacey and holding Willow forever.

'I'm going away. For a work thing, and for an

Edward thing. We're flying to New York in just two weeks,' I begin.

'But that's so soon! Not for long, though? Because of Lyla, right?' she queries.

'I know, crazy! We'll be there for nearly a month, and we're going to take Lyla. Kath is coming, too, and will look after Lyla while I work,' I say slowly and steadily, almost afraid to make eye contact.

The pause that follows feels eternal. Lacey is gathering herself, and I'm not sure if she's going to throw the pillow at me or plump it again.

'Obviously I'm really happy for you all,' she lies, kindly, 'but I'll miss you so much.' Her eyes fill up a little, but she smiles tightly.

That was a lot less stressful than I'd anticipated. Well done, Lacey, eh?

'I know. We'll miss you so much, too. But I can FaceTime you every day, and you still have Karl and your mum, who I promise will be fully on board with the bottle once she gets to do this,' I say, nodding down at Willow, who has now snuggled into me and fallen asleep.

'Karl works all day and is still in his golf group,' Lacey says sadly, picking imaginary fluff off her PJs, a couple of tears escaping down her face and dripping off her chin.

'Oh well, your mum is never too far away, is she?' I try. I wish I could say something to solve this. I hate seeing her this way.

'She makes me feel crap. Robin, I'm happy for you,' she lies again, fully crying now, bless her, 'but I really can't cope. I don't want to be even more of a burden than I already am—'

'You're not a burden,' I say desperately.

'But if I'm honest, I really, really don't want you guys to go. I need you. I need Kath! I've never felt so lonely in my whole life, even though I never get even a minute actually alone. I literally feel like everything is slipping through my hands like salt. Please don't go. Not just yet. Me and Karl will give you the money you'd have earnt there, or something. Please stay here, just this time, please.'

By this point, Lacey is a complete mess. She's doing that crying where you can't catch your breath and everything sounds thick and snorty, and you can guarantee that in about an hour you're going to have a raging headache. My heart breaks for her.

'It's not a money thing for me, it's a business thing,

really. Without this, I don't know if MADE IT will, you know . . . make it,' I begin trying to explain.

'I'll help! I'll support the business, but please, just don't all go for so long,' she sobs, probably knowing that's not really any help but clutching at straws.

'Oh Lace, I wish that was a thing we could do. I'm sorry, I never normally go away, and I won't be going away again for a really long time.' I'm almost crying myself now, seeing how hysterical my best friend is.

'I just need everyone to stay together. This is too much. This is . . . I . . . It's all . . .' Lacey peters off with a series of short, sharp breaths and great, huge sobs.

'Stop!' I cut her off, a light bulb suddenly flashing on in my head, hopefully just in time. 'Lacey! Why don't you come out too? It's a bit out there, but fuck me, you need a break, and a change of scenery might do you good,' I say, looking around the grey room full of baby garb.

Lacey blinks at me through puffy red eyes.

'What, just drop everything and fly across the world in two weeks' time? Leave home for weeks and weeks?'

'Three weeks, and yes. Why not?'

'I've got a baby,' she says, dumbfounded, as though I've just told her to swim to the moon or something equally absurd.

'Yes, you have a baby, but you're not a prisoner, are you?'

'What will I do on the plane? I'll be that person everyone hates, with the crying baby. Or what about during the day, while you're being a fabulous career woman? Just walk around by myself, all day?' she says, now sort of angrily crying. I know this isn't really her, but I want to shake her and make all this go away.

'On the plane you'll use a baby sling, carry Willow close or sit her on your lap. Kath, me and Lyla will be there too, so that will be lots of support. In New York Kath will be looking after Lyla, so I'm sure she'll help you too, and, let's not forget, your actual sister who flipping lives there! You could even stay with her! You'd have twenty-four-seven Team Childcare on your side!' I say enthusiastically as all the cogs of how good this plan actually is click into place. This might really solve this! Piper will put her up, she only needs one air fare, the trip might snap her out of this funk, Karl can golf himself senseless! This is *amazing*! I almost feel a bit dizzy!

Lacey sits for a moment, taking it all in, nodding, and then, wonderfully, the most enormous smile slowly spreads across her face.

'Oh. My. God,' Lacey says, with more life in her than I've seen in ages. 'Fucking. Yes.'

SEVENTEEN

THE NEXT TWO WEEKS are a blur of anticipation, anxiety, packing and phone calls.

Lyla is absolutely dancing on the ceiling at the prospect of New York. I've never done a big trip like this with her; our only holidays have been little UK minibreaks. Simon was a bit huffy when I told him I was taking Lyla away for three weeks and missing the last week of term. But his attitude evaporated when I asked him if he fancied having her for all of that time – managing her end-of-term social whirl, laundering the approximately eight tonnes of uniform, PE kits, lost property and goodness knows what else she keeps at school, plus explaining that he'd have to be the one to break it to her that he wanted her to spend three weeks enjoying whale song and gong baths with him and Storie, while I painted the town red in New York. He relented pretty damn quickly and seemed happy when I said he could spend some extra time with her in the school holidays, and he muttered something about a yurt and an organic family festival Storie fancied.

Kath has rung multiple times asking how many cases of her lavender creations she can bring. She plans to see if little shops and boutiques will stock them while she's out there. After attending her first WWW meeting and reading every tip, trick and comment on the Facebook group, this is her master plan for expansion: Lavender Lovies is going stateside. Problem is, I've had to make several calls to the airline to see how much three extra suitcases would cost, and if we can bring scented lavender powder and aromatherapy oils on the plane. 'Tell them I'm not making an actual bomb, just a *bath* bomb,' Kath said in the background while I was talking to Meghan from Virgin Airlines. Nothing makes a phone call to an airline more exciting than a middle-aged woman saying 'bomb' repeatedly.

Lacey was also fretting, but mainly about the flight with a tiny baby, which I can understand. We've moved our seats to the bulkhead so she can have a skycot, and reassured her that between her, Kath, Lyla and I, we've got it covered.

I haven't let on to Kath and Lacey, but, as is becoming a thing lately, I'm feeling a bit tense, too. I've barely seen Edward these last two weeks, let alone spent quality time with him. We feel like ships in the night.

Edward is flying out a couple of days before us for work and he'll be staying at his apartment to start packing up his stuff for The Big Move. Natalie and Martin fly out the day before us to get the keys to the house and, I suspect, to have a less chaotic travel experience than coming with all of us. I bet they're flying first class.

The pressure of ensuring that everyone's OK, packing my own kit and thinking about the actual job at hand is getting to me. I wish I could just sit down and chat all this through with Edward, like regular couples do, but with managing everything, there just hasn't been time. I take a deep breath, channel Gloria, remind myself that I'm a badass and crack on.

And so, before I know it, we're running through the terminal at Heathrow, bags and snacks flying everywhere; five women on a mission to catch a plane, take America by storm and live our best lives.

As it turns out, Kath has cut down her lavender haul, Willow is a natural at air travel, Lyla has taken full advantage of a tiny screen full of films and snacks being brought to her seat, and I have taken full advantage of the complimentary fizz. I mean, I sort of needed to after our ridiculous top-speed airport dash, thanks to sleeping through my alarm, but let's not focus on that. We're smashing it. One way or another, we are smashing it.

Nobody is more surprised than me when we land in the United States of America with (once we were on the plane, at least) no fuss, no drama and not a jot of stress. How the hell did *that* happen? Perhaps I was foolish to be worked up, and this is going to be the dream trip I'd hoped it would in the first place!

Yes, yes, yes – New York, here we come!

Part Two

IT'S A HELLUVA TOWN

EIGHTEEN

JULY

AFTER JUST A COUPLE of lavender- and baby-related delays at the airport, we are in an Uber people carrier to the Greenwich Village area and are all bursting with excitement, despite our tiredness from travelling. New York is just as I'd last left it. A cacophony of heat, noise, people, building works and smells. The scenery changes from industrial airport skyline to little wood-clad houses in the suburbs, a huge freeway flanked by vast graveyards (cue unknowingly insensitive comment from Lyla: 'Wow, Kath, imagine if Derek was in one of them – you'd never find him!') and then, finally, the city skyline, at which we all whoop and cheer.

Pulling up to our could-have-been-on-*Sex-and-the-City*-house, we clamber out of the Uber with all of our luggage and look up, gawping for a couple of seconds. Then Kath puts down her bags, throws up her arms and shouts, 'NEW YORK! WE HAVE ARRIVED!', which, as you'd imagine, leads to even more cheers, Natalie opening the door and joining in with the cheers and Lyla going from hyper to positively hysterical. Hurrah!

Unsurprisingly, since Natalie, the most effortlessly stylish woman on earth, OK'd it, the house is beautiful. Located just a couple of minutes away from a subway station, so perfect for us to make it uptown, it's a stone's throw from a restaurant called Rosemary's Pizza and an array of cute little craft and gift shops. The house itself is a tall terrace with deep red bricks and wrought iron railings swirling up the front steps to the bold black front door. Wow. I knew Stuart was a whizz at finding a good deal on flights and accommodation, but this place is incredible!

'I'm jealous now! I thought I'd be getting the best deal staying at Piper's in Brooklyn, but I almost wish

I wasn't!' Lacey says, holding Willow, who also seems utterly enchanted with her new surroundings.

'It's all right, lovey, we're right by the underground station so we'll see you every day,' Kath says, patting her arm and admiring the window boxes.

'Yep! And you can come for sleepovers and share my room!' Lyla offers excitedly.

'You're already sharing with Auntie Kath, you little monkey!' I say, tickling her. We'd decided she would stay in there so I could work on my laptop in the evenings, and wouldn't disturb her too much with early work starts when she's jet-lagged.

Looking up at the house, I'm so excited myself I don't quite know how to handle it. I want to jump up and down on the spot and shout, 'This is my life! Look', but I hold it together. Instead, I quickly pull my phone out to text Edward. I'd already texted him at the airport to say we'd arrived, but this feels like extra news.

Hey! Guess what! Our house is amazing! It's sooo New Yorky. Obviously, since we're in New York, haha! Fancy leaving work early and coming over right now?

'Are you going to come in, or should we leave you to stand looking like excited meerkats all afternoon?'

calls Martin, with a smile, through the open door at the top of the brownstone steps.

'Martin!' I shout. 'We made it!'

'Always on brand!' he replies. 'Do you need help with your cases?'

The house is as stunning inside as it is outside. We leave all the cases by the front door and walk around, marvelling. The ground floor is entirely open-plan. The front door opens on to an entry hall, which blends into a living room space complete with fireplace, two big pale blue squishy sofas with matching armchairs (yes, it really is that big!) and a TV. Beyond that is the most urban-farmhouse kitchen I've ever seen. The units are all teal wood with oak worktops and little pots of herbs growing on the windowsill, but the appliances are sleek and silver and oversized. There is a central island with a hob and fan overhead, and tucked into the corner a dinner table and chairs next to a window overlooking the garden. I say garden, but it's actually just a patch of concrete.

'There's no grass in it, Mummy!' Lyla says, surprised.

'They don't need grass here,' Kath interjects. 'They have a special place called Central Park that I'm going to take you to. It's the biggest park you can imagine, with lakes and swings and meadows and even a zoo and a castle!'

Lyla's eyes light up. I love seeing her this animated. I was a bit worried that taking her out of school a week early was really terrible of me. Valerie had overheard me talking to Finola and Gillian in the run-up to the trip and said, 'Never mind about her education, eh? As long as Mummy's having fun', and tittered her false, high-pitched laugh as she strutted off with Corinthia looking sadly back at Lyla. They seem to have really bonded lately. I must arrange that sleepover when we get home. Anyway, until then, we're here, and day one seems to be a success.

Natalie and Martin take us upstairs to show us the bedrooms. The master bedroom, which they have moved into, has views of the street in front from full-length windows. Kath, spotting their en suite, having learnt from WWW that every day is an opportunity, says, 'Natalie, you know you could use one of my lavender bath bombs in your bath. They're very good for relaxing, and I know how hard you work.'

'Hey! I work hard, too! I'm looking after you lot!' Martin jokes, as he deftly leads Kath out of the room and onto the landing with us. Our rooms are the two, slightly smaller back bedrooms with views of the 'gardens' and backs of other houses. Exposed brick and sanded floorboards make the rooms feel so stylish, before you even get to the abstract prints hanging up and the crisp white bedding. Lyla has taken the initiative to look at both rooms while we are still in the first, and declares which one she and Kath will have.

'We're going to have the next one because it's got a little fireplace!' she shouts.

'I don't think you're going to be lighting any fires in this heat, my love, it's boiling outside!' I laugh.

'Yes, but just in case we want to do any magic or cast spells, we can light a fire if we need to,' she says, matter-of-factly.

'Of course, I see your point. I'll have this one then. Thank you,' I say, equally seriously.

On the top floor, the attic has two rooms: a shower room for us to use and a little box room that Natalie and Martin have already put their cases in, so I assume we'll do the same.

'Ooh, couldn't Willow and I just camp out here?' Lacey pleads as she looks round with all of us.

'Ahhh, I wish you could, too, but Piper's place looks nice from the Skype tour she gave you, and it'll be lovely for her to spend so much time with Willow. She hasn't held her since she was born. It'll be amazing,' I say encouragingly.

'I know! And as soon as she goes to work I'll head over to you, so Willow can hang out with her new best friend,' Lacey says to Lyla, clearly trying to be chipper and wiggling Willow in her direction, making them both smile.

'Great! Well, let's all get unpacked,' Natalie says. 'Tonight, Martin and I thought we could head out and explore the surroundings, get our bearings, ready for a couple of rest days this weekend, and then it'll be a busy start to the week on Monday, Robin. Did you bring your A-game?' she asks in a surprisingly convincing American accent.

'I sure did, partner!' I chirp back, as all-American as I can.

'Mummy, that was terrible!' Lyla says, shaking her head as she goes through to her room to unpack.

I roll my eyes at everyone, as if to say, 'Wow, sorry about my not-even-a-teenager yet', and plod downstairs with Lacey and Willow to wait for Piper's taxi to arrive.

When Willow was born, Piper flew out for the

weekend to meet her niece and celebrate with the family. Lacey said that during that time she felt 'off her face' on sleep deprivation, hormones and everything else going on, so while the rest of the family might describe those first few days as newborn baby bliss, Lacey certainly doesn't.

'I'm so excited to see Piper with her niece this time!' she says, jiggling Willow up and down, looking out of the window.

'Weren't you excited before?' I ask.

'I was, but everyone wanted to hold her. I'd just had her, and I didn't feel like I'd had enough time with her. I felt like people were just snatching her off me every ten minutes,' she says, looking down at the baby in her arms.

'Like the Child Catcher from *Chitty Chitty Bang Bang*?' chimes Lyla unhelpfully as she bounces into the room and takes up watch for Piper at the window.

'Lyla, this is an adult conversation—'

'She's here!' Lyla shouts, and Lacey peers round her, straining to see her sister, finally spotting her running up the steps.

We all rush over to the door to greet her like excited Labradors who haven't seen their owners all day.

'Hi!' she shouts as soon as she sees us. 'You're all here! I can't believe it!'

Piper is Lacey's little sister. She graduated from art school just a couple of years ago, and after a brief stint living at home and feeling completely stifled, she moved out to New York and found a job curating in a trendy art museum. Piper is the epitome of cool. She has all the physical attributes of her sister – petite, naturally blonde, blue eyes – but she has a daring side to her and isn't afraid to embrace that. She's effortlessly fashionable, too. She's the kind of woman who could wear an oversized T-shirt with a metallic belt and look fresh off the runway, whereas if I did this, I'd look like I'd forgotten how clothes work. Essentially, Piper is the woman we all, a little bit, want to be. Except not, because Instagram has taught us life is about self-acceptance and not caring and— Wow, her legs are so freaking *shiny*!

Swept up in the joy of her arrival, we all gabble our hellos back, but she cuts us off.

'Right, never mind all of you boring people – except you, Lyla, you're obviously an exception – hand me this baby before I explode with how much I've missed her!' she says, reaching over to a slightly perplexed-looking Willow and a happier-than-I've-seen-her-in-weeks Lacey. 'Oh, my sweet mercy, this child is too much. I think my ovaries just popped.'

'What's an ovaries?' Lyla asked.

'I'll tell you later. Let's let Piper come in properly so she can sit down.' I bustle everyone over to the sofas.

Piper, as usual, looks phenomenal. Her skin is glowing, her nails well-manicured, she has long hair extensions and make-up that even Skye would be impressed with.

'You look so well,' Lacey says, sitting down next to Piper on the sofa, Lyla and I taking the two armchairs either side.

'Thanks, Lace. You look . . . wow . . . are you getting enough iron?' Piper says, almost in shock when she catches sight of just how tired Lacey looks.

'I just got off a plane, and I have a baby – of course I'm not getting enough iron, enough sleep, enough anything!' Lacey laughs unnaturally, looking round the room for someone to affirm her.

'It was the same with Lyla,' I add, sensing her need for a bit of comradery.

'I know, but you just look so, so tired. Like, *ill*

tired. Like worse than when you had that really awful bug before your wedding. Remember? Where you almost looked a bit grey?' Piper continues, not sensing my fierce telepathic rays telling her to shut the eff up because Lacey really doesn't need this right now.

'Yeah, OK, yep, I get it, I look like shit,' Lacey says, slapping her hands on her knees and getting up to start collecting all of Willow's bits and pieces that have already been strewn about.

'You don't look like shit, Lacey!' Lyla announces, horrified that anyone would insult her but also gleeful that she's getting to say a swear word.

'Language!' I snap.

'No, you don't look sh—, *bad*, you just look a bit worn,' Piper says, more quietly this time, with an apologetic look.

'I'm fine,' Lacey lies. 'It's just been a long flight, and I'm a bit sleep-deprived. A few days with you guys, some sunshine and some American pizza and I'll be right as rain again!' she jollies along, convincing only Piper and Lyla.

'Well, great! We're going to have such a good time! I'm going to spoil you and this little cherub absolutely rotten!' Piper is clearly pumped to have them coming to stay.

'All I want is eight hours of uninterrupted sleep and I'll be happy!'

'Done! I'll cuddle this little squisher all day! How hard can babies be, eh?' she laughs, looking at both of us, expecting laughter in return, but instead getting two tired mums staring back, unsure whether to slap her or cry.

It takes longer to get Piper to stop cuddling Willow than it does for Lacey and I to gather up all their paraphernalia – bags, buggy, baby sling, suitcase, small handbag, denim jacket, dummy, blanket, sun hat and sandals, but once everyone is in the cab and saying their goodbyes, I suddenly feel a little weight lift off my shoulders.

I love Lacey so much, but I'm glad she has Piper for support for a few days. Now it's time to focus on Kath and Lyla, my best ladies! And then, once that box is ticked, Edward . . . who can tick my box anyti— No, weird thought train. It's been a few days; I'm clearly missing him more than I thought!

By the time we've all unpacked the bags and Natalie and I have gone through our kit a bit, we're all absolutely ravenous and start grabbing bags and purses to head out for a mooch and to find some food. We're right opposite a pizza restaurant, so I'm gunning for this, but Natalie has suggested a vegan and paleo place on the square that we might all enjoy 'since we don't want to stuff ourselves'. Ummm. That's exactly what I want to do. Always.

Kath declines the exploratory wander, saying she's got a bit of a headache, but ever since Lacey and Willow left she's seemed a bit flat. She went for a lie-down earlier while Piper was here; I think she was tired from the flight. I ask her if she's all right to be alone, but she says she's going to 'long-distance FaceTime' Colin and read her book. I must try and find out what's really going on, but Lyla isn't showing any signs of fatigue or jet lag, so getting out of the house is going to be best for everyone!

Edward has replied to my message saying that he is tied up with some new suppliers for the stores and will be having drinks with them, so will come over tomorrow. I'm kind of miffed, but I do get it. We're all out here for work, so that does need to take precedence. I'm just a bit disappointed. I was so excited at the thought of seeing him tonight – we're still meant to be in that magical honeymoon period where everything is exciting and new, but we've barely spent any time together these last few weeks, which I'll admit is mainly my fault with work, WWW and popping in on Lacey more, but hopefully this trip will put that right. We're both back where we started, and there's something pretty special about that.

Natalie and Martin shut us straight down on the pizza option, but compromise away from paleo food when we see a little barbecue place just before it on the square. With dark grey interiors and industrial furnishings, we feel very hipster taking our steel bowls of pulled pork over to our table.

I've ordered myself a pulled pork rice bowl and Lyla opts for a mac and cheese side bowl, which I am secretly glad of because she never finishes the whole thing, so I can have a bite.

'Do you want to sit next to Mummy or opposite her?' Natalie asks as we find an empty table by the window.

'I want to sit right next to her because she's my best New York friend!' she says, reaching a hand round my thigh and wrapping herself in for a snuggle.

'Cherish these days, Robin, they are special moments,' Natalie says, smiling at the display of affection.

I'll absolutely cherish these moments, because these aren't always forthcoming. She's definitely a loving child, but I think being far from home has made her a bit clingy, bless her. I squeeze her back, affirming that she's my best New York friend too.

I look down at my sweet girl nuzzling into my tummy, up at my amazingly supportive and awe-inspiring boss Natalie, across to kind, laid-back Martin, who is the same kind of man I think my gorgeous Edward is, and smile wider than I have done in weeks. This really is a special moment. I'm here in New York City with all my favourite people, full to the brim of love and hope and potential. Christ on a cracker, life is good.

NINETEEN

TONIGHT IT'S MY MAGICAL NYC date with Edward. I can't wait to be with him again. I've woken up before 5 a.m., and just try to take everything in. I grab my phone to ping a text over to him.

Hey gorgeous, I'm up and raring to go! I've got such a buzz for New York already, and know today's gonna be a good one. I can feel it in my loins!

He's only working a half-day today, so the plan is to go out exploring with Lyla, maybe have a look in some of the little trinket shops we passed yesterday, and then Kath will take over with Lyla and I'll have some time to prep for work and see if there's anything I can do for Natalie (this is a work trip, after all), and then a New York City date night with Edward.

I can't *wait*. The sun is streaming in through my window and already I can hear the city. At home you might hear the odd cat and perhaps the binmen on certain days, but here is different – there's always sound. I quite like the feeling of knowing I'm always near other people; it's oddly comforting.

After sitting in bed with my laptop for an hour, I scrape my hair up into a bun and change into my bra, tee and comfiest jeans. A bit more formal than I would normally go for a Saturday morning, which is really saying something about my fashion standards, but I don't want to run into Martin, or Natalie, looking like a woman who's been raised by wolves or just escaped from an underground bunker *à la* Kimmy Schmidt.

Just as I'm leaving my bedroom, I hear a little whimper from upstairs. I stop and listen for a moment, wondering if I've imagined it, before I hear it again.

The door to the bathroom is slightly ajar, so I creep over with caution just in case it's Martin.

'Hello?' I call.

'Mummy, I'm poorly,' Lyla cries very quietly.

'Oh, my baby!' I say, going straight in and finding Lyla sitting on the fluffy mat, leant up against the side of the bath. 'My sweetheart, why didn't you tell Kath, or come and find me?' I ask, stricken that my little girl has been here like this, all alone.

'I didn't want to wake Kath up because I heard her crying last night, and I didn't know which room you were in and I needed the toilet and my tummy was hurting and I didn't know where I was and I, and I, and I didn't know where you were,' she starts stammering between sobs, getting worked up.

By now I've sat down next to her and pulled her in close.

'I'm here, I'm right here,' I whisper, stroking her hair and feeling how hot her head is.

'Are you going to go to work today and leave me?' she cries.

'No. I'm staying right here next to you. We're going to have a nice bath, have some Calpol, get better and stick together. Have you been sick?'

'No, but my tummy is bubbly and I had a big, slobbery poo,' she replies and I hug her in closer to me, almost wanting to cry myself for how little and fragile she feels right now. You can never say that motherhood is glamorous; before I was a mum, if someone had told me about a 'big, slobbery poo', I might have vommed a bit in my own mouth, but right here is the only place I want to be at this exact moment.

'OK, my bluebird. You've perhaps got a bit of a runny tummy from the travelling and all the cheese in your dinner last night. That's all right, we can sort that. We'll ask Kath to nip out and get some supplies, like mashed potato, and maybe some new sticker books, and we can spend the whole day in my room pretending it's our own private hotel and watch films on my laptop. How about that?' I say gently.

'Yes! And I can stay snuggled to you like a tiny bluebird, and you can make the duvet like a nest!' she says with a bit more life in her.

'Sounds like a plan, Stan! Now, let's run this bath and have a spa morning together. I'm just going to let Kath know you're poorly,' I say, standing up.

'She's sad about Eleanor,' Lyla says, with big glacier-blue eyes.

'Who?' I'm totally lost.

'Last night when she was asleep she sounded like

215

she was crying and she said "my Eleanor" and then rolled over,' Lyla says, completely seriously.

'Maybe she was dreaming about her friends, then. Do you remember that time you screamed in your sleep about "the giant TV remote" and I almost had a heart attack?' I laugh, making a mental note to ask Kath about the crying.

'Yes! That was so funny, Mummy,' Lyla laughs back, getting to her feet and having a look on the window-sill at the selection of bubble baths that we could use. 'Shall we use one of these, or one of Kath's?' she asks.

'Probably best to try one of Kath's soothing ones. I'll go and get it,' I say, nipping down the winding attic stairs.

Just before I make it to Kath's room, my phone pings in my pocket.

Feel it in your loins eh? I can think of something else you can feel . . .

Oh God. Of all the times to start a sexting sesh, this is not it. Diarrhoea and aunts who talk in their sleep aren't my idea of an aphrodisiac! Yesterday I was on top of the world, and now I can't catch three minutes to write a filthy text. How the mighty have fallen!

I knock gently on Kath's door.

'Oo-ooo, only me! Just wondering if we could use one of your lovely bath bombs?' I say gently, putting my head round the door.

'Hello, lovey! I was just waking up.' Kath shifts herself up in bed.

'Don't get up on our account. Lyla's a bit under the weather, so I'm going to give her some love and run her a nice bath. She said you were a bit down last night,' I broach, not wanting to flat out say 'you cried in your sleep', because it feels a bit intrusive.

'Did she? Not me! I'm absolutely gung-ho, lovey! Here I am, in New York City with some of my favourite girls! What's to be down about?' she professes, pointing to the bag with the lavender creations in.

'*Some* of your favourite girls!? *All* of!' I laugh, taking a purple bomb and heading up to Lyla.

We spend the whole day in my room, only really leaving to fetch food from downstairs (toast for Lyla, thanks to Kath popping out this morning before deciding she may as well make the most of the day and visit The High Line) and open the door to the delivery guy (spicy Thai crab cakes and lemon iced tea for me – man, I love this city!) Natalie, totally understanding that it's more important for me to spend the afternoon with Lyla than run through our plans, goes out with Martin to hit up Sephora and try out some all-day brunch spots, while Edward didn't mind putting the sexts on hold till the real thing later tonight.

By 5 p.m., the house is brimming with life again and Lyla is feeling much better, zipping up and down the stairs, playing hide-and-seek with Martin, showing Kath her art creations, watching Natalie and I prepare enchiladas for everyone and, when Edward arrives, opening the door to him with a warm welcome of, 'Muuu-uuummm, your boyfriend who you like to kiss and say slushy love poems to is here, and he's brought you flowers,' and running off giggling.

'Are you sure she's been ill?' Edward says, walking across the living room into the kitchen, handing me the most beautiful bouquet of roses and kissing me.

'Ahhh, flowers! You didn't need to do this!' I say, quickly kissing him back but feeling a bit self-conscious with everyone around.

'I did it for all the love poems you supposedly like to read to me,' he says, smirking and walking past to say hello to Natalie, stopping to give a big hug to Kath, who's now come down into the kitchen from a FaceTime session with Colin. 'Something smells good! What's cooking?'

I love how confident he is. I love how well he gets on with everyone (even now, he's sitting down next to Kath and you'd think the two of them had known each other all their lives). I love that he brings me flowers. I can't wait to hear how his trip has been so far. I want this for the rest of my life and then some, I think. But right now, I'm just looking forward to spending quality time with him tonight.

'Right, I'll leave you here with this lovely lot. I'm going to head up and get ready,' I say, giving him a squeeze and a kiss on the cheek, to which he responds with a distracted smile (he's leaning over the enchiladas) and a cuddle back.

'Get ready for what?' Lyla asks as soon as I've taken three steps away.

'I'm going out with Edward tonight. I told you that yesterday. We're going to have a little date,' I say, running my fingers absent-mindedly through her hair.

'No! I don't want you to go anywhere!' she says, suddenly distressed, her eyes darting between me, Kath and Edward, panicked at my potential absence.

Thus begin ten minutes of back-and-forth, soothing and cajoling Lyla, who is so worked up she is hiccuping. She seems a lot better physically, but clearly she isn't right in herself. I can't do it; I can't leave her like this.

I look over at Edward from my spot sitting squished in the big blue armchair with a distraught Lyla in my arms. Please understand, I think, please, please understand.

'Do you know what? I'm quite glad Lyla doesn't want us to go out because it means we'll get some of Natalie's enchiladas,' he says to me loudly, ensuring Lyla hears.

God, he's a good one.

I DIDN'T WEAR STILETTOS and perfume, we didn't kiss under the lights of skyscrapers and billboards, we didn't eat off an overpriced menu in an Instagrammer's dream restaurant – but our evening was lovely. It was like being in a big, warm family, all eating round the table, Natalie and Martin telling us about when their three boys, who are now graduating or just starting uni, were little and how they juggled work and home life, and me feeling better that it's not just us who struggle to fit it all in, and Edward giving my thigh a comforting squeeze under the table here and there.

By the time we'd all chipped in to clear up, I'd tucked Lyla into bed, Natalie and Martin had headed to their giant room to watch a film, and Kath had gone up to read, it was pretty late and my jet-lagged early morning was really hitting me.

'How are you still going? Aren't you jet-lagged too?' I say to Edward through a yawn as we head up.

'I'm a machine. Fuel me with coffee and a beautiful woman and I can go and go,' he replies, squeezing my bottom and making me race up the stairs that little bit faster, grateful that Natalie has been so relaxed about Edward staying over in the 'MADE IT house'.

SUNDAY MORNING IS EQUALLY as gorgeous as Saturday. Sunshine is already streaming through my window when I wake before 7 a.m. I nip up to the loo and there are no small children feeling poorly, which is a better start than yesterday. Even though we've started living together, I'm still very much in the 'make an effort' stage, so I wash my face to freshen up a bit, brush my teeth (goodbye death breath) and put a little bit of lip balm on before creeping back into bed with Edward for one last cuddle.

I can hear everyone starting to get up. Clearly we're not fully on New York time yet, so I slide out of bed again, pull on my comfy jeans and a T-shirt (I already miss the freedom of wearing joggers and being braless: my caged boobs want to sag free and easy, dammit) and head downstairs. Instantly I retract my desire for privacy, because in its place we have full access to Kath's cooking, and this morning it's smoked salmon bagels and freshly squeezed orange juice!

'Morning, lovey! I was up with the larks, so popped out for all of this! Did you know the shops open before ten a.m. on a Sunday here? It's magic! I really got to grips with everywhere yesterday. I feel like a native. I'll be eating hamburgers and riding in a rodeo before you know it!' she trills cheerily. I don't want to bring her down, so I don't bother to tell her that hamburgers and rodeos are not what I'd associate with a native New Yorker.

Lyla plods downstairs sleepily in her pyjamas and gives me a big arms-round-the waist cuddle. She's followed by Natalie and Martin, who are up, showered, dressed and presentable. They're having a day out at the latest exhibition at the Guggenheim, so want to get a 'good start on the day'. Edward and I had discussed taking Lyla to some of the city splash pads since it's another hot day, and Kath said she'd love to come too and have a look. Apparently there are loads all over Manhattan, all with delicious street food trucks nearby, so it should be a really chilled (and yummy) way to enjoy the city.

Just as they're leaving, Edward comes downstairs in a pair of joggers and an old T-shirt but still looks handsome – it's so unfair.

'Morning, all! What a gorgeous day!' he says, picking up a bagel and taking a healthy-sized bite.

'Good morning, Mr Worm!' Lyla giggles. It's almost become a term of endearment now.

'Good morning, Lyla! A lovely greeting from you this morning,' he says, surprised but I think chuffed.

'Well, that's because you're so nice to my mummy,' she says, swinging on the bottom of the banister.

'Am I, now?' he says, looking at me as though I've told her something. Natalie and Martin are by the front door about to leave, but are waiting to hear what sweet thing she's referring to, and Kath is smiling by the kitchen island as she whisks up some eggs for the pan.

'Yes, you are. Last night I heard you wrestling with her and she was saying, "Oohhh, Edward",' she begins. 'And then you said—'

'OK, Lyla, thank you very much!' Oh my God. I need to stop her. I know where this is going, and it is not a place I want to share with my boss, her husband and my aunt!

Lyla giggles almost hysterically and runs upstairs, leaving me absolutely speechless and Edward a shade of red I didn't think it was even possible to see on human skin. I want to die.

'Well, at least someone's having a good time!' Kath quips, breaking the silence and carrying on with the eggs as I head upstairs to tell Lyla off, or hide forever, and Natalie goes out the door, smirking. Poor Edward. This is going to be a long trip.

TWENTY

B Y MONDAY, JUST AS work starts, that amazing finding-it-easy-to-wake-up-early jet lag is gone, of course. I snooze my alarm for as long as I can before Edward uses both arms and a leg to shove me out of bed and tells me off for having no pep.

'It's because you're so dishy that I can't get out of bed,' I whisper in his ear.

'Babe. I appreciate the sentiment, but your breath smells like a rat's arse,' he says, wincing.

'How lovely of you. It's good to see we're still firmly in the honeymoon period,' I say, grabbing my towel and nipping upstairs for a quick shower and thorough teeth brush.

An hour later, in the Uber with our mini kit boxes (and reassurance from Edward that I now smell fresh as a daisy), we're headed off to the film franchise offices to have a chat with the new team face-to-face, to see if we can convince them that we should be on-set for the commercial shoot, and to offer any of their staff a free makeover or mini-facial to showcase our skills. Natalie is fully trained in a lot of the beauty therapies, and I'm pretty nifty at little hand massages and manicures, so between us we make a good team. I'm a bit apprehensive as to whether anyone wants their make-up doing at 10 a.m. on a Monday morning, but if I've learnt anything from my last trip, it is that anything goes in New York.

As we hurtle along Sixth Avenue, I can't help but feel that fizz of excitement in my stomach you only get from a place like this. It's ironic that we're working somewhere that's just like in the movies, so that we can work in the movies! I think about sharing that out loud with Natalie, but she looks so focused, I don't want to intrude on that with my musings, so keep it to myself, with a mental note to share it later with Lacey – she'll enjoy it.

As we pull up to an enormous skyscraper with one of those revolving glass doors, I take a big breath in. I remind myself that I'm Robin Wilde, MUA, Mother, Vice President of Women Who Win and that I'm going to smash it today.

We take the lift up to the thirty-third floor and step out into a stylish lobby, manned by an equally stylish receptionist.

'Good morning, Fierce Films, I'm Paige Toon, how can I help you?' asks the astonishingly chipper receptionist.

Without blinking, Natalie says smoothly, 'Morning, Paige, we're here to see Scott Turner and Lindsey Kelk about the make-up artistry for your commercial this week. I'm Natalie Wood and this is Robin Wilde. They're expecting us.'

'Perfect, I will give them a call and they'll be right over to collect you. Can I get you a drink or a snack in the meantime?' she asks, still perkier than the perkiest person I've ever met in my life.

'Just water, thank you,' Natalie replies before I can even enquire what kind of snacks they have on offer.

We sit and wait a few moments, admiring the office and flicking through our phones. We don't chat much because I think deep down we're both quite tense – we need to charm them today, plus make sure we've got everything lined up for the commercial. Natalie and I both know that if we mess this week up, there's every chance we'll wave goodbye to any future film work with Fierce, but I try to channel my wisdom from WWW and pretend I'm much more confident and able than I think I am. Fake it till you make it, after all.

'So, I'm really sorry but Scott isn't available right now. But Lindsey said she'll be with you in about thirty minutes. Did you want to wait here, or grab a smoothie somewhere and come back?' Paige asks, looking genuinely apologetic.

'That's a shame, Paige,' Natalie says, standing up with her kit. 'Do you know if Scott will be available at all today? We'd hoped to talk to him about the commercial, and I'm conscious the week will race by.'

'He's in with Lauren,' Paige says, looking weirdly afraid.

'Ah, I don't think I know Lauren,' Natalie questions carefully, cleverly trying to squeeze a little bit of information out of poor Paige, who is looking more nervous by the second.

'Lauren Sharp is our new Project Manager, heading up this campaign. She handles all the budgets, schedules, staffing,' she says, clearly aware that Lauren holds a lot of cards.

'OK!' Natalie says with a wave of confidence. 'I think I need to speak to Lauren at some point too, then! Instead of leaving for a smoothie, we'll wait for Lindsey, because we've chatted on the phone a lot and I'd love to put a face to a name, even if it's just to rearrange a time. In the meantime, while I just re-evaluate my notes, we'd love to offer you a hand massage or mini-makeover,' Natalie beams a mega-watt smile that I don't think anyone could say no to.

'Wow! Really? I don't have my purse with me right now . . .' Paige trails off, looking embarrassed.

'No, no, it's on us,' I say, sensing it is my turn to take control, as I see Natalie has opened her laptop and is stealthily googling 'Lauren Sharp Fierce Films' to get the low-down on our new contender to woo.

I guide Paige back over to the other little reception sofa with one hand, carrying my kit in the other and asking what kind of beauty treatments she usually enjoys.

In no time at all, I've given Paige a mini eyebrow tutorial, plumped her lips with a few of my finest lip liner tricks and shown her how to colour-balance dark under-eye circles with orange or red lipstick. We are having a great time, and she's shared that she's new to the city from New Jersey, this is her first job out of community college and she misses her 'mom' a lot.

Something about her vulnerability mixed with her eagerness to learn makes me connect with her. I feel like I understand exactly how she feels.

'I'm here with my aunt and my daughter for three weeks. If you want to come for a walk with us, or get some pasta or something, that would be lovely. My Auntie Kath is like a surrogate mum to me – maybe she could be a stand-in for yours, too! I know what it's like to feel like a small person in a big world,' I say, smiling at her, not noticing that Natalie and Lindsey are standing over me, waiting for me to finish.

'Oh! Sorry! Ha! Just chatting. But also doing a few little make-up techniques on lovely Paige here. Who was listening out for the phones at the same time!' I babble, suddenly feeling very exposed and like I've stepped over the mark.

'You've done an amazing job, as always,' Natalie says, smiling. 'Lindsey, this is my Creative Director and star make-up artist, Robin Wilde. She worked with me on the film shoot when we were last over, actually saved the whole thing when I was struck down with a gastro problem.'

'I've heard a lot about you, Robin,' Lindsey says with a knowing smile, which makes me wonder if she means my whistle-blowing antics on set last time or my make-up artistry.

'Aha! Thank you! I'm very pleased to be here,' I say enthusiastically, regaining my composure and giving Paige a little wave goodbye as she goes back to her station.

Lindsey leads us through into a small side office, where I listen to Natalie talk shop for an hour or so and discuss the situation, her ideas, what MADE IT has been doing and achieving in the meantime. Scott joins us, and she semi-rehashes as he nods keenly.

'Well, I know I'd absolutely love to have you guys involved again, but unfortunately the ball's not in my court, ladies,' Scott says, resigning himself to defeat.

'No, we thought perhaps not. When could we arrange a meeting with Lauren, please?' Natalie asks brazenly.

'Ah, she's always very busy,' Lindsey stalls.

'I know, at home when I'm running my office it's a nightmare trying to fit people in, but I'm sure she'll understand we've both travelled halfway across the world and Robin here, especially, has done such a lot for this company, and the industry, that it would be a shame to not squeeze us in,' Natalie says, maintaining a steady gaze at the same time as a perfectly courteous smile. What a skill, what a woman!

'Yes, absolutely, I'm sure. Let me go check with her assistant and I'll be right back!' Lindsey says, clearly a bit shaken.

Twenty-five minutes later, and Natalie's scored a morning meeting with Lauren, Lindsey and Scott the next day and is having a nice chat with them about the best places to try yoga in Midtown. Amazing!

As I close the door behind me when we arrive 'home' that night, I suddenly feel exhausted. Natalie has stayed out to have an informal chat with Lindsey and Scott, but I've come home because the adrenaline that carried me through the day has worn thin and I'm having pangs for my actual home. For the sagging leather sofa and my crisp blue John Lewis sheets (a little treat to myself when I moved into the new house all those months back), for my favourite mug I have my tea in and for the luxury of shlubbing about in whatever I want without anyone seeing or judging. Not that anyone here would judge, but Natalie is still my boss, yanno?

Like a tonic, Lyla comes hurtling over. 'Mummmyy! You're home! You've been gone ages! Me and Kath went on the subway to Central Park. There's a lake you can buy boats for, so we did and we rowed all the way into the middle. I actually think I saw sharks in there, but really quickly before Kath did. Lacey and Willow came too, but they didn't come on the boat, which is good in case one of the sharks ate Willow, which would mean—'

'Whoa, whoa, slow it down. I want to hear all about it but you're on fast-forward and it's too much. Let me get in the door and put my things down,' I say, trying to edge past her just to have some breathing room. I feel like I'm home again. 'OK. You went to

Central Park, amazing, you took a boat out on the lake, also amazing, Lacey and Willow were there, triple amazing!'

'I know! We did everything! We went into this big famous hotel that they have on that Christmas film about the little boy lost in New York, and we went down a gold escalator into the downstairs bit and bought ice creams,' she starts up again, as Kath comes through from the kitchen smiling and perches on the arm of the sofa to listen to Lyla's account of the day.

'Well, now I'm jealous if you had ice creams in famous hotels!' I say, pulling her in for a cuddle.

'Yep! We had ice creams but we had lunch first – pizza! We ordered one pizza but it was massive, as big as this.' She gestures with her arms as wide as they'll go. 'Then we wandered around, but that was boring and Willow didn't care about shops and build-ings, she wanted to go back to the park, I could tell, so we did. We went back into Central Park, which is massive, by the way, so it wasn't the same bit of park, and we found this amazing slide that was so fast. Like, supersonic fast. Willow fell asleep while Kath was feeding her, so I had about fifty hundred goes on the slide while Lacey and Kath talked on and on and on for so long, I thought maybe that's why Willow fell asleep!' She giggles and takes a big breath from all that talking.

'You cheeky monkey! I'm glad you had such a great day. I wish I'd come!' I say into her hair as I pull her in tighter and then let go to look up at Kath. 'Didn't Lacey want to come back? Has she headed off to Piper's?'

'She has. It was such a wonderful day, we saw all the sights, didn't we? I pushed Willow in her push-chair for most of it, and she was kicking her little legs, gurgling away! Lacey was looking a bit tired so I said she should go and look round all the posh department stores while I had the girls.' She smiles.

'Did you? Were you OK with two children in a big city? Very brave!' I say, surprised.

'Ooh, it was lovely. Willow is such a special baby, she reminds me so much of '

'Me!' shouts Lyla, jumping off me and throwing herself into Kath, almost pushing her backward.

'Of Miss Lyla Blue, yes!' She squeezes her. 'It was just lovely. I fed Willow two of her bottles. She loves them! I popped into one of the shops and picked out this little romper with a lacy trim round the legs like we used to have in the olden days. It was so darling, I had to buy it – lace for Lacey's girl! And Lacey thought it was unique,' she carried on.

'Did she? That's nice then,' I say, starting to feel a bit jealous of how much Kath dotes on Willow, which is utterly ridiculous considering how incredible she is with Lyla and always has been. I'm clearly overtired and being a cow.

'I think it was nice for her to get out and have a bit of time for herself. Motherhood has been a shock to her system. Her hormones are all over the place; she feels like she should be overjoyed at finally being a mother, and then feels guilty for not being on cloud nine. She's all at sixes and sevens, the poor thing. I really empathise.' She sighs, and gives Lyla a bit of an extra squeeze.

I don't think now is the time to tell her she means 'sympathise', not 'empathise', so instead, knowing Edward has a lot on and will be staying at his place tonight, I open my food delivery app (oh yes, I downloaded all the food apps on the first day), and start scrolling to see what we can have for dinner. Once again I think to myself, this city is fabulous.

TWENTY-ONE

TUESDAY IS A BIG day. Natalie is heading to her meeting with Lauren to negotiate our spot on the ad shoot. She knows that if she can establish our right to be there, it's the first step to making sure they honour our contract for the big-money film work. But she doesn't just want us to be there because we've got a deal – we need to be there because we're great at what we do. So while Natalie goes to the meeting, she wants me hitting the make-up counters of Manhattan, trend-spotting, sampling and generally proving that us Brits can match any of the local agencies.

It's a dream morning for me. By the time noon rolls around, I've got swatches of glitter shadow right up my arm, a bag full of samples, new product launches and all-American classic products – and, most importantly, I'm fizzing with ideas about how to use them. Still, when I get Natalie's call, the fizz turns to nerves.

But it's good news. At the meeting with Lauren, she's agreed to let us work on the sports commercial and we've said we're happy to assist. She'd already booked a team in, of course, so we've said we'll be willing to be there and help out and oversee how they use our original design work from the film. I think it's a bit of a step down for Natalie not to be running the show, but her attitude is gracious, as ever. I love that she's never too high and mighty to roll up her (very expensive) shirtsleeves and get the job done. I've said it before and I'll say it again: Natalie is one hell of a woman.

It means starting tomorrow, but we're both raring to go. Get this right, and Lauren has agreed to another meeting after the shoot to 'discuss our future'.

Natalie and I spend the afternoon looking over our designs, seeing how they can be updated to feel up to the minute, and, as we end the day with an iced tea, feeling like MADE IT has earnt a seat at the big table.

Full of energy from our triumph (OK, and maybe a little from all the sugar in my iced tea), I dash home so Lyla can quickly FaceTime Simon. It's late at home – and I think he has to smuggle his iPhone into the house so Storie doesn't complain about 'negative electrical energy' – but Lyla spends a happy half hour telling him about everything she's seen, done and eaten. It gives me a chance to catch up on a few emails to Gloria, planning the next WWW meeting, and to get my kit ready for the morning.

TRAVELLING TO THE SHOOT first thing on Wednesday, I feel like I've lost a limb, not bringing my kit with me, but we'll be using the other team's so there was no need to drag ours with us. As I watch the city whizz by it brings back the feelings I had when I came out here the first time. I'm fizzing with excitement, mingled with nerves, knowing we need to impress the production team – and I tell myself I've done it before; I can do it again. Although I have to shoot a sideways glance at Natalie just to make sure

I've not given myself my little pep talk out loud.

The advert itself is based loosely around the horror film we shot a couple of years ago, and how the villains and heroes in that film decide to ditch the fancy costumes and go for sportswear. Of course. Totally believable.

Our job is to turn the models into athleisure-wearing heroes that have been in a bit of a fight but still look hot. As you do. Since it's not every day I get to play around with latex, and watch Natalie absolutely nail it with the special effects kits, I have an absolute ball.

While I work on some realistic neck scars for my villain, Natalie sets to work making up one of our heroines.

'The brief says I need to look powerful but beautiful,' the model and, excitingly, rather well-known actress Sophie Richardson says.

Natalie studies her face for a moment, looks over at the table of kit (I can tell it's frustrating her to use someone else's kit as it's not our own, but she's handling all this so well) and says, 'You mean powerful *and* beautiful.'

'Ummm, no, for sure it says powerful *but* beautiful,' Sophie replies, confused.

'Well, I don't think a woman has to be beautiful in spite of being powerful, or vice versa, so give me that brief. I'm going to take this pen and change it and then we'll set to work changing the world. Or in your case, saving it. One pair of sweat-resistant leggings at a time!'

Once again, Natalie aces it. If ever there was a real-life hero, I think it's her.

At lunchtime, when the models sit down to eat with giant bibs on so they don't ruin any of the minuscule crop tops or leggings, and the crew tuck into the offerings on the catering tables, I pull my phone out of my pocket to 'check everyone's all right'. That's what I say out loud to nobody as though to justify screen time, but what I really mean is, 'ensure I haven't had any crisis-related messages from Kath about Lyla, scroll mindlessly through Instagram for ten minutes without blinking and then think about texting my boyfriend'. Happily, no crises from Kath, all the usual fare on Insta (mothers who've dressed their children in matching-but-not-quite-matching clothes, people who have ultra-trendy tiles in their new bathrooms, someone doing yoga on a beach with a caption about mindfulness, someone walking their dog on a beach with a caption about mindfulness, someone's candlelit bubble bath with a caption about mindfulness, and the honest mum who's taken a comedy shot of her recycling bin full of empty wine bottles. That gets a like from me), and then it's time to message Edward.

We've not seen each other since the maybe-too-loud quickie, and I want him to remember being excited and thrilled rather than embarrassingly caught out by an eight-year-old.

We still need to reschedule that night out in Midtown. I've packed a nice dress. Or maybe a night in at yours, and I can leave the dress on your bedroom floor . . . ? X

I click my phone shut, put it back in my pocket and head smugly over to the catering table. Before I've even put a meat-free, gluten-free wrap on my plate (I thought America was meant to be the land of junk food, but I've been severely let down once again), my phone buzzes. I pull it out of my denim skirt pocket (it's too hot for jeans, I feel too old for denim short-shorts and so I'm bringing back the denim-mini-with-T-shirt combo) and read it.

Dress on the bedroom floor. You on the bed. No one's going anywhere. Xxx

'There's either a sale at MAC or Edward has messaged,' Natalie says as she comes up to the table to scope out the goodies.

'Ha. It's Edward. I think we're doing something later,' I say as casually as possible, knowing full well my cheeks have turned bright red.

'Well, make the most of it. These first couple of years are the best. I actually feel like I'm having them again with Martin, now I've stepped back from work and hands-on motherhood a bit,' she says, pulling some grapes off their bunch and putting them in a paper cup to take back to her station for later.

'Yes, Natalie, you've really stepped back a lot, what with the trip out here, London Fashion Week, expanding the business, having your boys back from uni every reading week and travelling the world with your husband. So chill,' I joke.

'A rolling stone gathers no moss.' She smiles as she turns on her Chanel ballet flats and strolls back to her make-up station to sit and check her emails before we're called back for touch-ups.

I don't know how she does it all, but she does and I'm impressed.

I spend the rest of the afternoon standing to the

LOUISE PENTLAND

side of the set ready to offer touch-ups, but I'm a bit surplus to requirements since Natalie is on hand, too, and the rest of the team are already booked, so I have plenty of time to slip away and text Edward. I don't want to sound too desperate, but literally, I am desperate to see him.

This morning, Kath said she would be happy to put Lyla to bed. They're having another day out in Central Park today, since they loved it so much the other day ('We've got nearly a whole month to explore, so why not take our time,' she pointed out when I asked if she fancied a different park). I think Lacey and Willow might join them again, too, which will be nice. I need to schedule in some time with Lacey and Piper at some point. I know we've got a full three weeks, but it is going so fast and I want to relive our youth and pretend I'm young and carefree and don't spend my evenings rummaging through school bags to find the letter about the gymnastics competition or sewing badges onto leotards.

Natalie insists we take the subway home. 'It'll be cool,' she says nonchalantly. I don't want to disagree with her because she's my boss and I don't want to sound like a diva, but the thought of walking down

244

the steps onto a rammed platform to get into a steel tube at rush hour on a July afternoon doesn't sound all that 'cool'. By the time we get off at Christopher Street station, I'm sweating so much I think even my knickers are wet. Natalie, of course, has but a gentle glow, and her navy cotton shift dress looks like it's fresh on. She's basically an alien.

I'd planned to dash in, give Lyla a cuddle, grab my bag and hotfoot it to Edward's place (meaning we can be as vocal as we want with no children earwigging), but after that 'cool' journey, I need a full-body MOT, including maybe even a hair wash.

Just gotta clear up a few work bits with Natalie then heading straight over. Be with you by 7pm. Xxx

He doesn't need to know I got so hot my head sweated.

'Mummmyyy!' Lyla says, hurtling herself at me as I follow Natalie into the house.

'Oof!' I say, with the force of her. 'What a great welcome! You'll make Natalie jealous!'

'That's OK! One for Natalie too!' she says, jumping over to Natalie and giving her a big squeeze. 'Mmm, you smell like perfume. Mum smells like bins,' she says, chuckling to herself as she runs upstairs to tell

Kath we're home. It's not like her not to be in the kitchen or the lounge.

'Oo-ooo, had a good day?' I say, popping my head round her bedroom door. I'm startled to find her lying down on the bed fully dressed. She's usually such a doer, always cooking or crafting or playing, not sleeping. 'Are you OK? Are you ill?' I ask, panicked.

'No, I'm OK, lovey, just a bit worn out,' she says wearily. 'Maybe overdid it with all the walking,' she adds.

Kath's used to a lot of activity; she and Colin have regular walking weekends and she's enjoyed all of those, but maybe the mixture of that and the heat and having Lyla has been too much. I feel guilty for over-burdening her.

'Have you eaten? Shall I make you a cup of tea or something?' I say, still feeling a bit unnerved to see her so still and quiet.

'I'm all right, my love. Just pull the door to and I'll have a little rest.'

'OK. Well, I'm nearby if you want anything. Love you lots,' I say quietly as I pull the door shut and hear her say, 'Love you too' as I do.

'Is Kath poorly?' Lyla asks from behind me, looking worried.

'No, not at all! She's just pooped from a big day out with you! Why don't we go into the kitchen, make something yummy to eat and you can tell me all about your day? Let me just message Edward and I'll be straight down.' I inhale slowly as I pull my phone out.

Kath isn't well, she's lying on her bed and being a bit weird and quiet. I don't feel OK asking her to babysit tonight, and it's crossing the line to ask Natalie or Martin so I'll have to cancel. I'm so sorry. I wanted to come over so much. Wahhh xxx

All potential sexy vibes over. Typical.

Shall I come to you? And then come in you? ;) xxx

Oh God, he hasn't sensed the tone.

Aha, erm, probably not. I'm going to have Lyla in with me to give Kath some space. 100% on for something tomorrow though! I still have the dress! Xxxx

Righto. No problem. Awesome for tomorrow. I'll book somewhere, make a real date of it. Wear the dress. Then let me take it off ;) Xxx

I can't tell you how nice it is to have a man who's so into me. But it's even nicer to have one who can put his ego aside and not make a big deal of it when Lyla or Kath have to come first.

After changing out of my clothes and going heavy on the deodorant because this New York heat is ruining me, I head downstairs to make Lyla and I some dinner and chat with Natalie and Martin. It's lovely to have some laid-back non-work time with them and, as guilty as I feel to say it, it takes my mind off worrying about Kath.

After I've tucked Lyla into my bed with about three stories and a thirty-minute YouTube video of an adult's hands opening egg surprise toys, I nip up to the solace of the attic bathroom to give Lacey a ring and find out how today was. Lyla said she had played on the Alice in Wonderland statue 'for hours' (which in kid talk is about twenty minutes) while 'Lacey stroked Kath's arms and talked about adult things'. Sounds serious.

I try calling twice, but no answer.

Hey, sorry if you were having a nap. Just wanted to see how you got on today. Kath's a bit under the weather so I hope you still had a good time. Really missing you and Willow! And Piper!! Let's see each other soon please! Xxxxxxx

Immediately the dot-dot-dots flash up on my phone. Then disappear. Then flash up again. Is there anything more anxiety-inducing than knowing someone was going to say something and then didn't?

Hi hi! Sorry, just sorting a fussy Willow. Piper and I miss you too! We'll sort something! Love you! Xxx

Oh. I look at the message for a long time, trying to work out what I don't like about it. I think it feels a bit like I'm being fobbed off, but when I try to pinpoint why, I can't. Resigning myself to the fact that I'm probably more tired than I think I am, I sit on the bathroom floor, watch two YouTube videos of girls showing me how to 'shop' my wardrobe, text Edward that I miss him and head to bed, too.

TWENTY-TWO

THE NEXT TWO DAYS at work pass in a blur. Even without needing to be too hands-on on the shoot, it's great seeing our designs being brought to life again. Whenever I can, I flit back to the production office, in a flurry of being exceptionally charming (well, that's what they call my English accent); offering mini beauty sessions; talking a lot to lovely Paige and teaching her a few techniques on her breaks or when she's not having orders barked at her by Lauren or Scott; trying to list all the reasons why they should honour our original contract; and coming up with a stunt so amazing I could wow them all into choosing to keep us.

Kath seems utterly enthralled by Central Park. Despite trying out some of the other, smaller ones, she keeps going back there with Lyla and often takes Willow so that Lacey can go and have a look round the galleries and museums in peace. I've offered to go and meet her for lunch a couple of times, but she says she understands that I should probably stay at work or in the Fierce Films offices to show willingness (and be persistent!), so I appreciate that.

Things with Edward have been tricky. We've had a couple of daytime coffees together, but we're yet to have our big city date or any actual alone time. I guess living in a house with three other adults, a child and Lacey plus baby nearby, as well as having the pressure of the contract and him the responsibility of sorting the store, isn't exactly conducive to romance!

He seems understanding, though, thank God. He's been really kind asking after Kath, and I've got a night out with the girls to get the weekend started, squeee, but after that we've absolutely promised each other some alone time is on the cards, and oh baby, I cannot wait!

I can hardly believe we've been here a week. We were meant to have wowed the new team at Fierce by now and got our contract updated. I still feel a jolt of anxiety whenever I see Lauren on set, but at least the day ends with good news. The shoot has overrun and they want us back on Monday. Natalie's can-do attitude means she says yes to the extra day without missing a beat – even though I know she'll have to rearrange her plans with Martin and stay on in the city longer than she'd hoped. But right now, I'm not thinking about Monday. It's Friday night, and that means one thing: girls' night.

'Woowooo!' I howl up into the air as Lacey, Piper and I strut down the cobbled street towards Soho House in what I consider the sexiest saunter anyone has ever seen in their lives. It was on a night exactly like this that I met my gorgeous Edward, and my tummy does a little flip thinking about how well all that turned out. It would be so fun if he were here, I think, but then instantly remind myself I'm allowed to have time with my girlfriends and they were here first. I'm wearing super-tight, super-flattering black wet-look jeans that I bought in Forever 21 on Union Square after work last night and feel fantastic in, teamed with a gold tie-up, corset-style top that I've had since uni (though I wore it a little tighter back then) and have decided I'm bringing 'back'. It's surely actually vintage now, and that makes it cool by default. Plus, if you can get away with a gold corset top anywhere, it's SoHo, New York. I've teamed all this with the most beautiful Kurt Geiger heels, champagne-coloured and encrusted with little iridescent crystals, and I feel like I look amazing. I don't actually feel so brilliant on the inside, but with this outfit and my make-up carefully applied by Natalie as a nice favour, it's not hard to fake it to keep everyone's spirits up.

Lyla was in a terrible mood when I came home tonight. She seemed annoyed that Kath had 'only talked to Lacey all day' and that 'she just kept telling me to go and play'. She went on to pout that she wanted to go home so that Corinthia could come and stay over, and then when I told her to have a grateful heart for being in this fabulous city, she told me she wanted to go to Daddy and Storie's house. That was a low blow. I told her I wasn't interested in this silly behaviour and that adults are allowed their time too, me included.

I popped in to see Kath, who, again, was having a lie-down. I gently asked if she was OK and she just said she might have overdone it with the walking again, which I didn't quite buy, and had a sore throat from talking so much, but she was all right; she had had a lovely day and just wanted a bit of peace.

I considered not going out, but Natalie and Martin (who are babysitting Willow at our house tonight) insisted I go and have a bit of girl time and said they'd put Lyla to bed for me. Sensing my reluctance, I think that's why Natalie offered to do my make-up. It seemed petulant not to take them up on it, so here I am, shaking what my mama gave me (ha, she'd be horrified that I'm shaking my size twelve bum in tight trousers in New York!) and trying to make the best of it.

'Yoo-*hoo*,' cries Piper in reply to my earlier howl, clearly picking up the social cue to Have a Good Time. Piper looks phenomenal tonight in frayed denim short-shorts, white pointy-toed ankle boots and a slouchy white soft cotton tee tied in a knot at the side. She's combined this with a gold-chained tan bag, heaps of gold bangles and big beachy waves in her impressively long blonde hair. If I tried this look I'd come out an absolute mess, but somehow, as usual, Piper pulls it off with total confidence.

'Yeaaahhh!' Lacey semi-shouts, somewhat lacklustre. Tonight is really hard for her. It's her first night out since having a baby, she's in a new place, she's feeling a bit down and, as she said, 'To add insult to injury I'm still wearing my fucking maternity jeans!' Piper and I reassured her that she looked sensational; you can't tell they're maternity because her floaty black cami covers the stretch waistband, and it's only been a few months – she's supposed to still be living in maternity jeans!

I reach out and give Lacey's hand a little squeeze as we step through the door to the bar, knowing she'll need a bit of extra support, and she squeezes it back gratefully.

Three cocktails down and things haven't massively improved. We're all doing our very best, sitting with pretty-looking drinks and immaculately applied liquid lipstick, laughing about 'the olden days' and asking Piper all about her love life as though we're giddy schoolgirls finding out that someone went on a date to McDonald's and had a snog afterwards (mmm, cheeseburger breath).

'So, what are the odds you two have fallen so madly in love with the city you're both gonna move out here permanently then?' Piper asks, ordering another round of drinks – this time G&Ts, before we overdose on sugar and whatever else the cocktails are made of.

'Aha! I'd live out here if everyone else did. Although Lyla's made me feel super-guilty tonight for not arranging a sleepover with her new bestie Corinthia, and I must admit I'm starting to miss my mum friends,' I venture.

'Lacey's your mum friend now, though! Yummy mummies unite!' Piper cheers, sloshing a little of her drink on her thigh and wiping it off with her hand and laughing.

'Yes! You'll always be my number one, I love you so much,' I say, slurring ever so slightly and leaning into Lacey for a cuddle.

'I'm glad I'm still on my first cocktail. You two are a mess!' she says, mock disapprovingly.

'As soon as you've built your drinking game back up, we're forcing you to keep up with us!' Piper says, cheers-ing her.

'I'm so glad you came out, though. I've missed you!'

I say, still not releasing her from my slightly tipsy embrace.

'Miss her! She's been on set with you three times already this week!' Piper laughs. 'I'm going to the loo. Anyone coming?' she asks as she hops off her bar stool and we shake our heads.

'Why does she think you've been on set with me?' I ask Lacey, confused and sobering up at the revelation.

'Oh, it's no big deal,' Lacey says, trying to wave it off.

'OK, great, so tell me why she thinks that, then,' I push.

'Well, as well as our trips to Central Park, Kath's been offering to take Willow out a few times. On the first day I did go and look round a gallery in peace and it was really cool, but I'm just so tired and fed up, I don't want to look round anything.' She shrugs.

'So what do you do, then?'

'Just stay at Piper's, watch telly, sleep and stuff. I don't have any photos to show her from my day out, so I just say I've been hanging with you and it's no phones on set. Don't tell her, please, she'll just worry or be annoyed,' she says, completely deflated.

'I won't, but now I'm a bit worried. I thought things were getting better, Lace. What did your GP say when you went? Maybe you could talk to them about this when we get home. There's support out there, you don't have to do this by yourself.'

Lacey looks at the floor, then says in a voice so quiet I can barely hear her: 'I haven't been. I know I said I would, but I kept putting off making the call and then we decided to come here. I thought the trip might help, but now I've realised we've come all this way and, well, I'm still me. It's the same me, same problems, just a different place. Or it would be, if I could make myself leave the house.'

'Lacey, have you been out at all?'

'Yes! Kath and I took the girls all round the north of Central Park, which was, you know, nice. She must have told you. Willow slept in her sling, and since the pushchair was empty, Lyla crawled in and fell asleep all curled up with gangly arms and legs.' She smiled. 'Here, I've got a picture of that!' And she flashed open her phone, which distracted me for a moment.

'OK, that's the cutest thing I've seen all year,' I coo, looking at my baby girl asleep in the sunshine. 'How long was she asleep for? The trip must be really catching up with her.'

'Over an hour, both of them. I really want to tell you about it, actually. There's something—'

'No!' Piper says, jumping back up onto her bar stool and indicating the phone in my hand. 'You're not going to be those mums who are granted a rare night out but spend it showing each other pictures of their kids! Willow's great! Lyla's great! We're out! Let's paaartyyy!' she shouts, throwing her hands in the air so wildly a group of men next to us cheer.

CLIMBING INTO BED THAT night, I know I'm going to regret it in the morning, especially since I'm supposed to be seeing Edward. Tonight was ace. Well, maybe not *ace* ace, but still pretty good. Piper was in high spirits, I forced myself to be (I'm shattered, but I was *out* out and in a gold corset, so it would have been rude not to get involved, right?) and Lacey was a bit flat. I get it, though. If I were in my maternity jeans and feeling low post-baby, I don't think a bustling nightspot like Soho House would have been my first choice either. I'm pleased we managed to get her to stay out until almost midnight, though – a good chunk of time without the baby.

I take a big gulp of water from the glass next to my bed, pull my false lashes off and flick them onto the bedside table (knowing full well I should do a full face cleanse before I sleep but having no intention of doing so) and resolve to spend some proper time with Lacey as soon as possible to help her feel a bit better. And Kath. And Edward. And Lyla. It'll all be fine. It'll all be—*zzzzzz*.

TWENTY-THREE

As EXPECTED, I REGRET the cocktails (and the gin) the next day. I wake up feeling like there's a drum thudding in my head and sand in my mouth. Sadly, though, I don't have the luxury of being alone, so I have to clean myself up and put a brave face on it in front of my manager, my aunt and my daughter.

We spend the day flopping about and watching movies. Lacey comes round first thing to collect Willow (who has been good as gold), but doesn't stay to chat, and though I may be a bit paranoid because of the hangover, she seems really shifty.

By the afternoon, I've geed myself up a bit and call Edward. He doesn't have much time free because he has to meet a designer for 'drinks and a chat' that evening, but we make the most of it. Lyla and I hop in a cab down to Battery Park, where we met Edward and spend a happy hour riding the fishy carousel (the most beautiful thing you've ever seen – a carousel with, instead of ornate horses, fish of different colours, all glowing and dancing to the music) and staring out at the Statue of Liberty.

I'm feeling all kinds of bliss when he leans in for a quick hug and whispers, 'Let's have that alone time soon.'

How we've been here this long and not managed a solo date yet is beyond me.

On the taxi ride home, I give Lyla a big squish. 'That was super-fun, wasn't it?' I say, feeling quite jubilant despite the low-level alcohol poisoning.

'Yes, but I wish it was just you and me. I want some Mummy time on my own,' she says, looking out of the window.

All jubilation evaporates. I can't bloody win.

THE NEXT DAY, SUNDAY, is the day Natalie and Martin are supposed to leave for their tour of the East Coast, but with the shoot running over, they're staying on an extra couple of nights. I had originally planned for it to be a 'home day', spent just relaxing, but this morning I decide to get out of their hair and head into town.

I ask Kath if she fancies joining Lyla and me, but she declines, saying she fancies a look round the markets as research for Lavender Lovies. I understand. I figure she'll enjoy a bit of solo adult time after being around us all for so long.

Having nothing planned, I'm at a loss as to what we can do. Lyla has spent a week trudging up and down every park, playground and splash pad in the city, and I don't fancy a full-on museum day. Against all better judgement, I decide to ask my mummy-hungry eight-year-old what she wants to do.

'Lyla,' I say, once I've beckoned her into bed with me that morning for a big snuggly cuddle, 'If you could do absolutely anything at all today that's just you, me and this city, what would it be?'

Lyla smiles from ear to ear and looks at the ceiling while she thinks.

'I know!' she says, turning excitedly to look at me.

'OK! What?' I'm catching her enthusiasm.

'I want to go to near the big park and go in the American Girl dolls' shop. I want to buy a big dolly that looks exactly like me and the matching clothes, and then I want to go in the special little girls' salon they have and they can make my hair all curly, and then I want to go with you and my brand-new doll and get those giant milkshakes with doughnuts and sprinkles on top,' she says without once pausing for breath.

I thought about her proposal. I've seen those dolls, and I'm sure they're, like, a zillion dollars. I can't imagine the children's salon would be budget-friendly either, and the milkshakes probably contain a week's worth of sugar, not to mention additives that will no doubt send Lyla absolutely berserk.

But, as the youth say (or maybe they don't anymore, since I know the phrase), YOLO.

'Lyla Blue Wilde . . .' I pause for effect, watching her jump up onto her feet, towering above me. 'Your wish is my command.'

'YESSS!!' she screams, bouncing up and down on the bed, causing me instant regret for saying yes to the milkshakes.

And so Lyla and I spend the most perfect afternoon

in Manhattan on our own special mummy-and-daughter date. I load the salon, the doll and all her gubbins on my credit card, schlep all the way over to the milkshake place and enjoy every second of lavishing my time, love and resources on my little girl.

I knew she needed it, but perhaps not realised how much I needed it, too.

TWENTY-FOUR

ONDAY! OR AS MY dad would say, 'Two days to Hump Day', and Mum would roll her eyes saying, 'Robert, please!' as if he'd said, 'Three days to ShagSexWankSnog Day'. I must give them a call soon. When I told Mum last month about this trip, she'd told me to buy a sew-in pocket to keep my valuables close, because 'New York is full of ruffians'. Mum doesn't like to travel unless it's on a cruise ship (that she barely steps off) with Steve and Amanda from the Rotary Club. When I was little we did have a few holidays to the South of France, but Mum, ironically, thought the French were rude, so we stopped going. Kath and Derek always seemed to be travelling and I absolutely adored studying their photos and hearing all about their trips. They made everything feel like an adventure. They went to Austria to see the hills where *The Sound of Music* was filmed, and Kath still has a home video of her dancing with Derek, singing all the songs. And when I was about thirteen, they went to Athens, which is where Kath bought my memory box – this beautiful box covered in shells, which I've used to store photos, letters and ticket stubs in ever since. She also brought us back matching little gold headbands that she'd bejewelled with faux leaves and iridescent beads, so we could be 'like Greek goddesses'. Kath really knew how to have fun, and still does.

As I left her this morning, she seemed her cheery self and back to normal. She said the early night had really sorted her out and she was looking forward to a day exploring Chelsea. Relieved to see her back on her feet and Lyla skipping around her, I left for the subway and Fierce Films with Natalie, relaxed and ready to take on the day.

We knew this one last unplanned day of shooting was our best hope of getting a meeting, a contract, a win before we left New York. But despite our eager smiles and willingness to help, Lindsey and Lauren are there to 'oversee' the work and I think put everyone on edge.

'Morning!' I trill. 'Looks set to be a lovely day!' One of the few positive things my mother taught me was that if you couldn't say anything nice, go for a bit of weather chat.

'Does it? Looks to me like we're running over because nobody has been keeping track of timings,' Lauren snaps, leaving me completely startled. What on earth am I supposed to say to that?

'Lauren, let us sort this. You have plenty of MUAs, but if there's anything else we can do, we're here, an extra pair of hands, ready and willing to get stuck in,' Natalie says with such grace I want to squeeze her. If ever there's a woman you want in a crisis, it's Natalie.

'Oh, you're going to go and chase up the caterers, are you, who haven't supplied the breakfast for today?' Lauren retorts.

'No, no, you don't have to do that,' Lindsey follows up, embarrassed. 'That's not their job, Lauren,' she says, quietly pleading with Lauren not to be so rude.

'It's not our job, but an army marches on a full stomach, so give us the details and we'll make it happen!' Natalie declares with a smile and I nod because, quite honestly, I want some breakfast.

An hour later, and we're stepping out of an Uber with armfuls of trays of pastries and a boot loaded with fruit platters and juices. Turns out the breakfast was waiting and paid for but the delivery guy had cocked up. All it took were two glam delivery girls (us) and a taxi, and the problem was solved, but you'd have thought we'd found a cure for cancer with the response we got. Even Lauren smiled.

No sooner have we stepped back to admire the platters we've laid out on the tables than we hear a deafening crash from behind us, where the make-up artists have their workstations laid out. A clumsy runner (who won't be a runner for much longer, I reckon) has knocked into one of the tables from behind while fiddling with a socket and the entire thing has toppled over. Palettes are smashed, loose powders spilt and brushes are scattered all over the floor. The American artistry team look ashen as Lauren slowly turns round and takes it all in.

'Oh my *God!*' she screeches.

'Don't worry!' I say brightly, going into automatic mum-trying-to-prevent-a-toddler-from-an-almighty-meltdown mode. 'Many hands make light work!'

I walk over to the stations with Natalie following.

'If you guys carry on with the cast, we can tidy this up and clean the brushes. We can even fix a lot of these palettes' smashed powders, if you have any rubbing alcohol,' I say in the cheeriest it's-all-OK tone possible. Natalie nods and begins picking things up as Lauren looks on with what I can only hope is an impressed glare.

As soon as we've put that fire out, I receive a call from Lacey in tears, saying she can't face going out today but equally can't face being in all day alone with Willow.

'Could you ask Kath to help you?' I suggest.

'Mmm, I don't think so,' she says oddly.

'She won't mind, she loves spending time with Willow, which is why she's helped a lot so far,' I say, confused.

'No, it's OK, I don't want to bother her. I'll be OK, I'm fine, really.' I know she isn't fine (that fabulous word again) but I don't have time to argue because, lo and behold, Kath's also trying to get through.

'Hellooo,' I chime.

'Lovey, I'm ever so sorry but you're going to have to come home or I'm going to have to drop Lyla to you,' she says immediately.

'What? Why? Are you both OK?' I panic.

'Yes, lovey, absolutely fine. But I think it's the change – my hormones have gone haywire and I need a little break,' she says as though this is totally normal.

'Um, right . . . I can't leave this very second, but I can be home in an hour, will that be OK?' I ask, feeling stressed already at the logistics of this.

'Yes, thank you, I just feel out of sorts, nothing to worry about,' and she hangs up.

Nothing to worry about but I need to go home immediately? I feel anxious about bailing on Natalie on the last day of the shoot, and I can tell she's a bit annoyed, despite my success earlier with the clear-up. She asks if Lacey can shoot across town to help, but judging by her earlier call, I don't think she's in the right frame of mind. I consider asking Edward, but he's been so busy lately, only seeing me for small chunks of time and constantly promising alone time that we never seem to be able to make happen. Suddenly I feel very isolated, and like the weight of every single thing is on my shoulders. For the first time in a long time I can feel my throat tightening and tears pricking behind my eyes. Sensing an imminent breakdown, Natalie tells me to go home and see to Lyla, and I slope off to order an Uber. Sod schlepping home on the subway. I need to make a call.

It arrives in under three minutes (New York, you win again). I let the tears fall down my cheeks and dial Gillian, international charges be damned.

'Robin, if I were there I'd scoop you up, find the nearest café that serves giant slabs of chocolate cake and we'd put the world to rights. Please don't fret over all of this, you're doing so, so, so well,' Gillian soothes after I gab on about all of my problems and how crap I feel at every role I'm trying to juggle.

'Oh, Gillian, if only you could! Everything here is gluten-free, sugar-free, dairy-free, fat-free!' I wail, not caring a jot what the Uber driver must think of me.

'I'd call that fun-free, then!' Gillian laughs, trying to cheer me up. 'But seriously, though, I can't believe you feel a failure when you're doing so much! I keep telling everyone how amazing you are. We all missed you at Women Who Win. Gloria talked about "Playing Big".'

'Bloody hell, I dread to think what she means by that!' I say, wishing my brain wasn't instantly flashing to an image of her with the headmaster in the school supply cupboard.

'Ah-ah-ah! Mind out of the gutter! She was talking about how we shouldn't limit ourselves to what we think we should be or should do, but to play a big game. She talked about you as an example,' Gillian enthuses.

'What? How am I an example?' I ask in shock.

'Oh, I don't know, maybe because you have climbed the career ladder in a profession you love, secured amazing high-profile deals for your company, you've travelled to America twice for work, you're a good friend to all of us and you do all this while being a single mum and having quite a hunk of a boyfriend!' Gillian retorts.

'Did you all talk about Edward?' I say, a bit wobbly at how nice that was.

'Well, no, I added that bit in because it's true. We just spoke about your career and juggling motherhood alongside it. You're a great example of playing it big. You don't let little obstacles stop you, you set your sights on the goal and you just go out there and get it! I know you don't think so, but you're an inspiration, Robin!' Gillian coaxes. 'It's easy to find things to admire when we look at our friends, but so much harder to see those things in ourselves.'

'Ohhh, I don't know what to say now. I feel silly for ringing you all snotty and crying. You're so good to me.' I have so much love for Gillian I feel like I could cry all over again.

'Even our inspirations have a cry here and there, don't worry. I won't bring it up at the next meeting!'

'Thank you!' I say, smiling at her even though she can't see me.

'Now, get off this ridiculously expensive call, wipe your eyes and go and have your day. Work will find a way to right itself, Kath sounds like she's a bit homesick, Lyla needs a big cuddle and Lacey has Piper on hand. When you're home, maybe we'll all have a nice Mummy Day at the park and plan when Lyla can come for a couple of sleepovers with Clara, so you and Edward can have some much-needed alone time. Everything, I promise, will be OK,' Gillian says with absolute conviction.

'Gillian Magraw, I don't know how you do it but you are one of life's great fixers, and I love you.'

As I get out of my Uber and walk up the steps to our house, I feel renewed. I feel more energised than I have in days, and I know I can face whatever life throws at me. At least for a little while, anyway!

AFTER I GET IN, Kath goes straight out for a walk to 'clear her head'. It's the firmest I've ever felt her be with me – she's angry, almost – so I don't question her or stand in her way. I keep trying to think of anything I might have done to upset her – I don't want her to think I've ever taken her for granted or don't appreciate everything she's done for Lyla and me. But I draw a blank, and know that right now, Lyla has to be my focus. The two of us go to the attic bathroom, run a deep bubble bath and play spas for the afternoon. I paint her nails, do what feels like a hundred tiny plaits in her hair so it will crimp, give her arms and legs a little lavender massage and then sit with her while she has a long bath, telling me every single thing that's in her head.

We talk about all the things she's seen in New York: about how she'd wanted to go to the American Girl shop and pick a doll that looked just like her, with all the accessories; about the little playgrounds they have found, and how the Milky Way bars over here are called the same thing but don't taste the same as the ones at home.

I spend the whole afternoon in the bathroom with her. Not because I need to, but because I want to. When I'm with Lyla, I feel home, wherever we are. I feel as though my roots are deep and I am sturdy because I am doing what I was put on this earth to do: to be her mummy. I don't much fancy opening the door and facing Natalie being annoyed that I left the shoot, or Kath being a bit strange, or Edward being narked that I can't carve out time for him. Just for one afternoon I want to spread my branches wide over my little girl, shield her from everything and be there, with her, home.

TWENTY-FIVE

ZOOMING BACK TO THE Fierce Films offices today, I think about how much I'd like to be back in that bathroom now. My tummy is swirling with nerves and Natalie has a steely look on her face. This. Is. It.

Yesterday, after I left, Natalie secured a meeting with the team to talk about our next steps. We spent all of last night throwing ideas around and honing our pitch. Well, I say all of last night, but in truth, as soon as Lyla was in bed I'd called Edward to tell him, thinking he might want to celebrate – but he said I should probably just get an early night to be fresh for today.

Now I'm glad of the evening I spent with Natalie. We're as ready as we'll ever be. This is our chance to secure the job and, more importantly, secure MADE IT. I don't think I've ever felt so much pressure, but there is no way on earth I am going to let Natalie down. If I do, well, it doesn't bear thinking about.

Looking around the giant New York boardroom, I take a nanosecond to wonder how my life has brought me to this moment. Three years ago I was a part-time make-up artist, part-time mess and now here I am, in a room with the head honchos of Fierce Films, with panoramic views of the city around me and a cup of very strong coffee.

Natalie opens.

'Thank you for taking the time to meet with us. It's been a pleasure getting to know you all this past week.' She pauses, expecting some response, but is left with blank stares. She continues: 'Lauren, I hope you found our work to be professional and enthusiastic?'

'I did, it was awesome, but obviously we already had our team in and had those designs, so we thank you so much for your help but we really are all set,' Lauren says with a false smile and dead eyes.

'I would very much appreciate it if you could all,' Natalie says, gesturing at Lauren, Scott, Lindsey, the finance guy and the woman from legal, 'take a moment to reconsider. We worked successfully on the 2017 film and were promised the contracts for the next films. The right thing to do, we believe, would be to honour that, and we'd be thrilled to get working on the next set of designs for you,' Natalie says as smoothly as she can, but I sense a waver of anxiety. I wish I could give her a little thumbs up of encouragement like I do to Lyla in school plays and assemblies.

'And I appreciate you had that agreement, but that was with the old management. The firm's changed hands, and we're running things in a different direction now.' Lauren totally shuts Natalie down.

I look around the room. Everyone except Lauren, who looks angry as per, and Natalie, who actually looks completely downtrodden, looks bored out of their brains.

'Lauren, I'm sure we can find a little room for movement on this,' Natalie tries.

'I'm sorry, Natalie, but we cannot. We want to thank you for your time and your dedication but at this point in our journey, we don't have space for MADE UP,' Lauren says. I almost feel Natalie flinch at Lauren's disrespectful error.

Natalie does something she never, ever normally does. She sighs. 'OK. Well, thank you again for the work in 2017, and we hope to see you again in the future.'

What? Natalie's thrown in the towel? No! I can't let this happen. I desperately try to think of a hook or a reason we have to secure this job. Something witty, or something we didn't think of last night.

I can't. I've got nothing. We're going to lose this job and MADE IT's going to lose staff. We're going to have to lose Skye, or me, or I don't know, but I can't let this happen. I take a deep breath and suddenly, just as I think my head's about to explode, I remember Gloria's tips.

'Actually,' I venture, just as everyone is shuffling their tablets and laptops into their bags, 'I have something I'd like to say.'

The people around the big black boardroom table look up, waiting.

Channelling my inner confidence, and Gloria's third tip, I sit and wait a moment in silence. It's awkward as fuck, but oh my God, I can see I have everyone's full, undivided attention. Gloria was right!

I remember her first tip, 'If you don't ask, you don't get', and give it a go.

'Lauren, you say you have an American team on hand. This team haven't worked on the franchise in the way we have. We know the narrative, we know what's expected of the design and the artistry, and we know we have what it takes to do a fantastic jo—'

'And that's awesome, but we—' Lauren interrupts, but I interrupt her back.

'I'm sorry, Lauren, I haven't finished what I want to say.' There's now a stunned silence in the room.

'I'd like to ask you to take this American team off the job and do the honourable thing of giving it back to us. We've proved to you once in 2017 that we have the skills to do a phenomenal job, and we've proved to you this week that we have the drive and determination to succeed. So, could you please arrange with your legal and financial colleagues here to reinstate us?'

It's a bold move and I'm almost shaking, but I don't care, I'm not done yet.

Lauren looks at her colleagues, who nod that it can

be done. In true Lauren fashion, she says, 'Maybe I can, but what if I don't like your attitude?'

Oh, wow. I've had enough. Armed with Gloria's second tip, 'What's the worst that can happen', I make the riskiest choice of my career to date. I'm going for it.

'Lauren, you'll have to forgive me for being frank. I'm jet-lagged, I've left my homesick daughter in a rented house with a menopausal aunt and I haven't had any proper time to see my boyfriend since coming out here. That's not to mention my probably postnatally depressed best friend who's holed up in Brooklyn and who also flew out to the "land of opportunity" with us.

'Now, you have every right not to like our attitude, but I'll be damned if we walk away from this table having not given it our all. I have given this project everything. I have literally shed blood, sweat and tears over this job!'

I notice the woman from legal make a slightly disgusted face at the thought of my blood and sweat, but carry on.

'Natalie and I have flown over from England at our own rather great expense to show you and your team what we're made of, and let me tell you, Lauren, we're made of stronger stuff than you might think.

'We have swallowed our pride and done catering runs, cleaned up your team's equipment, given make-overs to everyone and smiled, even though you have, on occasion, acted appallingly. Quite honestly, it would be not only a disservice to us if you withdrew the contract, but a disservice to yourselves!

'You want to make great movies, right? Then hire the best fucking team you know! Us! MADE IT! This job is ours!' I finish, thumping my fist on the table and breathing so heavily I don't realise that I've actually stood up a little bit.

I sit down and suddenly feel panicked. What the hell have I done?

Natalie looks round with wide eyes, Lindsey looks like she might want to snog me, Scott looks afraid and Lauren is clearly taken aback. I bet nobody in her life has spoken to her the way I just did.

At least if we're going to go home, we're going to go home having given it every last drop.

'Wow,' Lauren begins. By this point I don't really care what she says to me. In a few minutes I'll be out of the office and will never have to see her again.

She continues, a smile spreading across her lips. 'You've got fire in your belly for this job. I like it. I like a woman who gives a damn.

'Natalie, you're clearly a woman of integrity, and your Roxy here has spunk.'

I won't bother telling her my name's not Roxy.

'Thank you,' Natalie says, unusually stuck for words.

To the amazement of every single person in the room, Lauren throws back her head and laughs.

'Roxy, that was one hell of a show! I love it! Natalie, I'll be in touch. That's a wrap, guys!' she says and leaves the room.

Essentially, that was the weirdest, scariest, most unconventional business meeting I've ever been in, and I've never wanted a glass of wine, a cuddle and a big fluffy blanket more in my entire life. What on earth just happened?!

TWENTY-SIX

THROWING ALL CAUTION TO the wind, Natalie says we can expense a cab rather than get the subway. We ride home, gabbling excitedly about how that all went, replaying it over and over, laughing and talking with almost manic levels of hysteria, so that, by the time we get back to the house and tell Kath what's happened, we've almost gone full circle and I feel as tight-tummied and sicky as I did when we left the house this morning.

I think I need a hot shower and a lie-down to reset myself, but Kath and Lyla have a *lot* to say about their day.

Apparently, after a morning running around The High Line and taking photos in front of trendy painted brick walls, Kath and Lyla went for a wander into SoHo.

'Well, we were just taking it easy, and Lacey didn't fancy it today. She wanted to potter around Williamsburg with the buggy, so we were just having a look at all the lovely town houses, weren't we?' starts Kath, with a grave look on her face.

'We were deciding which one we'd have if we lived here,' Lyla confirms.

'OK, that sounds really nice,' I say, taking a glass out of the kitchen cupboard to fill with water, wondering where this is going.

'We walked and walked and found a couple of little playgrounds and we had great fun playing in those, didn't we, lovey?' Kath continues, talking to Lyla.

'Yep! We found two! They're just in little gaps where you think a building could fit. Like baby playgrounds with a slide but fun, because you can still see everyone going past, and Kath could sit on the bench and watch me. I made her take seventy-hundred photos to send you because I looked so cool,' Lyla adds. I wish I had the innate confidence of a little girl. When do they lose that? How can I help her keep it?

'Well, yes, the little parks were great fun. We stayed for about half an hour in each.' Kath pauses.

'OK, this sounds really nice.' I'm baffled by her anxious expression.

'After we'd been in the second park, I was getting a bit tired, so we thought we ought to find some lunch and head back.'

'Yes, OK, good thinking,' I encourage.

'But before we did, we found a shop called Rainbow Dreams. Like I said, lovey, I was so tired, and Lyla thought the window display looked really fun with frilly dresses on the mannequins and bright feather boas and such.' Kath looked at the floor and Lyla looked back and forth at the both of us.

'OK . . .' I say, completely lost.

'I wasn't looking, really. Maybe if I'd had my prescription sunglasses on I'd have seen better but I didn't, and we just went in. I really wasn't looking because when we opened the door—'

'There were hundreds of great big plastic *WILLIES*!!' Lyla shouts with absolute glee.

'WHAT?' I shout, spitting the water I've just sipped all over the kitchen sink. 'What the hell do you mean?'

'I'm so sorry, lovey, I'm so sorry, I didn't realise it

was an, er, adult shop. As soon as we opened the door we realised, and I turned us right back round, of course, and we went to Chelsea Market, where they had a lovely pop-up Esty shop selling—'

'Rewind, hang on, you *accidentally* went into a sex shop?' I ask, stopping her waffling on in a panic.

'What's sex?' Lyla asks with a mischievous glimmer in her eye, clearly loving every moment of this drama, because at eight, bums, willies and poo are the pinnacle of comedy.

I take a deep breath and assess the situation. I've just aced one of the biggest meetings of my life; I am in New York City with some of my favourite people in the world; I have a beautifully inquisitive, funny, bright daughter full of life; I have a loving aunt who spends her time caring for all of us; a delicious hunk of a boyfriend and a sparky-when-not-a-bit-down best friend who's just had a miracle baby. Do I really need to be cross that my young daughter has seen a bunch of dildos? No, not really. Would it be better if she wasn't now asking what the big plastic willies were for? Yes, yes it would.

I sigh.

Kath looks as though she might cry.

'Right!' I say with uber-confidence. 'Lyla, sex is something we can talk about when you're a bit older. It's for adults. Those plastic willies were for adults too, and are a bit silly, and we can have a little laugh about them but that's it. It's not something we need to talk too much more about.' Knowing full well I'll be talking and laughing about it with my friends for years. 'Kath, it sounds like you had such a fun morning, and I'm so grateful that you took Lyla to those playgrounds and found such a silly shop! Let's none of us worry about this. Let's get ourselves ready and take Kath out to the pulled pork place she missed on the first night, and think about what adventures we can have at the weekend when my work is finished.'

I can honestly say, I don't think I've ever seen such clear relief on anyone's face quite like I do this evening on Kath's.

Once we're home, after a lovely hour and a half out in West Village, having more of that yummy pulled pork and a mooch round the vibrant streets nearby, I put Lyla to bed with a great big cuddle, pour myself a giant glass of wine, leave Kath to her crafts and go upstairs to FaceTime Lacey, who's texted to say she's feeling a bit down. What a surreal day. I wish I had the energy to pop round to Edward's and celebrate everything that's happened today, but I'm just exhausted, and we haven't had a lot of chat since Saturday, so I don't fancy tackling that. Happily, as soon as my head hits the pillow, I'm asleep. Bliss.

TWENTY-SEVEN

NATALIE AND MARTIN LEFT yesterday. They plan to tour the East Coast for a week before flying back. We all said we'd miss each other, but I secretly suspect they'll be glad of the space. The original plan was for Edward to come and stay now they're gone, but we're not really speaking much, so I've no idea what's going on there. I'll be damned if I'm going to beg a man to spend time with me. I'm Robin Wilde; I'm better than that. Aren't I?

Edward and I have barely seen each other. I messaged and said I feel like I'm constantly chasing, and he said he feels the same and things feel a 'bit much' right now. I was in a foul mood, and perhaps a bit too firm when I said, 'Well, I'm a package deal and you know that.' I can't help but feel defensive with anything that involves Lyla. Lyla, my gorgeous little Lyla, who I think is picking up on mine and Kath's angst and is pining for normality.

Lacey has gone quiet and doesn't want to take Willow out much. She hasn't been round and isn't having her regular days out with Kath and Lyla. I'm worried she's sinking again. Kath has been having a lot of headaches, early nights and 'turns', which she says are menopausal. I don't want to query that, but it seems out of the blue considering she was so OK a few weeks back. Well, OK-ish. OK but busy. Busy and distant.

Do you know what I'd really like? For each day to stop being such a flipping roller coaster! One minute everything's OK and I feel ready to handle anything; the next it's fallen to pieces and I feel like I'm in pieces too!

But I've not got time to brood on it. I've been working so hard, and finally now I can concentrate on Lyla. Sure, I'd imagined it would be me and my girl gang seeing the sights – but if it needs to be just me and my Lyla Blue, I'd better make the most of it. Still, as we explore the Museum of Natural History, or when we let our hair blow in the breeze on the Staten Island Ferry, I can't pretend I don't miss Kath and Lacey being by our sides, and I keep thinking of funny things I'd laugh about with Edward if he were here.

Frankly, it's an awful week. I don't tell anyone how I'm feeling except for the odd furtive text here and there to Gillian, because I don't want to add more weight to anyone else's shoulders when I can see that everyone else is pushing through their own stuff too.

I get through to Friday exhausted from solo-parenting Lyla round the sights of New York, and decide a quiet evening is in order. With Kath having one of her rests and Lyla glued to the iPad in my bedroom (a mum's gotta do what a mum's gotta do), I lie down on the squishy lounge sofa and shut my eyes. Peace. Perhaps I'll allow myself a full nap and then wake up feeling—

DING-DONG!

What. Fresh. Hell.

I open the door to be faced with an even paler than

usual Lacey, Willow asleep in a sling and Piper looking ashen.

'Robin, Lacey's got something to tell you,' she says, stepping over the threshold and heading straight into the main room, leaving Lacey and I staring at each other in the doorway. I'm too shocked even to ask what, this is all so weird.

'I'm going to leave you both to it,' Piper says, diplomatically moving off into the kitchen area and busying herself making a coffee. Although I get the sense I'm going to want something stronger after Lacey's said whatever it is she's come to say.

Lacey sits down carefully with the sling and baby still attached.

'I don't really know how to tell you this, so I'll just say it all and then you can do what you like. Just know that I didn't mean to find out, and I love you and . . . I don't know, I'll just start,' she says with determination.

I nod, absolutely baffled and really scared. I know everyone's been acting strangely, but this takes the biscuit.

'So, Kath and I were sitting opposite the Alice in Wonderland statue in Central Park the other week, you know, the night we went out,' she begins, and I nod, signifying for her to continue.

'Lyla was playing just a few metres away from us. I'd been feeling even more dreadful than I have in weeks. I had a bit of a lift when we arrived here, but that wore off and I just sank down again. I'd started to think some really dark things, Robs,' she continues, almost teary. I reach my hand over to her chair and squeeze her knee.

'It's OK, we're here,' I whisper.

'Everybody said the first bit of motherhood would be difficult, but I thought since I'd wanted her for so long, I wouldn't feel it. Wow, I was wrong. I don't feel like I've caught my breath these last few months. I've seen how good you all are with Willow, especially Kath, and I just felt like maybe I'm not good enough. Not good enough for Willow, that she deserves a better mum . . . a different mum.

'It finally spilt out of me that day. I was telling Kath all this, and she was just listening and I felt so at ease. Lyla was playing on that big bronze statue of Alice in Wonderland and had made lots of friends, so was happy for ages. I stopped talking for a few minutes and said, "Robin would love watching her play all over that, wouldn't she?" I was feeding Willow a bottle at the same time and, I'm ashamed to say, not really paying attention to anything other than her and Lyla, so I didn't really notice Kath getting a bit weepy.

'She was looking straight ahead at Lyla and she said, "She would. It's not right when a mother isn't allowed to watch her child grow".'

'I thought it was a bit intense so I said, "She is seeing Lyla grow, Kath. It's just a few days she's busy for. She's at work, isn't she?" and I was a bit concerned, you know, because she seemed upset now.

'We paused, then I carried on talking about Willow, and that I thought maybe I would see if Mum could have her for a few days a week or something when we got home, because maybe, like I said, I wasn't the best option for her.

'Kath didn't reply, but looked away, fiddling with her shawl – you know, the multicoloured one with all the beads on it?'

I nod. I can just imagine the scene as Lacey is describing it. New York in July can feel hotter than the molten centre of the earth, so Kath wearing a loose orange cotton strappy sundress, red glittery sandals with tiny shells stitched onto the straps, a pastel technicolour crocheted shawl with a gold pompom trim, her signature glass bead necklaces and a giant floppy sunhat (also trimmed with gold pompoms) sounds about right.

Lacey continues. 'By now the silence had become super-weird, so I asked Kath if she was OK.

'"Oh Lacey, I'd love to talk about this but it's too big, it's too much", was all she could say.

'Robin, it was such a strange vibe, but I knew she had something she needed to let out, so I encouraged her gently. I told her to start at the very beginning and see how far she managed. I could see things were serious, but I had no idea where it was going to go.

'So Kath began, twiddling her thumbs on her pompoms, she was so nervous. "It's not a story that's easy to tell. I've barely told a soul, but now it's like I just can't hold it in. I mean, of course I told Derek, and he was so good. He was always so good about everything. I wish I'd known him even earlier. I try not to think of it, of any of it, and usually I can manage, but since Willow, it's, well, it's as though a film is playing in my head and I can't find the remote to turn it off." By now she was crying, so I just tried to make her feel as loved as possible. I mean, she's done so much for Willow, and she's been like a second mum to me.'

Lacey looks nervous and pauses to adjust the sling around Willow. Then she carries on.

'Kath took a deep breath, looked over at Lyla, who was squatting down playing with this little girl with butterfly clips in her hair, and just let it all out.

'"Lacey," she said. "I'm going to tell you something very close to my heart, and I hope you can understand that I'm not ready to speak about this with anyone else," she said. She was so stern, not like her usual self, and so I promised not to share it. I felt awful straightaway, because she's your auntie and I know I should have come to you first, but I couldn't. I didn't want to upset her, I didn't want to upset you. I felt really upset myself. I just—'

I can see Lacey is getting distressed, and I'm now feeling very anxious about whatever it is. I'm starting to feel a bit sick, too, thinking the worst and not even really knowing what that is.

'Lacey, it's fine, you're here now. Just tell me what she said. Try to repeat exactly what you can remember,' I urge.

'OK, yes, sorry. So, she told me this story. She said, "I'm the youngest in my family. You know I'm fifty-four, don't you? And that Robin's dad is sixty-five?" I said I didn't know the exact numbers, but yes, I knew Robert was a bit older.

'She went on, "We came from a very conservative home and were raised with conservative values. My father, Robin's grandad, who, God rest his soul, has passed on now, was a very serious man. He worked for the local government and considered it his civic duty to be an upstanding citizen. He'd seen his dad come back from the war, after fighting for king and country, and he greatly admired him. He was proud to be British, proud to work for the country and proud to uphold his values."

'I said he sounded like a good man, but Kath said, "That's debatable. Mum was nice, but she would never stand up to Dad. I don't know whether she was afraid of him or afraid of herself, but she could never seem to get out of his shadow. I think given half the chance she would have been so colourful and full of life, but Dad saw anything like that as 'silly' or 'childish', and he wanted Mum to stand next to him as the perfect wife."

'"Straight after they married, Mum had Robert and things went well. She was a typical 1950s housewife. She cooked and cleaned and raised Robert while Dad worked his nine to five and felt important for it. They had one holiday a year to a nice resort in the Algarve, he bought Mum the same bottle of perfume every year for her birthday, and if she wore lipstick any bolder than a frosted pink he'd tut. I'm not sure you'd have liked him", Kath said.'

I'm amazed. Here is Lacey, telling me things I never knew about Auntie Kath and my own dad. People I thought I knew inside out. Not to mention my own grandparents.

'I was intrigued,' Lacey says. 'And even though a part of me was worrying about what was coming, I told her to go on. Kath told me that ten years later, her mum found out she was pregnant again, with Kath. "I was a bit of a surprise," Kath said. "Not really in their rather staid life plan", was how she put it. "They loved me," Kath went on. "I was well looked after, and I think Mum enjoyed having a little girl after all those years of Dad and Robert. We didn't have an exciting life, but it was what I knew and I was happy. Much to Dad's pride, just like Robert, I passed my eleven-plus and was accepted into the grammar school. You might not think it now, but I was considered to be very intelligent." I told Kath I thought very highly of her,' Lacey says. 'I was encouraging her to go on. Now let me see if I can remember exactly how she told me the next part.

'"I wanted to earn a little bit of money to pay for things like magazines and clothes and all the bits and pieces that youngsters wanted back then, so I applied for a job at the local fish and chip shop, and got it! Dad wasn't thrilled, because he thought it 'wasn't becoming for a lady to work behind a fish counter all night', but Mum persuaded him it was good for me to have a little bit of independence. Robert had been afforded so much more because he was a boy, and it was all right to differentiate back then. He'd already finished university and had his own digs with his engineering chums and had flown the nest."'

Some of what Lacey is telling me matches the little Dad has told me about his childhood, but I've never heard it from Kath's perspective. Lacey looks less anxious now, concentrating instead on relaying everything Kath had said.

'Kath told me how she loved that job in the chippy,

and how well she got on with the customers. "There was one young chap who came in a lot and took quite a shine to me. Ian. He was tall and handsome and had a job at the local garage as a car salesman. I thought he was so debonair, of course. He was twenty, five years older than me, and we started courting.

"'It was all secret. I didn't dare tell anyone because I knew Dad wouldn't approve, and even if Mum did she wouldn't go against Dad, so we snuck around. He'd take me out in all these cars he borrowed from the garage, he'd come into work to talk to me and we'd have a brilliant time. I was so carefree, so stupid.'"

'What else did she say?' I sense Lacey is working up to the heart of Kath's story.

'She asked me what it is that always happens when you're naive and think you're in love. "I got caught out, as they say. I missed one of my monthlies. The smell of the haddock turned my stomach and my skirts were too tight. I told Ian first. I thought he'd give me one of his dazzling smiles and tell me it would be all right and stick by me. I stupidly thought all men had the same morals as Dad, only maybe without his severity, and that perhaps Ian would offer to marry me, but he didn't. He told me to get rid of it. I cried and cried, but he said he couldn't take me on, couldn't cope with a baby and that I should have been more careful." Honestly, Robin, she was sobbing by this point. But luckily Lyla was still busy playing, thankfully oblivious.'

I feel a wave of outrage for what my aunt has been through, as Lacey keeps doing her best to tell me exactly what Kath said.

'Kath told me she just had to accept it. "That was how things were then. We've come a long way in forty years, you know. Still a way to go, but I'm not sure you young things know what a difference has already been made," Kath told me.

'I felt desperately sad,' says Lacey. 'But I knew I had to ask her what happened, if she'd had to have an abortion.'

I can't get my head around what Lacey is telling me. Kath? An abortion?

'I asked Kath if they were legal by then, and she nodded. "They were, but it was still a huge taboo and I'd left it a long time. I think I was in denial. I'd tried to hide it as long as I could but though she was timid and unassuming, Mum wasn't stupid and she figured it out. When I admitted it to her, sat on her chintz-covered sofa in the front room, she cried into her teacup. I asked if I could put a cot in my bedroom and look after the baby there and see about more shifts at the fish and chip shop, but she was adamant that Dad would never have it and that the 'shame' would kill him."

'I asked Kath about the father and she went quiet before carrying on. "Ian was long gone, and wouldn't answer any of my letters. I tried phoning him a few times when Mum was out, but he told me to stop contacting him and I didn't know what to do. I didn't know if I had rights, or if there was any support available for girls like me, so when Mum said there was only one option, I took her word for it.

'"We hid it from Dad for as long as possible, which wasn't very hard because he wasn't the attention-giving, doting dad you get today, and then we told him I was going to do a three-month secretarial course in Desborough. He was made up with that. A 'fine skill' for a lady like me, he thought. So we packed my bags and Mum took a taxi with me to the train station." Kath paused and looked up at the sky. "She didn't even come with me to the home."'

'The home?' I am struggling to absorb all this, but Lacey looks lighter for sharing it with me.

'The maternity home. Kath told me she stayed there for about a month before the contractions started and she gave birth to the most beautiful little baby. "She had light blonde hair that stuck up in wisps just like Willow's, and the lightest blue eyes you've ever seen. She was perfection. I held her and brought her up close to me and wished I could tell her how much I loved her and have her remember it." Kath was crying as she got to this part, Robin.'

I notice Laccy holding Willow all the tighter as she goes on.

'"I had her for six weeks," is what she said. "Every day I held her, washed her, fed her, stroked her and nuzzled my nose into her neck. They told me not to get attached or to name her because it would only make it worse for both of us, but I couldn't not. Nothing could have made it worse. She was my beautiful baby and they took her. They took her out of my arms and told me this was for the best. It was best that I stopped feeding her my milk and it was best that I didn't pick her up so much and it was best that I didn't give her her name."'

I can feel hot, angry tears building behind my eyes as Lacey tells me everything Kath has been through. How can the kind, funny, loving woman sleeping upstairs have once been a frightened, abandoned mother?

'"She was beautiful. She was the most beautiful creature, and my heart physically hurts every day that I didn't keep her, that I didn't run away and hide or keep her with me." Oh, Robin. I didn't know what to say. I was barely able to breathe. I just kept saying I was so sorry, just so, so sorry,' Lacey says.

'"They said she wasn't mine, and that a proper God-fearing, respectable family would take her and love her – but she *was* mine and I *did* love her. She was perfect and she was mine. I don't even know if they got the note I snuck in with her favourite blanket, telling them how I loved my Eleanor Edith Wilde. I loved her then and I love her now. My baby. Mine."' Lacey is choked with sorrow as she repeats Kath's words.

I'm totally overwhelmed, with tears running down my cheeks. 'Has she ever looked for her? Did you ask her that, Lace?'

'She said not. "Mum always said she was better off

with her new family, and it was best we all put it behind us and let the past be in the past. Dad died never knowing Eleanor had existed, and Robert's never said anything, though I think he suspected. Maybe Dad did too, really. I never became a secretary when I came home. I just sat in my room crying every day until Mum said enough was enough and it was time to find a job. I'd missed my last exams, so I took up a training course in hairdressing, and from then on that was my career.

'"It wasn't a bad life. I met Derek when I was twenty-two, and he knew what had happened and he loved me, let me talk about her, but it made things all the more painful that we were never able to have our own children. When Robert and Angela had Robin, it was a little bit like my chance to have a daughter of my own. Angela was never particularly maternal and Robert didn't have the gusto to step in – he's so like Mum – but I loved it. Taking her out, showing her how to make little paper dresses for her dollies, baking with her, all of it. I would always think of Eleanor, where she'd be now, what she'd be doing. She'd be thirty-eight by now. She might even have her own family. I think about her every day. Every single day. And I hope she's happy. I hope she'd understand that I didn't want to give her up. I know it's too late for me to tell her that, but I hope she knows.'"

'Oh, Lacey. Our Kath. I can't imagine it. And she's kept it hidden all these years. But why has it all come out now? Why couldn't she tell me?'

For a few moments, Lacey and I sit and let the tears fall down our cheeks in silence. I have never felt more in shock than I do right now.

Slowly, bit by bit, I start to process it.

'Kath is a mother,' I say to Lacey, who is holding Willow tightly, rocking her back and forth ever so gently.

'Yes. It makes so much sense now. She's always been so maternal.'

'I wish I'd known,' I say, staring at the chintzy rug laid over the bare varnished floorboards. 'I wish she'd felt able to tell me.'

'Are you cross? That I know?' Lacey asks worriedly.

'No. I don't think so. This is too big. It's not about me or you or how we feel – we need to help Kath. I can't imagine how her heart must be breaking right now,' I say, feeling such sadness.

'Or how broken it already is,' Piper says, walking back into the room, clearly having heard everything.

'We've got to do something,' I say indignantly. 'She can't live like this.'

'You're right,' says Lacey, glad we're on the same page.

'You are right, but let's keep this here for now, let's not go at Kath all guns blazing. Let's take it easy, keep things on the DL and work out what the best thing is, going forward,' Piper says, the calm voice of reason we all need to hear right at this moment.

'I've requested a bit of leave from work, and I'm going to come home for a month and help Lacey out, aren't I, sis?' Piper continues, looking at me. 'Once I'm back, we'll work out what we're going to do about Kath, OK?'

Relief washes over me harder than I thought it would. I'm glad someone is going to look after Lacey and I can relax a little bit, and I'm happy that someone other than me is going to think of a plan, because right now my mind is swirling like one of the rides at Coney Island – I can't get off and I'm ready to throw up.

Poor Kath, my poor, poor, lovely Kath.

TWENTY-EIGHT

LACEY, PIPER AND WILLOW say their goodbyes and head out to the subway. It was the most surreal goodbye we've ever had, all still in shock from the conversation, letting it sink in and working out what we're going to do next. I don't think I really said much, I was in such a daze – it's a lot to process.

I already felt like I had a lot on my shoulders, but now I feel like someone has picked up an entire planet and placed it on them too. This is a lot. How Kath has spent every day thinking about this, I don't know.

This is why she's been so teary, so involved with Willow – it's all slotting into place.

Just as my mind is whirring with all the little things she's said and done over the years that now make sense, and racing with all the things that could happen in the next few years, like maybe even finding her daughter, the doorbell rings again. It's Edward, though I'm so lost in my own thoughts I barely even meet his lovely eyes. I still feel a million miles away, caught up in a spiral of questions and concerns.

'Am I glad to see you!' he says, kissing me on the cheek and walking in as soon as I open the door.

'I've had the most manic day. All I've wanted is to come here, see my beautiful girlfriend, maybe give her a bit of a smooch and relax,' he says, swinging me round and giving me said smooch.

'Edward,' I say, pulling back, really not feeling in the spirit of things.

'Sorry, sorry!' He lets me go. 'The store has been on fire for customers this week. People wanting bespoke makes, people requesting particular designers, people wanting advice. It's been so intense.' He's clearly picking up on my wan face, and carries on. 'On top of that, I've been handling a lot of UK stuff over email and trying to keep that all going, and not having a chance to see you, and squeezing in a few of the New York guys for drinks. It's been a lot to juggle.'

Erm, yes, I do bloody know. I don't say anything, just blink at him wondering if he's listened to anything I've said over the last few weeks about also having a lot on, or if I've done such a convincing job of saying 'I'm fine' that he really hasn't noticed at all.

'So anyway,' he continues, 'I could really do with going out, maybe getting a steak and just letting it all out,' he says, holding both my hands, willing me to say yes.

'Oh Edward, I'd absolutely love to go out for steak and convo, but I can't. My head's spinning. There's so much on right now and I don't have anyone to look after Lyla. I can't,' I say, trying to excuse myself so I can just take a minute to process the day's revelations.

'Can't Kath watch her for a couple of hours?' he says, sounding annoyed. Surely not.

'Not really, she's done a lot this week. I don't want to ask her,' I say uncomfortably. I feel so awful for not being the girlfriend he wants and needs me to be, but I can't ask Kath for any extra favours or help right now – not when I know she's the one that truly needs the support.

'So we'll just stay in again, shall we?' he asks, definitely annoyed.

In an instant, I've gone from overwhelmed with the Kath news, mixed with guilty for not being able to give my all to him, to enraged that he's annoyed about this. See what I mean about the roller coaster?

'Edward, don't be like this. I'd love nothing more than to go out for food but I can't right now, I've got such a lot on,' I begin, trying to contain my frustration.

'We've all got a lot on, Robin! You're not the only person leading a busy life, or the only person with responsibilities to manage,' he says.

I can't believe he's having a strop about this.

'Yes, I know I'm not, but I—'

'But you what? But you have a child, so you're more important?' he says, making the hairs on the back of my neck stand up. How can he use that against me?

'How dare you!' I'm aghast.

'Look, I'm sorry, I just found out the Manhattan store is struggling with staffing, and—'

'Well, I just found out Kath had a daughter and had to give her up for adoption!' I shout, completely at the end of my tether. I know instantly that I shouldn't have just dropped that bombshell on him. It's a lot for anyone to take in.

He stands stock-still. We haven't moved from the front door where I greeted him five minutes ago, and all the anger and frustration in his face evaporates. His kind, caring demeanour returns and he takes both of my hands gently. Oh, I've needed this. Just for a moment, I need to be looked after.

'I'm so glad she finally told you,' he says quietly, looking into my eyes.

Utter. Boiling. Rage.

'How do *you* know?' I say with such venom in my voice I surprise even myself. Edward takes a minute step back.

'I haven't known long. She told me a few days ago. It was that first night. You'd gone out with Natalie, Martin and Lyla for dinner, I'd grabbed a cab over to surprise you and just found Kath in a terrible, terrible state. I was so worried something horrific had happened, an intruder or something, so I told her I wouldn't leave until she told me what was wrong. She did, and then asked me to go home. I didn't know what to do, it was a lot of information, so I thought it was best I just remove myself from the situation, respect her wishes and go back to mine. I told her to tell you . . .' he trails off.

'The whole trip you've known this huge family secret and haven't thought to tell me?' I say, prickling with irritation.

'What? "Thought to tell you"? I've wanted to tell you every bloody day, Robin!' he says, heating up himself now.

'So you just didn't have the guts to tell me then?' I almost shout, exasperated.

'Are you joking? Not have the guts? When I've had the guts to take on this relationship in the first place, potentially be a father, move across the world, step into a family, be understanding of your time constraints? There's hardly been a single fucking moment to even say hello to you, let alone tell you your auntie had a secret fucking baby!' he roars.

Wow. Now I'm stunned. I can't believe this is our first proper row. I don't want to believe any of what he's saying, but suddenly my confident facade is crumbling and I want to curl up into the tiniest ball possible and cry until I can go home to my house, my sofa and my friends.

'This is too much. I think you should go,' I whisper,

looking at the floor, the wind completely knocked out of me.

'No, I'm sorry, I didn't mean those things like that,' he begins, reaching out to me.

'No, it's fine.' It's definitely *not* fine. 'I just want to be, just be,' I say quietly.

'OK. I'm sorry. Call me and we'll sort it,' he says, opening the door.

'Yep,' I say as he closes the door and leaves me alone.

I take two steps back, sit on the bottom stair and cry so hard I give myself a migraine. This is not how New York was supposed to be. New York was supposed to fix everything and everyone. Once again, I've fucked everything up.

Part Three

'I'M FINE'

TWENTY-NINE

I'M THINKING EDWARD WILL make a dramatic entrance at the airport, come running over at the last minute with a bouquet of roses, loudly declaring his love for me and tell me he's bought a ticket to come back with us. Onlookers will weep and cheer as Edward lifts me high into the air and shouts, 'I love this woman!' All those 1990s romcoms setting unrealistic standards of romance in my head have a lot to answer for. I might just stick to gritty murder documentaries from now on.

I also think we should have sorted all this out by now. After the row in the town house, Edward rang to say maybe we should 'cool things off for a bit'. I couldn't swallow my pride and I didn't want to beg, so I just said that hideous little word, 'fine'. I was desperate to scream, 'No, please don't cool off, I need you, you're one of the happiest things in my life, I don't want to be alone again, what if The Emptiness comes back, what if everyone sees I'm not really a badass "girl boss", but that I'm just winging it till someone notices I'm a bit crap underneath?' But obviously I didn't. Just 'fine'.

So that's it. My last week in New York has been spent pretending. Pretending to Kath that I don't know her secret. Pretending to Lyla that I'm happy. Pretending to Lacey that Edward is just 'really busy at work'. But maybe that's one of my top skills – because I think I've pretended so well, they all believe it. I went toy-shopping with Lyla (we bought even more accessories for the beloved doll), I went round to Piper's and hung out with Lacey and Willow when she didn't feel like going further than the end of the block, and I even went to Central Park with Kath, wondering if being back there would mean she'd tell me her secret too. But she kept quiet. And so did I. Touché.

If you looked at my Instagram, you'd think this last week has been magical. Even Skye would be impressed. I hope it has been magical for Lyla, at least. You'd see the shots of her beaming a mile-wide smile at the top of the Empire State Building, or wearing a Statue of Liberty hat at the Waterside, and even a picture of all of us trying on I ♥ NY T-shirts. Well, all of us except Edward.

There's one piece of good news to come out of this week, though. Just as we were packing up, and I was wondering how much we would be charged to lug home all of Kath's lavender creations – she's clearly had too much on her mind to get her business mojo flowing as well – I got a call from Paige at Fierce Films. When we'd left, I'd given her a pot of Lavender Lovies hand cream, and she said her room-mate had seen it and loved it so much, she wanted to buy all the stock for the cute little Williamsburg craft market she has a stall at. Kath was bowled over. When we took a cab down to the market, we could see at once that Kath's wares would fit right in. And even better, when we showed Paige's flatmate the phone cases, she placed an order there and then! Hurrah for little victories.

But now our time is up and we are heading home. Every step further into the airport makes me want to whip round and check to see if he's here, behind me, desperate to make things right. But he isn't.

Piper has stayed with us right up to check-in at JFK, reminding us all it won't be long before she'll be back in the UK, too. We wave our bags through with their little tags on, we queue for security, look at all the boards to see which gate we're boarding at and walk through into the main hub of the airport and wait. What a difference a few weeks makes! Last time we were at the airport we were loud and excited (and late); now it feels like we can't wait to leave. We're a subdued little group.

The wait is a symphony of sounds and smells and lights and trying to soothe Willow, who isn't appreciating the DJ the airport have employed to make departures feel like a low-rate midweek club night. Why *do* this? Pump relaxing spa-like pan pipe sounds through the speaker system – don't have an actual DJ on the decks at the side asking us if we're ready to 'have a real good time'. I was having a real good time a month ago, and then I came here, discovered I had a cousin somewhere I never knew about and lost my boyfriend, thank you very much, DJ Kashid. Perhaps if he knew that he wouldn't be bashing out 'No Limits' so loudly over the din of Willow screaming.

'What do you keep looking for, Mummy?' Lyla shouts over the music as we walk to find a food place we all like.

Oh cool, I was being subtle, then. The music bellowing and Willow screaming and the duty-free lady spritzing perfume into our path and dragging an eight-year-old along on a wheelie suitcase are all too much, and it is as though my brain has turned to soup and dribbled out of my ears.

'I'm, yes, no, I'm not,' I stammer.

I look round again – not for some Prince Charming this time, but for some support. But Kath is distracted, held up behind us in her patchwork maxi skirt, putting Jo Malone-spritzed sample sticks into her crocheted handbag. I look to my right, and although Willow has stopped crying, thanks to the dummy popped firmly in her mouth, silent tears are rolling down Lacey's cheeks, as she tries very hard to keep looking forward and focus only on the far-off distance, instead of how hard she's found it saying goodbye to Piper and how completely drained she's probably feeling.

I give myself a good mental shake.

'I'm just looking around to check we've got everyone. Kath! Keep up, we don't want to get separated, not even for expensive perfume. Lacey,' I say, reaching out and squeezing her arm lovingly, 'you're doing a brilliant job. I think she's going to nod off soon.' I look at Willow, snuggled up in the baby carrier against Lacey's chest. I try not to think about how sweaty that must make her tits; she doesn't need to think about that either right now.

'What if she screams on the plane and everyone thinks I'm a shit mum?' Lacey asks just as I swing to the left to look at a menu outside a café, moving the wheelie case too sharply and making poor Lyla topple off onto the floor with a thud.

'Then we'll be shit mums together, who are doing our bloody best but need a long sit-down and a large glass of wine!' I say firmly in comradery as I scoop a good-spirited Lyla off the floor, catch the eye of Kath to beckon her over and then smile up at Lacey. 'You're not a shit mum. Everything is going to be fine.' Realising I've said my favourite word again, I cave and have one last look round for Edward.

'I don't think he's coming, Robs,' Lacey says, this

time squeezing my arm and checking Lyla is out of earshot. She's clearly picked up on the tension, despite my trying not to burden her with it. 'Fuck him. Fuck them all,' she says forcibly, as though trying to convince herself as well as me.

'Who are we fucking now?' Kath asks casually as she wafts little paper sticks saturated in different scents in our faces, making us wince a bit.

'Steady on, Kath!' Lacey laughs, taken aback by her profanity.

'Lovey, I've been around the block more times than all of you put together. If you can drop the F-bomb, then so can I!' she says, still beckoning to us to smell her sticks.

'What's an F-bomb?' pipes Lyla, as she picks up the wheelie case and steers it back towards us – and right into my ankles.

We're all a bit stumped. Nobody wants to answer with the truth, but I think we're all a bit too frazzled to think of a good reply. You know when you see contestants on a quiz show, struggling to answer the most basic question while you yell it at the TV? It's like that: we're all contestants not having the foggiest clue what words should come out of our mouths.

'What is it, then? The F-bomb? What sort of bomb is it?' Lyla continues relentlessly.

'Right! Can we please all stop saying either the F-word or the B-word? We are in an airport, and Kath, nobody is fucking anybody,' I say sternly, as soon as Lyla makes another loop away from us.

'Well, that is a shame then,' she says airily as she steps up to look at the menu too.

This is going to be a long flight.

THIRTY

AUGUST

THE PAST WEEK BACK at home feels like it's been so much longer than seven days. Lyla and I are both still struggling with being back on British time, and while she can afford to relax and enjoy her summer holidays with Simon and Storie (who are having her this week), I've been setting my alarm, heaving myself out of bed and trying to make myself look half decent in spite of my dry skin and giant eye bags. I never thought I'd be envious of Lyla spending time with her drippy dad and his mushroom-foraging girlfriend, but I am.

My magical movie moment with Edward at the

airport didn't happen, obviously. Instead, I spent the seven-hour flight taking it in turns with Lacey and Kath to walk a grizzling Willow up and down the aisles and trying not to cry myself. I'm not sure which was harder: settling Willow or convincing Lacey it was all going to be OK.

On top of that, while Kath was on walking duty, Lacey wanted to know if and when I was going to talk to her about the adoption, what I was going to say and how I thought she'd take it. I didn't have the heart to tell Lacey to just button it and let me be sad in peace and deal with my own problems, so I told her I'd have to have a really good think about it but that worrying now wasn't going to help. That seemed to appease her.

Edward's idea of cooling things off 'a bit' seems to be 'a lot'. I've barely heard from him – only once really to say his work is keeping him out there longer because they're struggling to hire a new manager. Very convenient . . . Well, I'm not going to beg for him back. He's a great guy, but so are plenty of other people and I shouldn't have to change myself or my life to suit a man. It's the modern world. I'm a working woman. I've got this. If I say that enough times I'll convince myself, right?

The one good thing about this week (aside from Tuesday, when I found an entire family-size bar of fruit and nut behind all the cereal boxes), happened at work.

Sitting at my desk and staring at my screen for so long, I developed a headache, which made me think maybe I haven't actually 'got this'. It's exhausting work, telling yourself everything is fine. But Natalie called me into her office, giving me the excuse to leave my mindless scrolling.

'Robin, I wanted you to be the first to know,' Natalie says. 'We've had the promised retainer payment from Fierce Films. It's official – MADE IT is safe. And a huge part of that is down to you. I've added a bonus to your salary this month – you've earnt it.'

I should be delighted, I think as I go back to my desk, and while I'm relieved the business is going to be OK, since Edward's gone I can't seem to feel things in full colour.

Skye looks up from her 'space' and notices my despair.

'Are you all right, bae?' she asks, jolting me out of my mind-wander.

'Bae is the one that means babe, right?'

'Yes. Bless your heart,' she says gently.

'Why are you being so nice to me?' I ask, narrowing my eyes.

'Because I'm your friend and I care about you,' Skye says, looking at me with such kindness I almost cry.

'Wow. Thank you, Skye. That's really very nice of you. You're my friend too, and I appreciate—'

'And if I were your age and had just been ghosted, I wouldn't know what to do with myself. But I'm here for you. If you need a makeover to help you get back out there, I'm happy to help you. We could make a night of it, couldn't we?' she says, speaking to me like I'm already in a home.

'Right. First, Skye, I'm not that old. I'm thirty. I know this is madness to you but I'm actually, techni-cally, a millennial too. We are the same. Second, I don't fully know what "ghosted" is, but I'm assuming dumped, and that's not what's happened at all, we're just having a bit of space. And third, I too am a make-up artist, so I think I'm OK for a makeover, thank you.'

'I know, sweetie, but I'm Head Make-Up Artist,' she says, as though she hasn't heard a word of what I've just said.

I don't feel like it's worth explaining to her that I am Creative Director, which is more senior than Head Make-Up Artist. My brain is too full of sluggish emotion to take Skye on, so instead I just glaze over a bit and say, 'Yeaaah, thanks, Skye,' allow her to waffle on a bit more about her mum, who has recently found love again (without pointing out to her that, again, I'm only thirty and not old enough to be her fucking mother), and that is all because she has a great attitude and uses the 'forces of the universe'.

'Honestly, Robin, you should look into it – *The Secret*,' she finishes.

'Yeah, I'll do that,' I agree, hoping she'll just get bored of this soon. I'm tired in every single way possible.

'I'd say you should come out tonight and I'll help you hook up, but you've got your women's club, haven't you?' she says, clearly not running out of fuel.

'Yes, I have my business networking night, Women Who Win. I also don't want to "hook up" with anyone because, like I said, I'm not single, we're just having some space. And I do actually have a lot to do. We've not got long before we need to send our pitch to Mara for her spring/summer show next year. And we really need to impress her again so that we become her go-to artists and don't have to keep bidding for the work.

'I'm really trying to immerse myself,' I say, nodding at my screen, thanking the lords above that she can't see my browser is open to the M&S children's section rather than any work. 'Also, as you know,' I say, trying to sound on my game professionally, 'I'm heading up the expansion project. I've confirmed the venue for the live tutorials and I think—'

'Isn't it just your friend's florist's?' Skye says, still full of pep and energy. Maybe she's on some magic vitamin tablets I need to invest in.

'Er, yes, Dovington's. It has a huge room at the back that the manager says we can hire for six months and convert how we see fit. I thought the floral element would be beautiful,' I respond with pomp.

'I mean, yeah, any room with good lighting and mirrors would be cool. But like you said, having all the plants and stuff would be good for Insta! We could set up a flower wall, too, with proper ring lights and a tripod for people to frame the perfect shot!' she declares excitedly.

'Thank you, Skye, I'll have a think about that and get back to you,' I say, writing GET FLOWER WALL on my notepad and underlining it. What a brilliant idea. 'I really do need to focus now,' I say, looking back at M&S on my screen.

'Right, right, got you. Gotta get in the game. Zone into your headspace. Find your vibe,' she says, nodding earnestly.

'Yes. Thank you, Skye.'

She's a good egg, really. On days like this I wish I could dial her down a bit, but I have to admit it's nice to be around someone with such enthusiasm. I'm glad she doesn't know how tough things can be or how close we nearly came to losing the job out there, and with it a whole bunch of staff – maybe even her. Ignorance is bliss, and I'd love a bit of either right now . . .

THIRTY-ONE

RIVING OVER TO THE school at 6:30 p.m. with no Lyla always feels a bit weird. I know she'll be having a great time with Simon and Storie, harvesting honey or bowing to the moon gods, but I miss her. How is it that children are the things that exhaust you most but fulfil you so completely? What a paradox.

I give Lacey a ring as I'm driving.

'Hellooo,' she says over the sound of Willow squawking.

'Oh, sorry! Have I called at a bad time?' I say apologetically.

'It's always a bad time now I'm not in New York!' Lacey laughs drily.

'I know! It feels like ages ago already, doesn't it? Are you glad to be home, though? Glad to be back with Karl?' I ask, hoping she says yes.

'I am, I really am, but I thought that would help and . . . I dunno. It hasn't really. Willow, please just take this bottle!' she says distractedly.

'Help what?' I ask, trying to figure out what she means.

'Just help me feel a bit more up. A bit more normal.' It all tumbles out. 'Before New York I thought I was just bored and tired and full of new hormones. In New York I thought I was a bit flat because I missed Karl and it was hard solo-parenting and I felt for Kath's situation. But now I'm home, I still feel down,' she says with no Willow sounds in the background, so I assume she's happily having her bottle now. I feel a pang of missing her after being used to seeing her so much.

'So,' she continues with a big intake of breath, 'I've booked an appointment with my GP. I really have this time . . . and I'm actually going to go. It's tomorrow morning. I'm going to talk to her about how I'm feeling, and see if I can get some support. I think that's the best thing to do,' she ends so confidently I can't help but smile.

'This is amazing! Yes, Lacey! Yes! What spurred this on?' I ask joyfully.

'Well, I've got Piper on my case twenty-four-seven!' she replies. 'But I think being in America helped, too. Everyone is so relaxed with talking about these things. The mums in the playgrounds were openly chatting to each other about how shit they feel. One mum, who I'd never even met before, with a little boy on the climbing frame, turned to me and said, "Why does nobody tell anyone how boring motherhood is?" and laughed. And then I laughed! It *is* boring, Robin! Why didn't you tell me?' she asks, laughing too.

'Ha, ha! I don't know! It's not something anyone ever says. What sort of a mum would I be if I went round saying that sometimes looking after my kid is a bit dull?' I ask, laughing along with her.

'An honest one!' she shouts, startling Willow, I think, because the squawking starts up again.

'Aha-ha, you might be right! It's the dreaded Mum Guilt, though, isn't it? Keeping us all silent for fear of someone thinking we're crap at our new jobs! Listen, I'm at Women Who Win, so I'd better dash, but I'm so glad you're going to talk to someone, and I'm going to take a leaf out of your book – motherhood is hard! MOTHERHOOD IS FUCKING HAAARD!' I yell into my car.

'YESSS! YOU ARE A GOOD WOMAN, ROBIN WILDE! YOU'RE THE FUCKING BESSST!'

'SO ARE YOU, LACEY HUNTER!' I shout back, and we hang up.

Nothing invigorates you quite like a good scream down the phone to your best friend, eh? Even if you do now feel a bit self-conscious that Reena Patel, a new reception mum who recently joined WWW, might just have heard you swearing at the top of your lungs. Oh well, I'm sure she's been there too!

It's a Friday night in the middle of summer, but the hall is packed with women ready for our meeting. This is our fourth meeting, and by now our numbers have risen to around forty, so news of our community is spreading well, which is a joy to see.

So, at my request, tonight's topic is The Juggle Struggle. It feels apt, and I've invited Natalie to speak, because if ever there's a woman who's mastered how to find the right balance, it's her.

I rang Kath earlier to ask if she wanted a lift to the meeting, but she's spending the evening with Colin. I'm going to find time this weekend to check in on her because I know she's hurting right now and I hate that I'm not helping her.

I take my usual seat with Finola and Gillian, and just as Gloria finishes her welcome, and is about to invite Natalie to speak, Storie wafts through the front door and sits with us. Just what I need. With forty or so women in here, it's so hot.

Natalie is giving an amazing talk about the history of MADE IT and her own career progression. I want to listen attentively, but I can't help thinking about all the things I need to do this weekend, and my To Do list for the week ahead. Every time I think about a thing I need to do I think about how I'd like Edward to be at home waiting for me when I come in, or how, rather than 'finish *Luther*' being my Saturday afternoon plan while Lyla's at her dad's, I'd like it to be 'finish *Luther* with Edward'.

I wasn't paying attention and Natalie's finished, so we start to move on to the discussion part of the evening. Finola begins talking about how pleased she's been with her first few lessons at the stables, and how Gillian's 'top-notch computer advertising' has really boosted local awareness of what she's doing.

'Well done, Gillian,' Storie says. 'You're really using the electrical forces for good, to connect people with the animals, to blend man and beast.'

'I think there's a word for that, my dear,' Finola chortles, before Gillian can jump in and kindly thank Storie for her compliment, of sorts.

'So tell us, Robin, how on earth did you and Natalie pull it all off?' Gillian asks, beaming, eyes agog, just like Finola. Amazingly, even Storie is looking tuned in.

It's so warm in this room. I wonder if Lyla's OK with Simon by himself? I wonder if Kath has time to come over tomorrow? God, it's hot.

'Well, it's a big story. We flew out to New York not really knowing what would happen,' I begin, feeling my chest and neck itching and prickling with the heat. I blink hard and carry on. I'm fine. 'We knew we had a big task ahead of us, and so much was riding on getting it right.'

'I bet it was! I'm no businesswoman, but I'd wager a lot was on the line!' Finola encourages, smiling.

'Yes, everything was on the line, a lot was,' I stammer, feeling my throat go dry.

'And did Edward fly out with you, or was he waiting at the other end, anticipating your spirits rejoicing when they met again?' Storie says, somewhat dreamily and with no hint of insincerity.

I think of Edward and scratch my neck, trying to gather my hair up and off my skin. I swallow hard. I want him to be here. New York is too far away. I want to call him. I swallow again, trying to push down the wave of emotion that's welling up, and before I can excuse myself, I've got up and run out of the room. I don't really know where to go, so I run all the way to Lyla's classroom and into the toilets next to it. I burst through a cubicle door, slam it shut, sit down on the extra-small child-sized loo and let out great big heaving sobs.

In an instant Gillian and Finola have followed me here and are looking over the top of the cubicle door, such is its child-friendly size.

'It's too much, I can't do it all,' I sob.

'Sweetie,' Gillian soothes as Finola walks out

again, presumably not impressed by how pathetic I am.

'It's like I have too many tabs open in my brain,' I cry, struggling to catch my breath.

'It's OK, you're OK,' Gillian carries on soothing as the door opens again, and in walks Finola, followed this time by Gloria and Natalie.

They coax me out of the miniature cubicle and into Lyla's classroom, where we all sit on equally miniature chairs around a table.

'This isn't like you, Robin, you're my go-getter!' Natalie says with a concerned look in her eyes.

'You're our inspiration for being a freaking life winner!' Gloria adds. 'What's happened to bring this on?'

'I'm not a life winner, I'm not a go-getter, I'm not any of those things. I'm just a tired, messy, faking-it single mum with a job I don't deserve, a family I can't look after and friends that I'm failing. I'm shit,' I sob, putting my hands to my face in shame and self-pity.

Now it's Natalie's turn to get het up round a table, albeit a teeny-tiny classroom table.

'Robin Wilde, I will not let you feel this way! You are amazing! You really, really are a go-getter! I've seen you handle your friends, your family, your work, other people, and you are everything you want to be and more. I admire you every day! Nobody feels like they have it together! I certainly don't. It's a team effort, and we're your team. If things are too much at work, let me give more to Skye. If you need some time for family, take it and enjoy it. We're here to support you because we love you,' she says so passionately I want to cry all over again.

Gloria pipes up, 'You have to be kinder to yourself. How are you meant to look after others when you're not looking after yourself? What can we do to help you? You wanna night out on the tiles, as you Brits say?' She smiles kindly.

'I think our lovely Robin needs a bit of TLC and an early night,' Gillian interjects as Finola sits by her and nods sagely.

'How about I take you home and make you a nice cup of tea? I'll run you a cool shower and we can watch a bit of TV together,' Gillian says gently.

'That would be really nice, thank you,' I reply.

'Will you promise us one thing?' Natalie says.

'What is it?' I ask.

'That you try to remember that being a life-winning

go-getter also means taking time to care for yourself, and that asking for help is not a weakness, it's a strength. We all care about you,' she finishes, reaching out and giving my arm a little squeeze.

'I will, thank you,' I say, a fresh tear, maybe one of relief, rolling down my face.

THIRTY-TWO

TWO DAYS LATER

A FTER A FULL SATURDAY of rest and a lovely evening painting with Lyla (who had been fine with Simon and not accidentally poisoned by Mother Earth), I'm feeling a lot better.

Gloria has rung this morning to see how I'm getting on, and it feels nice to be checked in on when lately I've been the one checking in on everyone else.

I've arranged, surprisingly painlessly, with Valerie for Corinthia to come and play with Lyla, and so the both of them are happily singing and dancing around upstairs, living their best lives. It makes me smile to hear Lyla having such a good time.

I've not long flicked the switch on the kettle when the doorbell goes and Lacey saunters through without Willow.

'Oh, hi! It's just me, Lacey Hunter, without a baby in tow!' she laughs, waving her arms about as if to show they're empty.

'Ohhh my *Goddd*, this is amazing!' I sing back.

'Yep! She's having some daddy 'n' daughter time, and I'm having some me time. I went to the doctor this morning and she confirmed that yes, it's postnatal depression. You were right. I've got some medication and strict orders to have time for myself, so here I am, at your service. Gillian rang, and said you'd had a bit of a night of it?' she says, her old energy back.

'Well, first, you look great! Surely those meds haven't kicked in that fast?'

'Nope, but I've had Piper helping me, and Karl's fully realised I need more support. The meds will help soon, but for now I'm just relieved I was taken seriously, and that things are going to get better. Kath's agreed to have Willow one day a week when Piper goes home, and Mum's going to have her every Friday. I'm going to get things sorted, Robs!' She's the happiest I've seen her in a long, long time.

'I'm so, so, sooo glad,' I say, going over to the other side of the kitchen and giving her the biggest squeeze.

'Thank you. Now, what can I do to help you? Are you OK?'

We spend a good hour talking about the 'incident', which Lacey thinks was probably a panic attack, and about what I can do to make time for myself. I admit that my heart hurts for Edward, but that my pride is getting in the way of reaching out because I can't bear to be rejected again, even though Lacey thinks I should give it a try.

I can feel the tears rising, thinking about Edward, so we change the subject to Kath. We've decided we're going to bite the bullet and look for Eleanor, consequences be damned . . .

THIRTY-THREE

'IT'S HERE! I'VE HAD a letter. I have had a letter! It's from the agency! They know where she is. THERE IS A LETTER!' Lacey screams down the phone the following Friday morning while I'm in the office doing the paperwork for the week.

'OK, Lacey, calm down, I'm going to finish up here and come straight over. Stay. Calm.' I'm barely calm myself, feeling all of my internal organs flip around inside as I try and figure out a way to leave the office early without raising any alarms.

I consider saying Lyla's ill as an excuse, but I don't want to jinx anything so I go with the old faithful.

'Skye,' I say as I walk into the kitchen where she is apparently spending a moment meditating with some rocks. 'I'm sorry to bother you, but I need to go.'

'I'm meditating,' she says in a low voice, not opening her eyes.

'OK, well, I'll leave you to it but just so you know, the office is all yours for the rest of the day.'

'Thank you for the space,' she says, uncrossing her legs and standing up, packing her rocks into a little cloth bag. 'Where are you going?'

'I've got to go home,' I say earnestly. 'I'm not well.'

'What's wrong?' she asks, looking me directly in the eye. Why is she so comfortable asking me that? Why isn't it the olden days, where nobody spoke about anything and 'not well' was sufficient?

'It's my stomach,' I lie.

'Do you want to hold one of my crystals?' Skye asks very seriously.

'Um, I will, but I think I just need to be near my bathroom, you know?' I bluff, knowing that you can't argue with that.

'Oh, right, no, don't touch my crystals then, please, just take yourself home and get well,' she says, holding her stones behind her back as if I am about to snatch them out of her hands and rub them all over my fake-germy body.

'Cheers, Skye. Have a good weekend,' and with that I dash out the door, hearing Skye tell Alice and Stuart something about my 'bottom troubles', before I drive faster than I should to Lacey's.

'Fuck my fucking fuck, is this the letter?' I say as she lets me in. I'm totally hyped now, having had a ten-minute drive to really think this over.

'Yes! I haven't opened it because you needed to be here, but shit me, I'm beside myself. This is it! We're going to find her!' Lacey says, dancing about.

'She's not actually in the envelope, Lace,' I laugh.

'Ha, ha, just open it before I rip it off you!' she laughs back.

I hold the letter in my hand and take a moment to consider how life-changing this could be. For all of us. This is a big, big deal.

I slide my thumb under the folded corner and carefully tear it open. The letter is on official paper. My eyes scan it quickly.

'Lacey, they've found Eleanor. Oh my God. Wow. They don't say where she is or what her surname is now, just that they have her on record and a registering some years ago of her interest to meet her biological mother. What's more, they've contacted her, and she would be open to meeting with Kath. Oh my *God*!' I screech, delirious with joy, nerves and sheer amazement. How can one letter mean so much?

I GO HOME THE most conflicted I have felt in a long while. I am buzzing with joy to find this long-lost baby, but frightened to tell Kath in case it's not what she wants. Plus she still doesn't even know that I know about her daughter. From everything she's told Lacey, it really sounds like Kath would give anything to meet her, but what if we've got it wrong? Maybe she actually does want to leave the past behind her, and me showing up with all of this will be an overload. I wish Edward was here to discuss it with; he'd definitely have something supportive and useful to say on the matter.

I think about texting him but decide against it. If he's not interested in having me in his life, then nor am I. I'm not going to be the weak one this time. While I'm feeling strong, I pick up my phone and type a reply to my last text from Kath.

*Bit short notice but are you home and free for
me to pop round?*

*Yes! Have just made lavender cordial! Colin's
finished poking my pipes so everything's ship-
shape now! Just me! Come on over!*

I don't want to delve into what was wrong with the
pipes, or even consider that this might be an innu-
endo. She's home, she's alone, I need to do this.

'Hello, lovey!' Kath coos as she opens the door.
'Don't mind me looking so smart, I've been on my
rounds with the lavender creations so I'm in my business gear. Do you like it?' she says, doing a little twirl
in the hall as I step in.

I can see where she is going with this, but there's
no denying it looks absolutely bonkers.

'I found the suit in Oxfam for £17.99 and just did
the rest myself! Can you believe it?' she trills, so proud
of herself as we walk straight through to the kitchen.

Kath is wearing a lilac two-piece tailored suit. The
trousers are wide-leg with a firm crease up the front,
and the hip-length jacket is double-breasted with two
gold buttons over her stomach. Underneath she's put

on a little white cami. Seems all right so far. Probably was all right on the hanger. Kath, though, being the brilliant Kath that she is, has taken the embroidery thread to it and from the hems around the ankle all the way up to the knee she's sewn on trailing, swirling little stems and lavender flowers in sage green and deep purple. The lapels of the jacket have also been emblazoned with the embroidered flowers, but these have the added embellishment of tiny purple sequins on the bud and then delicate green bugle beads up the stalks. In addition to this, she is wearing more than her usual share of seafoam glass bead necklaces, her specs up on her head and a badge that says '#GirlBoss' that I think she might have been given at a WWW meeting. If there was ever a woman who threw herself into a project, it was Kath, and I love her so, so much for it.

'Kath, you look a million dollars. If this outfit alone doesn't make people want to stock your creations, then they're crazy!' I say, giving her a big cuddle.

'Now, this isn't like you! So cuddly! What have I done to deserve this?' she asks, squeezing me back.

I take a breath. There's no point dragging this out.

'I need to tell you something. Can we sit down at the table?' I ask.

Stirring my straw around my – surprisingly nice – lavender cordial, I struggle to find the words to begin.

'OK. I don't really know the best way to have this conversation, but I know it's important we do,' I begin.

'Whatever it is, I love you and we'll get through it together,' Kath says kindly, reaching over to squeeze my hand. I don't know if this makes it easier or harder to tell her what I know.

'Thank you. Equally, I want you to know I love you. I always will.'

Kath carries on looking at me, wondering where I am going with this, but, I think, suspecting.

'In New York, Lacey told me something. She didn't want to break a confidence, but she knew I'd want to know, want to be there for you, want to—'

'I know what you're trying to tell me.' Kath cuts me off before I can get any further. 'Yes, it's true. It's sad, it's hard, but it's history. I'm used to managing it and I don't need to talk about it. I appreciate your caring, and I appreciate that you think you are looking after me by encouraging me to talk about it, but I'm quite all right, thank you,' Kath says angrily, tears welling up in her eyes.

'Kath, no, I'm so sorry, I don't want to force you to talk about this if it's making you upset, I just want to see how you feel, and maybe—'

'I can't talk about it anymore because it hurts. I've been hurting a long time, but seeing newborn Willow look so similar, so like her, it hurt too much. Baby Lyla reminded me of her, of course, but there was something about Willow's wispy hair that stuck with me. But Willow's getting older now, and it's getting easier. I didn't know Elean— the baby, as she got older, obviously, didn't even have a picture. I've resigned myself to never knowing her. I don't know where she is, what she's called now. My baby is gone. We've just got to accept that and live our lives the best we can, and—'

I can't handle seeing Kath so despairing, tears rolling heavily down her face and splodging onto the lilac suit, turning it dark indigo where they land. It's like watching someone's heart break.

'We've found her. She wants you. She registered an interest to meet you!' I blurt out, saying anything I can to stop Kath spiralling down in this awful way.

I'd meant to build up to it gently, find the perfect way to introduce it, but the words race out.

Kath looks up instantly, her hands shaking and her eyes so wide I think I really should have said all that better, eased her in a bit.

'You've found my Eleanor?' Kath says, incredulous. 'My baby Eleanor?'

'Yes!' There's a huge smile on my face now, and my own tears are falling. 'We don't know where she is but the agency does, and if you want to meet her, all you have to do is say.'

'In all of my days I never thought I would ever see her again,' Kath whispers. 'I thought she'd hate me.' She looks blankly ahead.

'Kath, who in their right mind could ever hate you?' I say.

'The little girl who was given away. The little girl who felt her mother didn't want her, that she was unloved. You talk so often about Mum Guilt, but this is a Mum Guilt that has burnt a hole in my heart all these years. I let my baby go. I gave her away. I didn't fight for her, and I've never even thought of looking for her,' Kath sobs.

'No. No, no, no. You did not give her up, you placed

her for adoption. They don't use that language anymore because it's not right. You did what you had to do. I know it was unimaginably awful for you, but I know, and Eleanor knows, that it wasn't because you didn't love her. You were almost a child yourself! They were different times. You can't think like that!' I cry with her, feeling so impassioned that Kath feels this way. After all these years of heartache, she doesn't deserve to suffer such pain right at this moment, when we should be celebrating.

'I want to see her. I want to see my daughter,' Kath says, lifting her head up and looking me straight in the eye.

I STAY WITH KATH for over an hour, talking about her past, about Dad, about me when I was a baby, and Lyla, and now Willow. Kath briefly mentions how kind Edward was to her about it all, and I feel a pang in my heart for how much I want him to be back in our lives. I know I'm being stubborn but I don't know what to do now; I've left it weeks, and the monster feels too big to face. I've messed it all up, but there are bigger things to deal with here, like Kath and work and, to my horror, I've just realised tonight is the night I agreed Lyla could have Corinthia to stay over.

I say my goodbyes to Kath, reassuring her that everything's going to be all right, and she reassures me that she's going to be fine tonight (Colin's coming over again, and I have a feeling she's going to have a lot to talk about with him), and I drive home to have a quick tidy-up before I head out to pick up Lyla and Corinthia from holiday club.

As I wait for Lyla and her friend, I'm almost overwhelmed with how lucky I am that I get to do this. I think of Kath missing out on her little girl growing up – how she never got to be the mum waiting at the school gates. It makes me want to hug Lyla that little bit tighter, and it even softens my heart (only a bit, mind you) when I think of Valerie and her bullying ways. Maybe it's not so bad that Lyla has chosen Corinthia to be her friend. Don't all of us need a second chance sometimes?

THIRTY-FOUR

SEPTEMBER

I T'S BEEN FIVE WEEKS since I told Kath we'd made contact with Eleanor, but I think for all of us it's felt like longer. Life has ticked on: work's gone well (the Mara Isso SS pitch has been submitted, and my beauty tutorials are almost ready to go live).

In August, I threw a little birthday party for Lyla. How is she growing this fast? Didn't I just have a toddler about forty minutes ago? Instead of hiring the hall and doing a big full class thing, she just wanted to invite her 'most absolute best friends' for a movie night and sleepover and I wasn't going to argue with that – far less effort than crafting sixty billion mermaid decorations like last year! This year, though, we did have the addition of new friend Corinthia. Now I don't actually mind her – you can't not like a child, can you? (Well you can but you can't admit it.) But her mother, Valerie, is a different kettle of fish altogether.

As I opened the door to 'greet' her and let Corinthia in, she said, 'Sorry I'm not parked on the drive, I couldn't fit the Range Rover on it.' Good old Valerie. Never disappoints with a put-down. As she stepped over the mat to settle Corinthia in – saying, 'I won't step on the mat if you don't mind, it's a bit grubby and these shoes are Chanel,' – I noticed something different in the post. A birthday card with an airmail sticker on the front. Written on the back was *If undelivered, return to a slimy worm.*

Edward. He sent her a card.

After Lyla had opened it and tossed it to one side with all the other gifts and cards, I took a moment to properly look at it. No mention of me. No point dwelling. Life goes on.

Now, back at school for autumn, since the sleepover Lyla seems to have fully brought Corinthia into her little gang with her other besties Roo (Finola's son) and Clara (Gillian's daughter), and I've spent some much-needed time with Lacey and my mummy friends – like mother, like daughter.

Today, though, Kath the mother is meeting her daughter, and I feel so many emotions, I have already actually been sick. I decide not to tell Kath this as I arrive to collect her, because this is her day and I'm here to do anything I can to help it run smoothly for her.

Opening the door, I can tell Kath's made an effort.

'Oh Kath, you look absolutely gorgeous,' I say, almost breathless at how beautiful she looks.

Kath's selected a blush-pink silk shirt with little pearls for buttons that I suspect she's sewn on herself. She's tucked the shirt neatly into a long, flowy navy-blue skirt that of course has been 'Kath'd', but instead of pompoms, she's sewn little crescent moons in silver thread all around the waistband and hem, to match. She's wearing brown leather brogues with silver laces and, of course, as she wouldn't be finished without an extra flourish or two, she's wrapped herself in a handmade silver shawl that has a fringe of little silver feathers hanging from it. She still looks every inch Kath, but a coordinated, thoughtfully put-together version, and with her cheeks pink and eyes sparkling

with what I hope is excitement, she's looking absolutely radiant.

'Well, I want to make a good impression on my
daughter,' she says, clearly relishing being able to use
the word, picking up her mobile (in a Lavender Lovies
phone case) and slipping it into her handbag. 'I've
waited thirty-eight years for this moment. I'm ready,'
she says, so calmly I feel in awe.

'Then let's go,' I say, turning round and heading
back to the car.

We drive the short journey to the park we've agreed
to meet in and pause for a moment in the car park.
I'm giddy with excitement, sweaty with nerves,
anxious, happy, sad and scared all at once, so I can't
even imagine what it must be like for Kath. She's not
said much on the drive over, but nor have I. We've
sat in a comfortable silence, both aware that our lives
are about to change forever.

'She said she'd be waiting on the bench opposite
the swings, so shall we head over?' I suggest.

'Just a minute,' Kath says, looking straight ahead,
a quiver to her voice.

'It's going to be all right,' I say, putting my hand
on her arm. 'I love you, Lyla loves you and you've

given us all the love in the world. Now we have a chance to let Eleanor know that love is waiting for her if she wants it,' I add.

The walk over to the swings probably takes only a minute, but every footstep feels like a mile. As we approach, we see a woman with long blonde hair, tied in a plait, sitting alone with her back to us. The hairs on the back of my neck stand up.

'Kath,' I whisper, looking at her.

'I know,' she says. I think she's going to stop, and for a moment I even fear Kath is going to turn round and flee. But instead she picks up her pace.

We approach the bench, and the woman turns to us.

For a moment, the whole world stands still and every sound stops. This woman is beautiful. She has Kath's sapphire-blue eyes and a soft look to her face. Almost in slow motion, she stands up and puts her hand to her mouth.

Kath takes two steps forward and they fall into each other's arms and hold each other for long minutes. I can see tears running down Eleanor's face, and Kath just says, 'My baby, my sweet baby,' over and over again until I'm having to scrunch up my face so hard to stop myself from crying even more. I don't think

I have ever witnessed a more precious moment than this in my whole life.

They both sit down and beckon to me. I join them on the bench.

'This is my niece, Robin, your cousin. Though I think you must know of each other from making contact.' Kath takes the lead so easily.

'We know each other, but only by name. So lovely to meet you at last,' she says, leaning in for a hug.

I wrap my arms around her. Kath's daughter. Since Kath has been like a mum to me for so many years, perhaps I should have prepared myself more for how this moment feels to me. Not like meeting a cousin. More like embracing a sister. As I let her go, it's like looking into Kath's eyes.

Kath takes both of Eleanor's hands and looks into her face. 'I've so much to ask you, and so much to catch up on, but before we do any of that, I want you to know I've always loved you. I never wanted to give . . . to place you for adoption. I thought of you every day, lit candles for you on your birthday, looked out for you with every little blonde girl I passed, and missed you for all of these years. You were, and are, loved. I will understand if you're angry or resentful, and I won't begrudge you if you'd rather not have us in your life, but I just need you to know that, to me, you are my beautiful, perfect baby, and I will love you for as long as I live.'

At this, we are all flooded with even more emotion.

Eleanor is quiet for a moment. Then she takes a breath. 'I don't even know where to start, but I want you to know I'm not cross. My mum, my adoptive mum, I mean, only ever spoke highly of you. She told me about a young girl with blonde hair like Rapunzel who hadn't been able to keep me but who had loved me very much. She told me how you had generously given her the greatest gift anyone could ever give, because she'd never been able to have children of her own. I've always known you loved me. When I was old enough, my mum gave me your note that she found. I've always felt twice the love, because there's been you, far away but somewhere, loving me, and my mum, loving me each day.'

'Yes. Always loving you from far away. Your . . . mum,' Kath struggles, and I know this must be so hard for her to say, 'is clearly a marvellous woman, and one day I'd like to meet her and thank her with all my heart for raising you. Were you happy, as a child?' Kath asks tentatively.

'I was. I had the most lovely childhood. I grew up not too far from here. It was just me and Mum and Dad. They're still going, in their seventies now. I was good at school but was never particularly academic, much better at arts and crafts, really. I left to work in a school as a teaching assistant, and then a bit later on in my twenties I went to uni and trained to be an art teacher. I met a lovely man there, and we ended up getting married, eleven years ago now.' She smiles.

'How wonderful,' Kath gushes, still holding both her hands. 'An art teacher! I love making things,' Kath begins, but is interrupted by two little girls, one a bit bigger than Lyla and one smaller, running up to our bench from the swings, both with blonde plaits framing their faces.

'Mummy! Is this the special lady? Is this your special friend?' the younger one asks, breathless from the run.

'Yes! Girls, this is Kath!' Eleanor says, beaming at both of them.

And that's the moment Kath realises she has two granddaughters, her very own gang of Wilde women.

THIRTY-FIVE

ITHER SOMETHING'S IN THE air, or life is going pretty amazingly right now, because I take a moment to look around the room, and everyone seems so full of life.

The latest Women Who Win evening finished half an hour ago, and as we are clearing away, I'm telling Gloria, Gillian and Finola about my live beauty tutorials project for MADE IT. Since we got back, I've been finalising plans for it and soon, we have our first session. I've even delegated some of the work to Skye – which is a pretty big step for me, considering I'm normally the world's worst person at asking for help, and especially at work, after it all nearly went so wrong with Mara Isso last year. Geed up by the WWW meeting, the fact it's a Friday and the children are all at a sleepover with Corinthia (yes, I know, the frost has miraculously thawed slightly with Valerie . . . maybe she did find a good Sugar Daddy after all, ha ha), Gloria asks if we can pop in and see the 'incredible venue you've been raving about!'.

Our session tonight was titled 'Stop Worrying, Stop Saying You're Fine, Ask for Help', and I decided to take the 'stop worrying' element and run with it. I ping a text over to Lacey.

Hey babe! Bit of an ask, but is there any chance I could swing round and pick up Dovington's keys? I'd love to show Gloria and the girls the set-up we put in with the mirrors and lights, if it's OK? xxx

We've spent the last week totally transforming the back room. We still have the old oak table (because a) it's useful, and b) that room wouldn't be right without that battered, paint-splattered, trusty old table that Lacey and I have spent so many hours at), but round the edges of the room, instead of the huge metal shelving units, we've painted the walls the palest shell pink, added huge mirrors framed by movie star-style light bulbs and trendy see-through acrylic chairs. Each of the eight stations has a little shelf under the mirror for students' palettes and brushes, and at the head of the room there's the tutor's station with a similar camera-to-screen set-up to the one we had at the second Women Who Win session, so the students can see what they are being taught.

Since Dovington's is a florist's, Kath suggested we should have floral art on the walls, and so for the last few days, she and Eleanor have spent time together in here stencilling the most beautiful wild flower murals, twisting and turning around the mirrors and up to the ceilings. And yes, I've even started on Skye's great idea of the flower wall, for our clients to get the perfect Insta.

Spooky! I was just talking about the classroom! Kath popped in with Eleanor. Told me about the painting. We were gonna head over and have another look, anyway! Meet you all there in 20? Xxx

So, half an hour later, I'm standing in one of my favourite places in the world with three school mum friends that I couldn't admire more; my gorgeous auntie and her new-found daughter, who seems so like her and so bonded with her already; my best friend, who, thanks to having a month of Piper staying with her and to reaching out for help from her doctor, seems so, so much better; beautiful baby Willow; and Karl, who's put the golf on hold so that every weekend he's home with his family. Apparently, he's even put in a request for flexible hours, so he can be around as much as he can while Willow's tiny. And as we stand in Dovington's, I can see a glimmer of pride in Lacey's eyes – this is her business, and it will be waiting for her whenever she's ready to step back in.

Although I'm not related to all of these people, they're my chosen family. I spend a moment thinking about the people in my life who make it what it is and who've been there through thick and thin.

'What a summer it's been, eh?' says Lacey, rubbing her shoulders a bit as the nights are getting longer and cooler.

We stand and look at Eleanor holding Willow as Kath coos.

'Shit me, Lace. What an adventure!' I reply, still not over how much Eleanor and Kath look like each other.

'Thanks for sticking by me when I was a bit, well, weird,' Lacey says quietly.

'You weren't weird, Lace, you were really poorly. I'll

always stick by you – always have, always will, here till the bitter end,' I say, smiling. 'It's not like I've not been through enough, and you've always had my back, too,' I add as Karl walks over and gives Lacey a kiss on the forehead.

By now, Finola, Gillian and Gloria have looked round the room and admired all our hard work.

'This place is swell!' Gloria enthuses in her lovely American drawl. 'I'm gonna book myself a lesson straightaway, if it means I'll wake up every day looking like you!'

'Aha-ha, that's very kind of you, but don't scare away future customers with promises like that!' I laugh.

'Looks like you've got all your ducks in a row now, Robin!' Gillian smiles, giving me a quick congratulatory hug.

'Except the situation with that nice chap you had on the go, my dear,' Finola adds.

There's a wave of tension in the room.

'She doesn't need a man if she doesn't want one,' Lacey says supportively, slightly irked by Finola's bold statement.

My heart hurts. I know Finola was only trying to be kind, in her usual blunt way. And sometimes it does me good to have friends help me face things head-on. And she's right: I do want Edward. In fact, overwhelmed with emotion after Kath met Eleanor, I decided I should, ahem, grab the bull by the horns, and that Edward deserved to know the happy news. So we've texted a little bit and had a couple of stilted FaceTimes, but all we've spoken about is Kath and Eleanor, and how Lyla is settling in to the new school year. Nothing personal, nothing about us, and I don't know how to find the words to change that. I miss him. I miss everything about him, even the socks in the duvet. In fact, even Lyla has asked after him a few times, wondering where her favourite worm-man is.

'I do want a man, that man, but he doesn't want me. He hasn't come and swept me off my feet, has he?' I say, the vibe in the room feeling really intense all of a sudden.

'I'm sorry, I know I don't know the situation very well,' begins Eleanor softly, 'but just because someone hasn't come for you, it doesn't mean they don't want you.'

I make eye contact with her and see so much love and sincerity that I don't know how to react.

'It's OK,' Lacey says, sensing the tidal wave of emotion threatening to knock me off my feet.

'I'm fine. If he wants to sort things, he knows where I am. I'm not going to go chasing a guy. I'm absolutely fine, honestly,' I protest.

'What complete and utter tosh!' Finola erupts. 'Haven't you been listening in these Women Winning meetings? You young fillies saying you're "fine" all the time when you're not. You've got to stop doing this. Sorry, *we've* got to stop doing this! We've got to speak up and say what's what, so we don't find ourselves in a pickle, all depressive and miserable!'

Finola is so passionate, I'm taken aback. She's not out of steam yet, either.

'None of this "you're a girl and he's a guy rubbish". Robin Wilde, you are a woman. It's the modern day, and no man is going to ride in on a white steed and rescue you.'

'Except maybe Edgar, because you actually do have a white steed in your stable, don't you?' Gillian adds meekly, and a ripple of laughter goes round the room.

'Well, yes, dear, but our Edward chap certainly doesn't, and you'd better take the reins on this, Robin, because he's not going to. We all know you love him, we all know he loves you. You just got a bit busy, lost yourself in everything after your terrible, terrible loss last year . . .' She continues talking, but I feel a sharp stab in my heart when I realise how right she is. '. . . And lost sight of what was right in front of you. I don't like to see you sad, and I don't want to make you feel set upon, but my dear, you need to go and get that man back!' Finola stops, taking a breath and looking around her.

We all look at each other, nobody really knowing quite what's just happened. Finola's spoken such sense, being so vocal, bringing up the loss of our baby.

'I, um . . .' I begin.

'I'll pick Lyla up from Val's tomorrow and have her for a night,' Gillian offers, stepping forward.

'And I'll have her the next night,' Lacey says, looking at Karl for confirmation he'll be there and getting a smile and nod in reply.

'And then I'll have her for a night after that!' Kath adds in.

'She can play with her cousins!' Eleanor smiles.

'So, you want me to go home, book a flight, find Edward and tell him I love him?' I say, laughing at how ridiculous this all is.

'Well, do you love him?' Gloria asks boldly, as only Americans can.

I think back to my thirtieth birthday party, held here less than a year ago, where Edward surprised me, tipped me backward and kissed me in front of everyone. I think back to telling him about the baby, and how he said he'd be there through it all and how he really was, even when 'all' wasn't what we thought it would be. I think about all the times he's let Lyla jump on him, pelt him with pillows and call him names, taking it with such grace and humour. I think about his kind, chocolate-brown eyes and his smooth, strong arms. I think about how happy I was when I knew I was driving home to him and how full he made my heart feel.

'More than anything,' I say, with eyes full of tears.

'Then get outta here!' she yells as the rest of the room erupts in a cheer and I shout, 'Yes! *Yesss!!* I'm going to New York! I'm Robin Wilde, and I'm going to get him back!'

THIRTY-SIX

A S THE PLANE TOUCHES down on the tarmac, I check my bag one last time for all my things, make a note to grab my cabin case from the overhead locker and march straight through customs (well, as much as you can at JFK) and jump into a cab.

This time, I don't marvel at the little multicoloured wood-clad houses, the giant sweeping cemeteries, the famous New York skyline or the bridges over the Hudson and the East River. Instead, I am totally and utterly focused on what I'm about to do next.

Booking my ticket last night, thanks to my bonus

from Natalie, I felt a sense of elation so strong I was utterly inspired to be this brave more often. I caught the first flight out, and with the time difference, it's now only Saturday lunchtime. How can you go from Friday night in a florist's being yelled at by your friends to reach for the stars, to Saturday afternoon, pelting down the streets of New York in a yellow taxi, about to do one of the riskiest things of your life?

I haven't phoned ahead to tell Edward I'm coming. Ironically, I didn't have the nerve. I just knew I had to make the leap, hope for the best and have a little bit of faith. Also, the three G&Ts I had during the flight have helped, too.

I push the buzzer to his apartment, hoping he's in.

'Hullo?' he answers quizzically.

'Um, yes, hello, hi,' I begin, suddenly faltering.

'Robin?' comes Edward's voice, crackling through the machine.

'Look, I know this is weird, it's a lot, *I'm* a lot.' I take a deep breath. I'm going to do this, *I am going to do this*, I say in my head, shifting my feet about. 'Edward, I love you. You're the only man for me. You're everything to me, in fact. And I—'

The door opens wide, with Edward, my gorgeous

Edward, standing right in front of me, head tilted to the side, smiling his gentle smile, and I'm lost. My mouth's gone dry, my eyes are teary, my heart is thudding.

'But I thought we were over,' he says, and I swear I see tears in his eyes. 'I thought your life was too full to fit me in.'

'I know it's felt like that at times, for both of us. But you need to know the truth. And if you don't, well, I've flown all this way because I just wanted to ask . . .' My voice has softened to a whisper.

'You just wanted to ask . . . ?' he nudges, reaching out to hold my hands, his skin warm and familiar.

The touch of his hand is all I need to find my voice again. And finally, the words are there. Loud and clear.

I smile. 'If you'd marry me?'

The End

ACKNOWLEDGEMENTS

Here we are again, the Oscar speech moment for any author, one filled with absolute pride in thanking the people who have made this dream possible and absolute fear that you'll miss someone vital off the list and cause eternal offence.

As my most wonderful manager Maddie once said, 'I'd like to thank all the *key* people'.

There. Nailed it.

Heh heh, I jest, let's do this for reals. Queue dramatic stage lighting and pass me my golden statue to weep over. I'm going in.

This book would never have been a book in your hands (or screens) without the hard work of many people. I would like to first give special thanks to Abigail, Dom, Maddie, Meghan and Hannah, my amazing team at Gleam Futures who always have my back, who always believe in me and also, who shift my calendar about so deftly on days when I'm having a little cry because I don't think I have enough time to write. You are like magicians to me and I love you all dearly.

OK, imagine now there's a confetti cannon going off and golden ticker tape tumbling down from the ceiling – thank you so much Bonnier Books UK! You. Are. Good. People! The publishing team have held my hand (not physically, that's not in the book deal) for the past three years and I've never known people cheer so loud for Robin.

Particular thanks go to my editors, Eleanor Dryden and Sarah Bauer. I don't think Robin would be the Robin she is without you. Eli you have championed me writing about the harder topics since our very first one-on-one in my old house, and Sarah you have worked tirelessly on *Wilde Women* and have invested in the characters so much that (and I hope you don't mind me exposing you here haha) you have a little crush on Edward! You are both brilliant women and I'm beyond thankful to have had you in my life, both professionally and personally.

The whole team at Bonnier have been pretty epic, actually, and not just because they always decant Maltesers into bowls for our meetings. I'd like to thank Katie Lumsden, Kate Parkin and Perminder

Mann. I'd also like to thank Clare Kelly for covering the publicity and for saying, 'We don't body shame here, you order a side,' when I went a bit gaga on the Wagamama's order after our Manchester book signing. I'd like to thank Alexandra Allden and Sophie McDonnell for the beautiful cover and illustrations. You have captured our Wilde women so perfectly.

Thanks go to Jamie Taylor and Alex May, who make the actual book and the 1000s of pages they send to me to sign.

Stephen Dumughn, Sahina Bibi, Felice McKeown, Nico Poilblanc, Stuart Finglass, James Horobin, Andrea Tome, Victoria Hart, Angie Willocks, Carrie-Ann Pitt, Amanda Percival, Vincent Kelleher and Sophie Hamilton, thank you so much for your sales and marketing wizardry!

And lastly in the Bonnier section, I'd like to give big squishy thanks to Laura Makela, Ruth Logan, Ilaria Tarasconi, Saidah Graham, Genevieve Pegg, Jenny Page, Natalie Braine and Jon Appleton.

Bonnier, you're the best. Here's to many more!!

Another round of thankful praise must go to my long-suffering family. For Liam, who took on far more than his share of the parenting duties whilst I was in the midst of writing, for Darcy who loves that Mummy writes so much she's set up her own class book club, and for Pearl, who can't yet read anything but does enjoy pointing to the dog in the farm book. If I didn't have my homey peoples, I'd be a wreck of a woman and would never really be able to do anything. I love you a lot famalam, thank you for always supporting me.

And so we come to the end of the Oscar-style speech, the lights have swivelled into an even more dramatic set up and I should probably let a couple of dainty tears fall gracefully down my face (though we know I'd never manage this and it'd be panda eyes and foundation streaks). I'd like to thank you, the dear reader, for taking the time to allow Robin into your life, to love her, to sometimes feel angry with her, to keep her going as you read through her books. I thank you for coming on her journey and for supporting her each and every step of the way. You are everything to these books and whilst I'm sad we've reached the end, I'm glad to know they keep going with every person who picks up a copy and begins their wild(e) journey.

Thank you.

Oh hi!

How on earth have we got here? The final thank you letter of the *Wilde* series. I fear I may shed a little tear. Except I probably won't because I'm writing this in the hairdressers and I already look a bit weird having my laptop out whilst I have a blow dry so I think crying would only add to that.

Much like Robin, my own life has been a bit of a #JuggleStruggle this year (hello, I'm writing this at the salon) and so often I have found myself using that toxic little F word – fine. 'I'm fine!', 'fine thank you!', 'yes, that's fine!'. Why do we do it to ourselves?

Despite the challenges of fitting in a lorra lorra work commitments, a growing family and vaguely trying to stay sane, I have loved writing Robin this year. Watching her grow over the past three books has been a joy to me and I hope also to you. She's pulled herself from The Emptiness to happiness with a few hurdles along the way but, with the support of her friends and family, she's done it. I don't think anyone could say they haven't been there in some way or another. Robin's definitely one of us.

I'd like to thank you for being there with Robin

through her ups and downs. For cheering her on and crying with her when things got tough. I meet so many of you at my book signings, out and about or just via online messages, and hearing your thoughts on the *Wilde* books always fills my heart. I have put so much of my own heart into these that to know you have enjoyed reading them – well, it's a lot. Thank you.

There won't be another novel out next summer (although I will be keeping myself busy, so keep your eyes peeled for something else a bit new – squee!) but I do find myself pondering what becomes of our Wilde women. Perhaps one day in the far-off future we'll revisit them, but for now, they live in these pages and in our hearts and I am grateful to you for keeping them alive as you read these books.

If ever you are feeling a bit flat or like the world has lost its fizz, please remember that your friend Robin has been there too and that there are always sunnier days to come.

Wishing you great big loves and thank yous,

You're flipping good eggs,

JOIN MY READERS' CLUB

Thank you so much for reading my novel!

If you enjoyed *Wilde Women*, why not join my Readers' Club*, where I will tell you – before I tell anyone else – about my writing life and all the latest news about my novels.

Visit www.LousePentlandNovel.com to sign up!

Louise
xxx

* Just so you know, your data is private and confidential and it will never be passed on to a third party. I'll only ever be in touch now and again about book news, and if you want to unsubscribe, you can do that at any time.

Coming soon from Louise Pentland . . .

MUMLIFE

*MumLife; noun: the inescapable swirling vortex of love,
guilt, joy, annoyance, laughter and boredom that
makes up the life of a mum.*

Louise Pentland has been through a lot. From a
traumatic birth with her first daughter, to single
motherhood, to finding love again and having a
second child, Louise's parenting journey has been full
of surprises. Discussing the realities most working
mums face, plus the impact of maternal mental
health, Louise is on a mission to make other mums
feel less alone. She beautifully reveals her own
imperfect but perfect route to motherhood, as well as
the loss of her mum so early in her life, how it
shaped her and the mother she became.

Reflective, uplifting and with her signature hilarious
wit, *MumLife* will share Louise's ups and downs,
reflecting on her route to motherhood and what she
has learnt along the way. This is the honest truth
about motherhood, from someone who's been
there and experienced it all.

*MumLife: What Nobody Ever Tells You About Being
A Mum* is available on 6th August